The Duke
Alone

T0002146

OTHER TITLES BY CHRISTI CALDWELL

Wantons of Waverton

Someone Wanton His Way Comes

The Importance of Being Wanton

A Wanton for All Seasons

Lost Lords of London

In Bed with the Earl

In the Dark with the Duke

Undressed with the Marquess

Sinful Brides

The Rogue's Wager

The Scoundrel's Honor

The Lady's Guard

The Heiress's Deception

Wicked Wallflowers

The Hellion

The Vixen

The Governess

The Bluestocking

The Spitfire

All the Duke's Sins

It Had to Be the Duke (novella)

Along Came a Lady

One for My Baron (novella)

Desperately Seeking a Duchess

Scandalous Affairs

A Groom of Her Own
Taming of the Beast
My Fair Marchioness
It Happened One Winter

Heart of a Duke

For Love of the Duke
More Than a Duke
The Love of a Rogue
Loved by a Duke
To Love a Lord
The Heart of a Scoundrel
To Wed His Christmas Lady
To Trust a Rogue
The Lure of a Rake
To Woo a Widow
To Redeem a Rake
One Winter with a Baron
To Enchant a Wicked Duke
Beguiled by a Baron
To Tempt a Scoundrel
To Hold a Lady's Secret
To Catch a Viscount
Defying the Duke
To Marry Her Marquess
Devil and the Debutante
Devil by Daylight

The Heart of a Scandal

In Need of a Knight (A Prequel Novella)
Schooling the Duke
A Lady's Guide to a Gentleman's Heart

A Matchmaker for a Marquess
His Duchess for a Day
Five Days With a Duke

Lords of Honor

Seduced by a Lady's Heart
Captivated by a Lady's Charm
Rescued by a Lady's Love
Tempted by a Lady's Smile
Courting Poppy Tidemore

Scandalous Seasons

Forever Betrothed, Never the Bride
Never Courted, Suddenly Wed
Always Proper, Suddenly Scandalous
Always a Rogue, Forever Her Love
A Marquess for Christmas
Once a Wallflower, At Last His Love

The Theodosia Sword

Only For His Lady
Only For Her Honor
Only For Their Love

Danby

Winning a Lady's Heart
A Season of Hope

The Brethren

The Spy Who Seduced Her
The Lady Who Loved Him

The Rogue Who Rescued Her
The Minx Who Met Her Match
The Spinster Who Saved a Scoundrel

Brethren of the Lords

My Lady of Deception
Her Duke of Secrets

Nonfiction Works

Uninterrupted Joy: A Memoir

The Duke Alone

CHRISTI CALDWELL

Montlake

This is a work of fiction. Names, characters, organizations, places, events, and incidents are either products of the author's imagination or are used fictitiously. Any resemblance to actual persons, living or dead, or actual events is purely coincidental.

Text copyright © 2022 by Christi Caldwell Incorporated
All rights reserved.

No part of this book may be reproduced, or stored in a retrieval system, or transmitted in any form or by any means, electronic, mechanical, photocopying, recording, or otherwise, without express written permission of the publisher.

Published by Montlake, Seattle

www.apub.com

Amazon, the Amazon logo, and Montlake are trademarks of Amazon.com, Inc., or its affiliates.

ISBN-13: 9781542033954
ISBN-10: 1542033950

Front cover design by Juliana Kolesova

Back cover design by Ray Lundgren

Printed in the United States of America

Found family is some of the greatest family one can ever know. When my son was born, we discovered family in other mothers and fathers who also had children with Down syndrome. It was during my boy's first hospitalization that a friend entered my life. She came and sat beside me. She brought me snacks and food and magazines. She promised when he was discharged, we would take our boys on a playdate . . . and we did. It was my boy's first playdate. When my family had to move, I promised my friend I'd someday return. It was ten years before I did. And when we did . . . she was there, waiting. Tamara, thank you for being not only the best of friends, the kind of woman I know I can always count on, but also my "found" sister. Val and Myrtle's story is for you.

Chapter 1

London, England
December 1813

Neighbors, servants, and passersby to Ten Yardley Court could—and had—long attested that the din emitted by the familial household of the Earl and Countess of Abington was enough to rival a raucous affair at Vauxhall and the most competitive, closest horse match held at Ascot, combined.

Then again, such was to be expected of a noble family consisting of three sons and three daughters born of Scottish origin, and the hapless mother and father desperately attempting to be heard over their unruly offspring.

It was why all had breathed a collective sigh of relief when that same family had announced plans to vacate their London townhouse and retire to the country until long overdue renovations to their home had been completed.

It was also why those sighs of relief had fast turned to groans of regret as the timeline of work had been shifted to the winter months, when all of London went quiet and the peers retired to *their* respective country seats.

The noise this particular evening was even more resounding than on most others. Which was saying a good deal indeed about the McQuoid household.

Or perhaps it was just that Lady Myrtle McQuoid, gone four years and returned only two days from Mrs. Belden's Finishing School, had been removed from her family for so long that she'd forgotten how voices swelled as her kin competed to be heard, and how booming laughter or high-pitched whines of annoyance rose above the blur of the chatter.

At that moment, Myrtle stood on the landing above the foyer and assessed the bustling activity below.

Servants scurried about with trunks and valises atop their broad shoulders, making a march to the wide, double front doors that hung open. Her younger siblings—a nine-year-old sister, Fleur, and a ten-year-old brother, Quillon—rushed about, giggling, as they hid from Myrtle's young cousins, also aged ten, who now visited for the Christmastide Season.

As they did every Christmastide Season.

They, along with the rest of their many siblings and parents, Mr. and Mrs. Francis Smith, Myrtle's aunt and uncle.

And just as at every family gathering before it, Myrtle's eldest sister, Cassia, broke off and paired herself with cousins Meghan and Linnie. Fleur and Quillon joined up with near-in-age twin cousins Andromena and Oleander. While Myrtle's eldest brothers, Dallin, the future earl, and Arran, rode and played billiards or did—as they referred to them—all the gentlemanly things with their male cousins, Brone and Campbell. Or, at least, Arran took part *when* he was not traveling.

Through it all, Myrtle remained alone. Invisible.

Nor was her forgotten state a product of the fact she'd been gone these past years. Rather, she'd always been left out of the melee. As a young child, she'd chafed at being the forgotten one. She'd hated the fun her family members had enjoyed, only because she'd remained on the fringes, wishing to be part of it all. Determined to *make* herself be seen, Myrtle had gone out of her way to carry out every wicked prank on her kin, and to be as loud as she possibly could.

Which also, no doubt, accounted for one of the reasons she'd been sent off to finishing school and not kept around with a governess as her elder sister had.

And hating that miserable finishing school, Myrtle had done absolutely everything within her power to prove herself a lady so she might get out of there as quickly as possible.

She'd stayed out of mischief—or at least carried it out in a clandestine enough way to have evaded the miserable headmistress's notice.

She'd attended to her lessons with a diligence and solemnity, laughing about the absurdity of it all only under the covers with the other girls, who'd hated that place as much as Myrtle had.

She'd dropped more flawless curtsies than she could count.

Had perfected her stitches and singing.

Well, perhaps not her singing. Mrs. Belden had cringed and banged her cane, accusing Myrtle of having the tones of a drowning cat trying to scratch her way out of a metal tub. And even as Myrtle had strenuously disagreed with that harsh assessment, she'd not challenged the miserable old biddy, but instead had focused on playing the pianoforte—at the *appropriate* tempo and volume.

She'd learned to perform steps of the quadrille La Boulangère and even the scandalous waltz—as best she was able to without a male partner leading.

Along with the rules of propriety and decorum, she'd been schooled on needlework and the practical study of household management. She'd learned and practiced her discourse with other students and instructors, in both English and French—always speaking on topics suitable for polite discussion when she made her Come Out this spring.

Through it all, Myrtle had conducted herself with grace and aplomb.

But this? This day and this moment were pushing Myrtle in every way, as through the roar of the household activity she threatened to erupt, undoing everything she'd done to get out of Mrs. Belden's.

From her central vantage point, she searched the bustling crowd of servants below.

A young maid approached, and to make herself heard over the din, Myrtle called out to her loudly. "Do you know where my mother is?"

"No, miss," the unfamiliar young woman responded, and then dropping a curtsy, she hastened around Myrtle.

Myrtle followed the maid's descent to the marble foyer, where Hanes, the family butler, stood in wait, directing the maid amidst the commotion.

Another servant rushed past—this time a footman.

Myrtle stretched out a hand, almost wishing to catch him like a spotted trout in her family's ponds and hold on so he'd have no choice but to look at her and answer. "Excuse me, I'm looking for my mother." Her mother, who ruled the roost in this household and, according to Myrtle's doting father, the world. "Can you point me toward her?"

He dropped his stare to the floor. "I cannot say, my lady." A ruddy flush stained his cheeks, and he stepped quickly around her . . . and fled.

Myrtle rocked back on her heels.

He *could* not say?

He could not. Nor could any of the previous six young men and women to whom she'd posed her questions.

And though she prided herself on being quite clever and intelligent, it wouldn't take *much* deduction from a person with even *half* her wit to gather that the staff had been instructed to avoid her.

Nay, more specifically, they'd been advised to hide their mistress.

Myrtle headed downstairs and attempted to wheedle an answer from four more servants before she caught sight of someone who could help.

No matter how inadvertently that may be.

"Aunt Leslie!" she called loudly, for her tiny, heavily rounded, bespectacled aunt and godmother was headed out one door and over to the adjacent chambers her eldest daughter was invariably assigned every holiday house party.

Bypassing a pair of servants with a trunk between them—with *Myrtle's* trunk between them—Myrtle rushed to intercept her aunt. "Aunt Leslie. Have you seen my mother?" she asked without preamble when she reached the frizzy-haired woman.

"She is in your chambers, packing," her aunt said and then let herself inside. "There you are," she said to whichever one of her kin she'd been looking for. "I told you we must . . ." Aunt Leslie's words faded as she shut the door behind her.

Knocked back on her heels once more, Myrtle stared at the panel. "Packing?" she repeated aloud.

Her mother?

Her mother, who delighted in having servants and wouldn't be able to pick out a trunk from a valise, suddenly found herself actively engaged in packing those very items—and in Myrtle's rooms, no less?

Though in fairness, it was also the last place Myrtle would think to look for her.

Sure enough, when she reached her rooms, Myrtle found her.

Them.

"Mr. Phippen is set to begin immediately," her mother was saying to her husband as she sorted through an array of jewelry set out on Myrtle's vanity, then instructed her husband to place the properly wrapped item in the valise.

Ah, they were hiding *together*.

Then again, Myrtle's mother had never much been one for being alone. Myrtle had often suspected it was one of the reasons her parents had wished for—and had—their brood of six children.

"The servants have already begun draping the sheets," her father said. "But for the chambers that will be in use this evening . . ."

She'd hand it to them: they didn't manage to look even a tad bit guilty.

In fact, they didn't so much as pause in their work and acknowledge her. Nay, they were far more engrossed in talks of whoever this Mr. Phippen fellow was.

"Who is Mr. Phippen?" Myrtle called out. When neither parent looked up and over, she folded her arms at her chest and resisted the urge to stamp her foot like she'd done as a small, stubborn girl. Not that they would have noticed anyway. "I asked, who is Mr. Phippen?"

That managed to force their attention over to her.

Her mother frowned. "Mr. Martin Phippen is only the best master builder in the whole of London and the one who'll be overseeing the renovations of our home."

Alas, Myrtle would have had to have been in London and truly part of the McQuoid brood to have known about the renovations planned for their *home*. It was just one more reminder of how much a stranger she was here.

Best builder Mr. Phippen forgotten, Myrtle frowned as her parents carried on as they'd been. "*You* are packing?"

Her parents looked up as one and stared at Myrtle as if she'd just entered the room.

"Your mama is quite capable, dearest," her father responded for the pair as Myrtle's mother turned back to the vanity table and the tiaras resting there. "Very much, indeed."

The attention they paid her proved brief, as with that avowal, husband and wife resumed their rapid discourse, leaving Myrtle in the state that had become increasingly common these last three years.

Oh, Myrtle didn't doubt for a moment that her mother could have single-handedly done the work of the Sixth Coalition to rid Boney of his quest to conquer the world. Neither, however, did Myrtle believe for one single Scottish minute that her mother had developed a sudden affinity for packing her own belongings.

"We must leave early in the morn," the countess was saying. "It will allow us just four stops until we reach Scotland . . ."

So they were off to Scotland. The place of her father's birth and their family's country estate.

Only, their London townhouse was where they called home.

Or that had been the case.

Those were the memories Myrtle held of so many of her favorite Christmases. In winter and even more so after the little season when the lords and ladies of London scattered to their country properties and the McQuoids had turned the town into a playground of sorts. In fact, some of the earliest memories she still carried went back to days spent skating on the canal in Saint James's Park or on the Serpentine River in Hyde Park.

Cupping her hands around her mouth, she raised her voice in a manner that would have absolutely extended her sentence at Mrs. Belden's. "I don't wish to leave London for the holiday."

When neither parent acknowledged her, she swept over. "Hullo," she said, waving her arms back and forth, forcing them to see her. "Did you hear me? I said I do not wish to leave."

Her mother set down hard the necklace she'd been examining. "You don't wish to leave?" she asked. "You don't wish to leave?"

And Myrtle really should have known by that repeated question that no answer was required, and that her mother was set to deliver a scathing lecture.

Alas . . .

She managed a tight nod.

Her mother shot an arm up, pointing skyward. "We have a roof that has begun to leak."

As if on cue, a single drop of water fell, landing with a surprisingly loud *plink* in the flowerpot that had been set beneath to catch it.

"The floorboards are rotting." To punctuate her point, Mother stomped the floor with her foot, and the oak panel dipped in a precarious way. "The walls are drafty." Even Mother Nature chose to cooperate with the countess. The wind battered the windows, rattling the panes and sending such a chill through the room that, despite a raging fireplace, Myrtle couldn't keep from hugging her arms to ward off the nip.

Her mother was not done with her, however. "Of all your siblings and cousins, you are the *only* one to make this difficult. Neither your brothers nor your sisters wish to leave for the holiday. Nor do your cousins. *They* are good enough to know that if these renovations do not happen at this juncture, then the household will *not* be ready for this London Season. Am I making myself clear?"

Myrtle had always been hopeless at conceding defeat. "Linnie and Meghan, and for that matter, Cassia, wouldn't know if they were in Scotland or the sea," she said, and not unkindly. Her female kin were flighty at best, empty-headed at worst.

Her mother frowned. "I suggest you heed your father's advice and gather up your Mr. Newberry books and marbles—"

"It is *Pride and Prejudice* in three volumes By a Lady," Myrtle gritted out. And it was a sin of the world that the real author must hide her identity away behind a pseudonym. But then, hadn't Myrtle learned at the hands of her own family that the last thing the world wished was a woman with a voice? "It is *Pride and Prejudice*, and it was given to me by Miss Cassandra Austen." The Austens were only Aunt Leslie and Uncle Francis's neighbors in Hampshire and her favorite family outside of her own. Actually, of late, including her own. "Furthermore," she went on impatiently when neither of her parents so much as acknowledged her, "I haven't read Newberry's books since I was a girl, and those pieces you refer to as marbles are in fact fossils Arran brought—"

Her mother gave a dismissive wave. "Whatever they are. If they matter to you, see them packed up, and either bring them in your valise or tuck them away here, as Mr. Phippen's men are set to begin work."

"At Christmas?" In feigned innocence, Myrtle batted her eyes. There were, after all, but two sacred times for the McQuoid mother: the London Season and the Christmastide one. "Never tell me you're having these poor men begin before the holiday?"

"Of course we would nev—" At Myrtle's triumphant look, her mother instantly clamped her lips together. She turned an entreating look on her husband. "Harold."

Just like that, his name a command, Myrtle's father, ever the peacemaker, stepped between them. He rested his hands on Myrtle's shoulders and steered her gently toward the door. "Why don't you run along, dearest, and pack up your marble collection."

"They are not marbles, Father," she said, her exasperation rising by several notches. "They are minerals. Minerals." She'd expect a collector of fine marble pieces would appreciate the difference and, at the very least, respect *her* collection.

"Yes, well, do have a care with them. Your aunt Leslie nearly shattered her neck on several pieces you left out."

Her heart fell. Left out? She'd had them in the Corner Parlor, that room so aptly named for its placement at the end of the townhouse that provided glass windows throughout and offered views in three different directions of London, and also light enough to examine those stones her brother Arran had given her right before he'd made his first journey abroad. "Did she break them?"

"Why don't you run along and see," her father suggested, his tone more hopeful than suggestive.

Run along and see . . .

As though she were a child.

She may as well have been for all the attention they paid her.

After all, every Englishwoman knew the only person less heard and seen in the world than a woman was a child.

She should go. She should just leave as they wished and see to her minerals. "They were in the Corner Parlor," she said as patiently as she could manage, unable to leave.

"And?" her mother asked distractedly as she packed several hair combs in that rapidly filling bag.

"*Annnd* the room is in abject disrepair." It was also one of the reasons those rooms had forever been her favorite. When Myrtle wished to avoid the natural noise that came from an enormous family whose every member had made it their life goal to needle her about something, she escaped there.

Except she inadvertently provided her mother an opening. "Which is why we've builders and are leaving for Christmas. Now run along and see to your marbles."

"Minerals," she said, her annoyance mounting. "They are minerals." And she wasn't a blasted child anymore.

Alas, it mattered not whether she'd managed to score the Regent Diamond; her parents had already forgotten her and gone back to packing her belongings.

As though she were a child who could not see to her own things.

Though in fairness, she'd never had any intention of packing her jewelry. She'd never had much interest in or need for shiny baubles to wear. To study. *Yes.* To don. *No.*

"And why, if we aren't celebrating the holidays as we usually do, must they join us?" she insisted.

Her mother gasped. "They?" She touched a hand to her chest. "Do not be rude. The people whom you refer to as 'they' are, in fact, your family."

"How ironic that you think I should require that reminder," she shot back. "I've been all but ignored since I've arrived from Mrs. Belden's." She curled her toes into the soles of her slippers, wanting to call back those words, which revealed too much. Words that made her look like the child they'd always treated her as.

And hating that she should so care that they'd both sent her away so easily, and that no one had seemed to either notice or care that she'd returned.

"*Tsk. Tsk.* You're not forgotten, lovey," her father said in a matter-of-fact way, as if in so doing he made that statement somehow true.

"Dear heart . . . would you please help me carry this piece to Myrtle's valise?"

With that request from her mother, however, in a great show of irony, Myrtle was once more truly and completely forgotten.

Gritting her teeth, she quit her chambers and found herself lost amidst a sea of servants racing and rushing about.

Heading down to the foyer, Myrtle went in search of those fine stones her brother Arran had given her. He'd insisted all people should have some artifact special to them.

All the while, she attempted to breathe deeply and calm her fury and outrage, because fury and outrage had only ever landed her in more trouble.

Why did she still allow herself to forget her role within her family?

She was not so self-absorbed that she didn't realize her big, loving family was one most of the young ladies she'd attended finishing school with would have traded their left waltzing arm for. But she was just selfish enough to wish that *they* wished to have her about. That they cared enough to remember this was her favorite time of the year, because they were a family together.

Her exuberant ways had seen her sent off to finishing school. But the Christmastide Season proved the one exception. With a family gathering that continued on for days, the festivities were a grand, jubilant affair. It was the *one* time when she was accepted, and when the high-spiritedness that had gotten her sent away was permitted. For an all-too-brief few days, she, the odd piece, found herself sliding her way back into the multifarious puzzle that was the McQuoid family.

Myrtle firmed her jaw.

And if that hadn't mattered to them, then she'd at least have expected—*hoped*—they'd remember her birthday was in just a few days, and she'd soon be a woman married and off on her own, and then her time, the memories she'd created in this household, would be just that—memories, not moments that she was part of.

Myrtle reached the bottom of the stairs, where the butler now spoke with a pair as different as days: one fellow stocky and short with beady eyes, the other tall, lankier in frame, and with a cap that fought desperately to constrain the wild mane of crimson curls atop his head. She'd never seen hair that shade of fire.

While the shorter fellow spoke with Hanes, the other periodically nodded and took notes but remained largely silent in the exchange. The two put her in mind of a lion and a badger.

"Mr. Phippen was asking whether the family's plans to vacate remain the same . . . ?" the short one asked.

"Ah, yes. Please inform Mr. Phippen they've since moved up their plans and will remain gone over the next two months."

"Mr. Phippen," she muttered. She'd be glad to never again hear that blasted name.

At least Mr. Phippen was enjoying the benefit of her family's focus.

The lanky fellow who'd gone silent as Hanes spoke did an assessing sweep of the foyer and the halls beyond and above; there was a keen intent to his study, his eyes lingering briefly upon the marble busts sitting on various pedestals throughout. That collection of rare stone her father had inherited from his father's father's father, valuable artifacts to which he'd only added over the years. Surely her father knew they were coveted for their worth and in need of greater looking after . . . than whatever this haphazard madness was.

Just then, that hard gaze locked briefly on Myrtle.

She paused, something cold in his eyes stopping her briefly in her tracks. A glimmer of greed and . . .

He smiled.

That grin reached his eyes, and he tipped the brim of a small cap before going back to whatever it was that trio now spoke about.

Frowning slightly, Myrtle gave her head a shake.

She was in danger of being the fanciful, imaginative creature her family had always teased her for being.

Though if she were being mature in the moment, she could acknowledge it was hardly the builder's fault her family had chosen Christmastide as the time for him to oversee the renovations.

Myrtle made a purposeful path for the Corner Parlor to retrieve those stones from Arran, a traveler extraordinaire, who'd been not rushed off to finishing school but instead allowed to explore the world in search of extraordinary artifacts, and who returned to the adoring praise and interest of all their family.

"But no"—Myrtle spoke quietly and crisply as she walked, her pace quick and furious—"my interests are equated to that of a child." Her relatives still saw her as the small child who'd called the marbles she'd collected as a girl the Elgin marbles, to everyone's amusement. Nay, to her family, Myrtle was the same girl who read Newberry's books for wee ones and mistook children's toys for valuable treasures.

But then, that's what happened when one sent one's daughter away: she remained frozen in their memories and minds as the same girl she'd been.

Reaching the end of the hall, Myrtle didn't break stride, turning the corner quickly enough to set her muslin skirts into a noisy rustle.

As she did, she caught a flash of movement as the door at the end of the hall suddenly shut.

That ever-important room where she'd once spent hours upon hours listening to the tales her brother had told about the pieces he'd added to that curiosity parlor.

Even now, they were likely packing those pieces up and preparing them to be carted away.

And yet . . .

Myrtle reached the door.

Unlike the din of activity on the main levels of the household, a thick silence hung over the room. It was the absolute kind of quiet that left the air humming and rang in one's ears.

Frowning, she leaned in and looked about.

Nothing.

Not the crack or flutter of a crisp white sheet.

Not the officer-like directives called out by the head housekeeper, Mrs. Stonington.

There was . . . nothing.

As she straightened, Myrtle's frown deepened.

This meant only one thing.

Her siblings and cousins were at their familiar game of hide-and-seek.

These rooms, however, had been and would always be off-limits.

Why, even the hoyden she'd been as a child sent off to Mrs. Belden's had known *that*.

"But nooooo," she mumbled. "I was sent away."

Rife with annoyance, she entered the room. "All right," she called loudly. "You've been foun—oh." Her announcement ended on a shocked little syllable.

A lion-looking fellow spun and faced her.

"Who are you?" she demanded when the man continued to stand frozen, his jaw slightly slack.

She really should ring for a servant. Though given that he was already alone with the items and the house was in uproar, it was more likely this fellow would have made off with her father's collection before anyone even noticed the household had been invaded.

She reached for the broadsword from the gleaming suit of armor stationed at the doorway, then heaved it up and pointed it at the fellow. "I asked you a question," she called, using all her energy to point the ghastly heavy weapon, praying he would fail to see the way it shook or the way she remained unable to hold it. Alas, he'd likely have to be blind to not note those particular details.

The stranger immediately shot his palms up. "Oi'm with Mr. Ph-Ph-ippen," he stammered, his coarse Cockney especially difficult to understand because of the speed with which he spoke.

"*You're* with Mr. Phippen?" She echoed that question about her nemesis. The man responsible for her family's wintertime flight.

"A-aye," the man stammered, misunderstanding the reason for her question. "'ires m-men and w-women from East London, 'e does."

"No. No." She lowered her weapon—or rather, her shoulders and arms broke under the strain she'd placed on them holding it. The still razor-thin sharp tip sliced into the hardwood floors, already weak from age and wear . . . and water.

The man gulped loudly and took a wary step away from her anyway.

"That isn't what I meant. I merely meant . . ." Her words trailed off as she continued to contemplate the man. "Why would Mr. Phippen himself not see to this particular room?"

"Delegates, 'e does, miss. 'e'll oversee the transfer of artifacts himself. I'm merely inventorying." With that, he picked up a notebook and a nub of charcoal she'd failed to note resting on the edge of a rectangular pillar, and held them aloft.

"Oh," she said dumbly. And yet . . . she didn't trust him to be in these rooms. Not because of his earlier, erroneous assumption that it had to do with where he was born. Rather, it had to do with the fact that only those who truly appreciated both the value of the items here and the history behind the artifacts should be handling them. This Mr. Phippen, grandest of builders in London, should have realized that.

Unless he wasn't as grand as people presumed. Unless her parents had been taken in by someone who—

"Miss?" The man's hesitant query cut across her silent thoughts.

He turned his book around, revealing crude handwriting hard to make out at the distance.

"Been hired to inventory the items and measure them." He picked up a carpenter's folding wood ruler, displaying the item for her benefit. "Oi'm in charge of selecting the crates and wrappings."

He spoke as a man proud of the role he'd been assigned. He said all the right things and had all the right tools to account for his presence here . . . and yet . . . "And you'll wrap those pieces yourself?" she quizzed, unable to shake her unease.

"Three of us have been assigned the role."

"Three," she repeated meaninglessly.

"Three."

Hmm.

And then something he'd said registered. "Mr. Phippen is overseeing *these* rooms."

The man hesitated, then nodded. "Yes, miss. Oversees all of them, 'e does. Involved in every aspect of the projects he takes on."

That may be, but these rooms were different, not for the walls and the floor and the windows, but rather for the items within. "My father wouldn't just leave his collection to a builder. He'd trust them to someone familiar with the artifacts here and how to handle them."

Mr. Phippen's emissary shrugged. "Oi don't know that, miss. Oi only know the work Oi've been 'ired to do and what was worked out, miss, between Mr. Phippen an' the earl and countess."

They stood silently for several moments before Myrtle cleared her throat. "Then I shall let you back to your task, Mr. . . ."

"Henries."

"Mr. Henries."

Did she imagine the way his shoulders sagged in relief? Or was it because of the cessation in her questioning?

As Myrtle dragged the broadsword over to its stand and heaved with all her might to get it back up and in place, she watched him.

Sure enough, he set to work, unfolding his measuring stick and just then putting it against the marble bust of a man. That mid–First Century piece from the early Imperial age of Julio-Claudian. Details she knew even without the gold plaque her father had commissioned for the front of the pillar, as he had for all the pieces in this room.

Reluctantly, Myrtle quit the rooms, leaving Mr. Henries to his assignment.

Her father must be getting on in his dotage, for the proud and exceedingly careful connoisseur of artifacts, a man who'd looked with the same reverent awe upon the items in this room as he did his wife, would not simply leave them for someone else to oversee. Nay, it was more likely he'd have handled the task himself . . .

But then, how much do you really know him or your mother, or any of your family, for that matter?

As she approached the sanctuary that had always been hers, the loud giggling within served as another reminder that all the places she'd called hers belonged now to her family, and that she was just a visitor amongst them.

Why, everything she knew about this place and how to treat the treasures within had changed without her knowing. Gone as she'd been, she'd failed to know that her papa had grown more lax in his allowance of whom he let see to his collection.

"Cassssssiaaa, do step away! He'll see you . . ."

Momentarily distracted by that curious statement from one of her cousins, Myrtle let herself into the Corner Parlor.

Clustered at the windows, her cousins Linnie and Meghan stood in a sideways line, using the curtain as a shield while Myrtle's elder sister, Cassia, peered around the edge.

"I know it did not seem it at the time, but you truly were fortunate to avoid a future with *that* one," their cousin Meghan was saying.

While Myrtle had been gone, Cassia had nearly wed? One would expect that discovery after discovery of just how much life had continued on without Myrtle would have left her numb to each way she'd been excluded from the family. And yet, it did not. "You almost made a match?" she blurted, and her sister cast a sharp look over her shoulder.

"It was Mother and Father's idea." She gave a little toss of her auburn curls. "I merely behaved as the dutiful daughter"—Myrtle narrowed her eyes at that less than subtle jab—"joining them when they paid a visit to welcome him."

With that, Myrtle was invisible once more. The figure who had fascinated her kin recalled their attention.

"Was he really as rude as my mother said?" Meghan asked earnestly.

Cassia looked squarely at the younger woman. "Worse," she murmured in ominous tones. "But it wasn't just that he had his butler turn us away three times . . . Oh, no. It was something far worse."

"W-worse?" Meghan stammered, breathless with fear.

Cassia gave a grave nod. "Worse."

As one, the McQuoid ladies looked outside.

Unbidden, Myrtle found her gaze following their stares below, and then saw him.

Attired in black from the top of his head to the dark wool of his jacket, trousers, and boots, amidst the white, snowy landscape, the gentleman had the sinister look of a fallen angel trapped in paradise. Why, even the queue that hung past his headwear bore the same midnight coloring. His arms laden with wood, he strode with furious steps toward the mammoth townhouse.

Not that most would consider London in winter a paradise.

Myrtle did.

At that moment, the hulking bear of a man stopped, then looked up.

At her side, her kin gasped and stumbled out of the way to avoid being seen.

Myrtle, however, remained trapped.

Never before had she witnessed such fury emanating from a person's eyes. The fiery sort that locked a person's feet to the floor and even stole all thoughts of fleeing from one's head.

Which was saying a good deal, indeed, as she'd seen other girls get on Mrs. Belden's bad side—and been on it herself.

Notoriously cold and heartless, the headmistress inspired terror in the hearts of students and staff within the institution alike. Why, even Myrtle, who prided herself on not being weak-kneed, had been moved to tremble a time or two.

Even with all that, Mrs. Belden herself would have quaked with fear at the sight of the man below.

Still . . .

Myrtle cocked her head. There was something *interesting* about him. Something almost sad.

He glared at her, a black, menacing look that reached all the way across the streets and space separating them.

Daring her to stay. Urging her to leave.

And she should.

After all, "do not stare, and always drop your gaze to the floor" had been one of the first rules ingrained in her by one of the instructors at Mrs. Belden's.

Despite all the *skills* she had mastered to get herself out of that place as quick as possible, "no direct stares" had also been one of the rules she'd been hopeless to master.

The stranger's frown deepened, and then whipping away from her direct look, the man stomped off.

"Do get away," Cassia urged frantically, catching Myrtle by the arm and speedily steering her to the back of the line. "You'll be seen," she whispered, taking up her place next to Meghan, while Myrtle remained behind even her flighty cousins. "Or did he see you?"

"I don't know," she lied. He had seen her. Myrtle was sure of it. "He was . . ."

It didn't matter that the words had left her head. She was already forgotten as Cassia whispered and talked to her like-in-age cousins. Myrtle wrinkled her brow. Yes, her place had fallen mightily, indeed. Pushed to the literal and proverbial end of the line.

". . . always heads to the stables with the wood."

"It's not wood; it's kindling," Myrtle pointed out.

Linnie cast an annoyed look over her shoulder. "How do you know that?"

Actually, she didn't. And yet . . . "What *else* would a servant be gathering wood for?" Myrtle shot back.

"*He* is no servant," her sister said with an exasperation that would have been more suitable had Myrtle been around to learn all these details herself. Including Myrtle in the discussion, she dropped her voice and spoke in haunting tones.

Pride demanded Myrtle leave where she was not wanted; curiosity, however, compelled her. "Who is he?"

"That is the Duke of Aragon," her sister explained.

A duke. No wonder, then, that their parents had made a pest of themselves welcoming their neighbor.

"And they say he gathers that wood and uses one log for each of his victims . . ." Cassia paused for effect. "Murder victims."

Their cousins let out quiet screeches.

"Better off without him, I'll say," Meghan whispered.

Linnie added a nod of support.

Cassia lifted her freckled nose a touch. "Indeed I am."

Myrtle stole another glance outside.

It was yet another unnecessary reminder that she was a stranger amongst her own family, that in her time away, a new neighbor had moved in, and one whom her parents had sought to join their family to. "And these stories about His Grace, I take it, have nothing to do with the fact he rebuffed y—er . . . our family," she swiftly amended when Cassia flung a dark look her way.

Their cousins gasped.

Cassia waved a hand, dismissing their outrage on her behalf. "Oh, no," she murmured. "The stories existed long before he proved discourteous to our family." She paused for effect. "Tales of the poor victims who faced his wrath."

Despite herself, and despite the fact Myrtle knew her sister had always been a storyteller and that some of her favorites had been those that had sent Myrtle hiding under the covers as a child, she shivered. Cassia had always been deuced good at spinning a yarn.

Myrtle reminded herself that she wasn't a girl any longer, and as such, she wasn't prone to bone-chilling stories. She folded her arms at her chest and stared pointedly at Cassia. "You're claiming a duke is a murderer?" she asked, not bothering to keep the incredulity out of that question.

"You find it hard to believe?" Cassia demanded.

"I find it more likely to believe that you and Mother didn't take too well to being snubbed," she muttered to the collective gasps of her female kin present.

Meghan took a step toward her, but Cassia held up a staying hand. "And just why do you find it so hard to believe, Myrtle? Because of his *title*? Because lords and ladies aren't capable of truly evil acts?" she challenged, and had Cassia been more defiant and less calmly matter-of-fact, it would have been easier for Myrtle to dismiss her sister's story.

Cassia looked back to Linnie and Meghan. As she resumed and her cousins went wide-eyed and silent, Myrtle knew this wasn't a telling solely for her benefit.

"He was once the most sought-after gentleman in all of London . . . until he wasn't. Because"—Cassia paused for effect—"he went mad."

Linnie clutched a hand to her throat and took a step away from the curtain, distancing herself farther from the stranger down below.

"They say he collects one log for each of his victims . . ."

Myrtle didn't want to be caught up in her sister's story, and yet she found herself latching on to that outrageous telling.

"He waits for his servants to displease him," Cassia continued in those eerie tones, but let the remainder of those words go unfinished.

And if they did . . . ?

"What happens when they do?" Meghan whispered in terror-filled tones, posing the very question that had formed in Myrtle's mind. "What does he do to them th-then?"

Clearly relishing their absorption, Cassia waited until all eyes were squarely on her. "Why, he practices his swing." Pretending she had something in her hand, Cassia brought it up and then slashed down in a wide arc, coming near her audience.

The young women—Myrtle included—emitted like shrieks and jumped.

"He's killed servant after servant, taking his rage out on his staff. And when he's done"—her sister paused—"he feeds them to his wolf."

Myrtle wrinkled her nose.

His wolf?

"A wolf?" Linnie asked incredulously.

Cassia nodded and pointed.

Despite herself and her annoyance at her sister's over-the-top storytelling, Myrtle found herself craning her neck around her kin and following Cassia's extended finger.

Sure enough, engrossed as she'd been in the towering stranger, Myrtle had failed to note the enormous wolf at his side.

She cocked her head.

It really was . . . a wolf. Or at the very least, an enormous dog.

"Why would he do that?" Myrtle asked her sister. "Why would a duke kill his servants?"

Cassia lifted both palms faceup. "Because no one would notice if a servant is offed. Other peers' absences would be remarked upon." She dropped her voice again. "But a servant who's gone missing will not earn proper notice, and as such, he keeps his victims to the servant station."

"That is rude," Myrtle said, even as she hugged herself tightly.

She realized what she'd done and swiftly let her arms fall.

"Not even his mounts are spared from his wrath," Cassia said in that same haunting way. Myrtle's sister looked out again toward the courtyard belonging to their neighbor. "They say he enters the stables daily and takes his annoyance out on the horses and practices his swing." Once again, she slashed her arm back and forth in a wide arc.

Oh, this was really enough. Myrtle rolled her eyes. "That is a lot of claptrap. *Who* says *that*?"

A frown formed on Cassia's lips, her disapproval at having her story challenged stamped on her face. *"People."*

"*Which* people?" Myrtle pressed.

"Lots of them," her sister snapped.

"Lots of nameless people?" Myrtle snorted. "And unknown victims?" Yes, the more she heard, the more it sounded a good deal like there'd been offended sensibilities on her family's part. "You should stick with the first part of your telling. The part about the horses is where it veers entirely off course. Everyone knows British gentlemen favor their horses and dogs more than they do people."

Cassia lifted her left shoulder in a dismissive little shrug. "Say whatever you wish to make yourself feel better."

"Casssssia!" Their mother's voice came from the hall. A moment later, the countess appeared in the doorway. She beckoned with a single hand. "I must speak with you about the travel arrangements for tomorrow."

And with that her sister left, her cousins dispersed, and Myrtle was left alone . . . with the window and the stranger and his wolf dog outside.

Myrtle lingered at the edge of the curtains; her mother's and sister's voices grew fainter until only silence remained. A silence made all the more eerie for the tale told by her sister.

A mad duke?

Myrtle dampened her lips.

This was nothing more than Cassia up to her usual storytelling, meant to elicit the precise response she'd had from Myrtle.

Well, Myrtle wasn't the same young girl who'd been marched off to Mrs. Belden's. She was a young woman, just months away from making her London debut.

Her cousins could believe that rubbish yarn her sister had woven all they wanted.

Myrtle, however . . . Myrtle had left fanciful and returned practical. She'd had to. After all, it had been her hoydenish ways that had seen her sent away to that miserable, if distinguished, finishing school.

No, she was decidedly not one to go about believing tall tales about her family's new neighbor. Or . . . new-to-her neighbor. It appeared she was the last of the McQuoids to learn about the gentleman.

Those assurances did not completely chase away the chill left by her sister's telling.

You are being ridiculous . . . There is no mad duke next door.

Before her courage deserted her, Myrtle stole one more peek, immediately catching sight of him. In an attempt to bring the gentleman into focus, she squinted . . . just as he disappeared into the stables.

He returned a short while later with his horse.

As any gentleman might.

"Murderer," she muttered. "Impossible."

And yet, her gaze crept over to the window, and she followed him as he rode off. She wasn't so silly as to believe all that.

The gentleman was likely only lonesome, was all.

And that was certainly a sentiment she could relate to. She'd endured four lonely years at Mrs. Belden's, where friends were few and far between, only to return and find, even with the household swarming with McQuoid kin and servants, she was lonelier than she'd ever been.

It would bring her great satisfaction to inform Cassia that not only was there an abundance of servants in their ducal neighbor's household but also that he was an entirely affable chap.

Enlivened for the first time since she'd returned home, Myrtle released the curtains, setting the fabric rustling . . . and waited for the duke's return.

Chapter 2

They'd been staring again.

Such had been the way since Valentine "Val" Bancroft, the Duke of Aragon, had moved into the sprawling limestone Mayfair townhouse four years earlier.

Just before his life had fallen apart when he'd suddenly found himself a widower.

From that moment on, he'd shut the world out and attempted in vain to bury the demons of his recent past.

Only to find demons of a different sort.

With a growl, Val swung his leg off his horse, dismounting.

Usually there were just two gawkers peering out the window.

Earlier that afternoon, they'd doubled in number. With two sets of eyes becoming four, as the damned nosy busybodies followed his every move.

Beside him, Lady neighed, loud in his disapproval.

That disapproval, however, was not with the nosy chits, but rather with Val. "Forgive me, sir," Val said, belatedly stroking the midnight-black mount on his withers as he did at the end of every ride.

Val glared blackly at the household across the street.

He'd some privacy . . . for now.

It wouldn't prove long-lived.

They'd be back.

Staring.

One would expect that, as a duke, all eyes turned upon him was something he should have grown accustomed to.

It'd certainly been the case.

He'd been one of society's greatest preoccupations: the whispered-about rake with both one of the oldest, most revered titles and a fortune.

His attraction had only redoubled when he'd become a reformed rake, a young gentleman whose wild ways—and heart—had been tamed by Lady Dinah Astley, the Diamond of the Season.

And then, when she'd been his wife, the *ton*'s fascination had taken a macabre turn upon the sudden passing of that same lady.

Only, it hadn't been so very sudden. There'd been piteous moaning that felt like it had gone on forever. And blood. There'd been that, too. Time, however, had existed in a blur on that day, where even with the passage of weeks, months, and then years since the event, he couldn't recall how precisely long or short each moment had been.

There'd been a sharp, bloodcurdling scream—hers—but then quiet moaning. The faint whimper of desperation and suffering sounds which haunted him still, and always would.

That and a lone crimson stain had blended with the fabric of a red satin, turning the material black.

Val briefly closed his eyes, not to blot out the vision in his mind—that would always remain—but rather from a grief that would not quit.

A soft whining pulled him back from the edge of insanity that always threatened to claim complete control.

Suddenly very eager to return inside and pour himself a healthy brandy to chase away the chill and memories, Val went and gathered up more of the wood he'd cut that morn. Bracing it against his chest, he reached down with his spare hand to pat his faithful dog, Horace.

With a quiet click of his tongue, he urged the creature on.

The four-year-old hound had been a gift from his wife upon their marriage and had been like a child to them.

The child they would have eventually had . . .

Oh, God.

Agony sluiced through him, stopping him in his tracks. Clutching the wood close, he welcomed the sharp bite of pain as, even through his garments, it bit into his flesh.

He stared blankly ahead.

This future had turned out to be so very different from the life they had spoken of together.

A—

From the corner of his eye, Val caught a flash of movement.

What the hell? It'd been a flicker of light and movement so quick and so brief that for a moment he thought he'd imagined it.

He thought it was a flash of sun, attempting to peek through the heavy cloud cover overhead.

And then he spied her.

More specifically, he detected the curl of fingers along the bottom of the stone windowsill, as the lady ran the length of his townhouse, peering briefly into each window she could reach before she moved on to the next.

Val remained completely unnoticed by the oblivious prier.

The prier who spoke to herself, less than quietly at that, as she conducted her even less than stealthy search of his home.

A growl worked its way up his chest.

He tolerated their staring.

He tolerated their whispering and gossip.

But he'd be damned if he put up with their invading his privacy and looking directly in his windows.

The lady reached the end, and then with her hands on her hips, she backed away. "No servants . . ." That whispering came quiet as the young lady rubbed her gloved hands together briskly.

He folded his arms at his chest. "Can I help you?"

With a shriek, the young woman spun, her foot catching a slick patch of ice, and she went flying up, and then came down in what could only be a hard fall.

She landed with a quiet groan.

There'd been a time when he would have raced ahead and helped her to her feet.

He'd neither the energy nor interest in playing the role of gentleman in Polite Society—or for society on the whole, ever again.

"Only if you know what to do with bothersome brothers and sisters and parents," the lady muttered.

He didn't. His father was dead. His mother knew better than to come around. He'd no sisters. A brother whom, but for an occasional exchange when he came by at Christmastide, he'd otherwise not spoken to in several years. "I don't."

"That is unfortunate, because I certainly don't know what to do with them. Marbles." She muttered that last word under her breath, giving her head a shake.

And if he'd been one to lean toward the curious, he'd have asked what in tarnation she meant by the word "marbles."

But he wasn't so curious as to be asking eager questions.

The only thing he was eager to do was be rid of her.

Collecting Lady's reins, he started for the stables.

"Are you the Duke of Aragon?"

Was he the . . . ? He turned back just as the young woman struggled to her feet; the way in which she winced as she brushed off her skirts suggested she'd indeed taken a hard fall. What in hell business could this one—or anyone—possibly have with him? As a rule he avoided all.

But especially strangers.

Apparently, no confirmation was necessary. "I have it on authority you are the duke," the jabberpot continued on, "and as such, I was looking for you."

In her fall, her hood had been knocked back, revealing a lion's mane of midnight-black curls, a bold tangle perfectly suited to the audacious creature before him.

He'd never seen a lady possessed of so many tight ringlets.

Or if he had, they'd always been flawlessly arranged in an elegant coiffure, held back with jewel-encrusted hair combs, and not an untamed mass of tresses that threatened to swallow a slightly too-pointed, faintly freckled face.

"Are you?" she pressed him.

That question cut through his study of the peculiar creature, and it took a moment for Val to register.

"Am I what?" he barked, his voice rough from lack of use, and also from his fury and frustration with life.

Others had run; with the exception of his stubborn butler, all the loyal servants who'd remained on had invariably fled when presented with those fury-encrusted tones.

This one merely smiled. "The Duke of Aragon. Are *you he*?"

He was and wanted her gone. "I am," he said coolly. Val opened his mouth again, prepared to tell her that latter part.

The lady beamed. "Splendid." She punctuated that exclamation with a little clap, as if she truly meant it.

Which was bloody impossible. One, she was a damned stranger. Two, the people he did know and who did know of him, because of his notoriously surly reputation, hardly sought him out. Lord knew his former friends and family had learned to keep their distance.

"I'm sorry," he said. "Who the hell are you?"

Anyone else would have been offended with his crass, harshly barked query.

Not this woman, who very well may have been a half-wit. She dropped a quick curtsy. "I am Lady Myrtle McQuoid." Myrtle McQuoid? With a name like that, the girl's parents clearly hated her. "I do believe we are neighbors."

The McQuoids, the big family next door filled with children of varying ages who always found themselves at their windows staring at his. “Splendid,” he muttered. They’d more spawn.

Lady Myrtle cupped a hand around her ear and leaned in. “What was that?” she called, using that as an invitation to come closer.

She looked to be five feet nothing, and her cloak hung large on her small form, revealing little of the woman under that emerald-green fabric.

And unlike her siblings, who made it a habit of running when he was in sight, this particular spawn came toward him.

Fucking hell.

At his side, Horace cocked his big head in canine confusion. “I feel you on that, pup,” Val said under his breath for his dog’s benefit.

“It sounded as though you said ‘splendid,’” she jawed. Of course she should also prove to be a damned jabberer. “Which is very kind, as I’m quite happy to meet—”

“I was being sarcastic,” he said tightly, attempting to disabuse the ninny of whatever illusions she’d built in her head to erase the fear she seemed to be absent.

The lady frowned. It was the slightest downturn at the corners of her lips, so faint, like it was a wholly unfamiliar movement for those muscles.

But then she smiled and started forward once more. “I’m generally very good at spotting sarcasm.”

“That I doubt,” he said under his breath.

“I’ve been known to be sarcastic myself, sometimes.” She spoke like she thought he should care. “Mrs. Belden insists it is rude, but I believe it to be quite handy to have many different forms of humor . . .”

And perhaps it was that complete confusion that kept him out here conversing with the silly thing. Nay, not conversing. Speaking with people was another activity he’d let die with his wife. Listening. He was, however, listening to the chatterpot . . . which was more than he'd done with, well, *anyone* that he could think of.

"I was not being humorous," he snarled, managing at last to put a nail in the coffin of the unending flow of words falling from her lips.

At his side, Horace took his cue and growled, taking a step forward.

Even with the distance between them, Val spied the way the lady trembled.

Good, she was afraid of Horace. Horace had a nasty bark and growl that he wasn't afraid to use the rare times anyone came near Val, but never had he bitten. Instead, the dog ensured people kept their distance.

Only, the young lady took a step closer, and another . . . and Val narrowed his eyes as it hit him like a long-ago fall he'd suffered from a horse: she was undeterred.

Val rested a hand on top of the enormous creature's head, staying his charge.

She licked her lips. "Is that your . . . dog?"

She displayed the same fear that all did around the lupine wolf dog. Val had always loved the pup, but he loved him all the more for keeping bloody humans away from him. This time proved no exception.

"He doesn't like people," he said brusquely.

Lady Myrtle chewed at the tip of her glove-encased finger, contemplating Horace. "*You're* a person, and he seems just fine with you."

My God, was she stupid, bold, or just a damned innocent? He'd wager she was a combination of the three all rolled together.

"I love dogs," she shared. She continued to make her way over.

"Does he *look* like a dog?" he rumbled, briefly halting her in her tracks.

Horace took up his cue, yapping softly, and there was a greater menace to that bark.

Undeterred, Lady Myrtle McQuoid resumed her march.

She reached his side and angled her head left and then right, peering at Val's dog. "I . . . He has the fur and mannerisms of a dog."

Apparently, she was as good at detecting a rhetorical question as she was at spotting sarcasm.

He'd opened his mouth to regale her with pretend tales of the dog's vicious past when she suddenly dropped to a knee and reached inside the pocket of her cloak.

The lady held out her palm, revealing a Queen's Cake . . .

"He doesn't like strangers or treats." Val bit out each syllable of those words.

Except damned if his loyal dog didn't suddenly turn traitor and trot over, making a liar of Val.

"Nonsense." Lady Myrtle cooed that pronouncement more for Horace than Val himself. "Who wouldn't wish to have a Queen's Cake?" She praised the beast, who looked all the more enormous next to her diminutive form.

"I wouldn't," Val snapped.

"Well, that is just fine, as that means there's all the more for . . ." She paused and looked to Val. "What is his name?"

Val stared confusedly at her.

Surprise filled the lady's saucer-size brown eyes. "Never tell me he doesn't have a name."

"Of course he has a name," he mumbled.

"Then what would it be? I don't think he can tell me." She instantly switched her attention back to Horace, who'd devoured the whole cake and now licked at the crumbs on the side of his mouth. "Not that you aren't the most clever of creatures," she praised, taking the dog gently by his enormous head and touching her tiny, slightly too-pointy nose to the dog's large black one.

Val rocked back on his heels. *My god, the McQuoids' latest daughter is mad.* Along with "stupid," "bold," and "damned naive," he'd throw "mad" into the proverbial mix.

Horace panted, his large, pink tongue coming out as he lapped at the young woman's cheek.

And Val went motionless, the tableau of lady and dog freezing him more than the frigid cold of the winter day could.

Horace's affections and loyalties had always and only been reserved for Val. Nay, that wasn't quite true.

There'd been just one with whom the wolf dog had been playful: the same woman who'd picked him out as a pup and gifted him to Val their first Christmas as a married couple.

And Horace had shown his affections and loyalties to only his mistress and Val. Never any others.

"My sister was adamant he was a wolf," Lady Myrtle was saying, snapping Val from his stupor.

"And you are of a different opinion," he said, not knowing where that retort came from. Confused as to why he engaged with her still.

"You see"—the lady dropped her voice to a whisper—"my sister is something of a storyteller. That is, Cassia. Not Fleur." Once again, she spoke like he should know who in hell these people were, and more . . . as though he should care. "Fleur is just nine. Not that she can't be a storyteller at the age of nine. She can. But that is not her way."

"I don't give a damn about your siblings," he barked, and apparently, he'd found the one person in all the kingdom unafraid of him.

And at last, he managed to kill that effusive smile. It dimmed, and damned if Horace didn't turn a frown his way, too. "Well, that is *quite* rude, Your Grace."

He was rude, was he?

"What in hell were you doing at my windows?" he said tightly.

"Looking for servants. My sister said—" The young woman instantly stopped speaking, clamping her lips in a line and letting her words go unfinished.

Good. At last, he'd silence from her. And he took advantage of it. "I don't care if your sisters like stories. I don't care if they write them, sell them, or anything else for that matter." He looked to his dog.

His dog.

Val patted his thigh once.

Horace cocked his head and remained locked at the McQuoid girl's side.

His planned tirade briefly forgotten, Val slapped his leg a second time—this time harder.

When his *faithful* pup made no attempt to come, Val swallowed a curse and stalked the remaining distance until he towered over lady and dog.

Up close, he appreciated the lady was an even tinier thing than he'd credited. Her curls were an even greater tangle, and her round eyes were even wider, giving her the look of an owl startled from its perch.

Hardly pretty but certainly interesting to look at, in a peculiar way.

Interesting to look at? Val started. Where in hell had that thought come from?

He recoiled. His face flushed.

"Come," he commanded, and his dog whimpered, stepping behind the young woman's skirts.

Val gritted his teeth. This was really enough.

The lady gave him a pitying look, and then leaning close to Horace's pointed grey ear, she whispered something that sounded a good deal like, "Your master is sad. Go be with him . . ." She nudged him lightly with her palm.

Alas, Horace did not budge.

The lady said something else, and at last, the dog trotted over, back to Val's side.

He clenched his teeth all the harder, the muscles of his jaw radiating in painful protest. "Do you know what I do care about, my lady?"

"Your dog?" she ventured.

"Yes." Flummoxed, he tried to right the remainder of his curt argument. "But that wasn't—" He gave his head a hard shake. "That isn't what I was talking about."

"Oh." She tipped her head back so she could more directly meet his eyes—she, the unlikely first person to do so after his wife's passing. That subtle angling of her neck only put her features on prominent display: an elfin nose and slightly too-large ears that peeked out from her hair. She gave those curls a slight shake. "You were saying?"

"I care about trespassers who've invaded my properties and made a pest of themselves," he hissed. He infused as much steel as he could into that pronouncement, and yet, even as he spoke, the lady nodded. "I care about people who peer in my windows and pry." The last words spoken seemed to penetrate.

She widened her eyes. "You are speaking of . . . me?"

Was he . . . ?

With a growl, Val leaned down and stuck his face in hers and snarled. "Are there any other people about, invading my properties and peering in my windows to pry?"

The young miss gasped softly, and she darted her tongue out, trailing it along a seam of thin lips.

At last, he'd frightened her.

Good.

Val, however, wasn't done with Lady Myrtle McQuoid. He wanted her gone not just today . . . but every day beyond this.

"You are not wanted, Lady Myrtle McQuoid. Do not come back here again . . ." He paused for effect, letting the prominent break linger. "Or else."

The lady drew back, pulling away from him.

Immobile with fear? Or rooted there by the same stubbornness she'd displayed this day?

Neither caring nor wishing to find out, he snarled, "Now, go!"

With that, the young woman took off running, tripping and slipping slightly as she went, but moving at a quick pace and managing to keep her footing, an impressive feat with the icy snow coating the cobblestones.

Val stood, staring after her retreating form as it grew smaller and smaller . . . He followed her flight all the way to the front door of her family's property, and then as a servant on the other side of that double doorway drew the panels open and let the lady inside.

And he'd confirmation she was, at last, gone.

For good.

With his nose, Horace nudged Val hard against his knee.

"What?" he asked defensively. "She was a busybody, peering in our windows. I'll not feel badly for running her off." Nay, the only thing he would feel badly about was that he'd entertained the nosy chit as long as he had. "We're better without her sort." Or any sort, for that matter.

He'd come to appreciate surliness and coldness for the armor they provided; they insulated him from people, which kept him safe from feeling anything. Feeling nothing was safer. He'd come to appreciate ennui as the gift it was. Loving and living and laughing had been highly overrated emotions that only left a person crippled with pain.

"Who was that, Your Grace?"

Startled, he peered over his shoulder.

He looked to Jenkins, having failed to hear the older servant's approach. The man was permitted greater freedom than most in the questions he asked. He was one of the few servants whom Val had kept on. The rest he'd scattered to his various estates throughout England. But the old man had come with Dinah from her family's home, and for that Val had remained unable to send him away.

"No one," he said, and it was an honest answer. "It was no one." That was precisely what the peculiar, long-winded creature was to him—nothing. "Why are you out here?" he demanded as he headed for his townhouse.

"I wanted to report to you on the current state of the household." Jenkins limped, managing to keep up.

"And that could not have taken place when I'd come inside?" he asked tightly, adjusting his step slightly to accommodate the fool servant's gout.

"Most of the staff has gone," Jenkins said when they reached the inside. "Only three remain for now: Cook and the footman, Thomas, will stay on. The remainder of the maids will depart in the early-morn hours, Your Grace."

And it was a testament to the older man's place in the household and the length of his tenure that he took the liberty of ignoring the question Val had put to him, and instead issued an enumeration of the staff.

"Good, they should have left a week ago," Val said, stalking—albeit at a leisurely pace—along the corridors, largely doused in the darkness he preferred. "And you should have gone with them." He reached his offices and, drawing the door open, let Horace inside first, then made for the drink cart.

A day like this called for brandy. This time of year invariably did, and had, since his wife's passing. But after the vexing visit from a nosy woman, with her busybody ways, he especially needed a drink more than ever.

The gall of her. Insolent baggage.

Jenkins hovered in the entrance of the room. "I would, however, like to propose"—as he invariably did—"that all be allowed to—"

"No," Val said, already anticipating the *suggestion*.

"Remain on."

"It is Christmas." That godforsaken, most hated, heinous time of year—for Val. The last thing he cared to have about was anyone, family or staff. Not at a season where people were invariably cheerful and joyous and all things he'd never be, and never wanted to be, again. "You should be with your family."

The butler bowed his head. "As you wish, Your Grace."

And executing a deep, deferential bow, the servant backed out of the rooms, drawing the doors shut behind him and leaving Val completely and blessedly alone.

As he wished it.

Jenkins well knew the happiness that had once rung in these rooms, and the darkness that had come after Dinah's death.

Jenkins no doubt remained on as he did because he perceived his master was broken and lonely.

What Jenkins, however, did not and would never realize was that all Val craved, the only thing he now wished for in this world, was to be left completely and truly alone.

And with all but a handful of his staff taking their leave this evening, Val would have that blessed solitude . . . if even just for a short, precious while.

Chapter 3

There'd been no servants.

At least not that Myrtle had been able to see during her inspection of the duke's windows.

She'd been able to assess only the lower level with its floor-to-ceiling crystal panes.

But she'd seen enough to gather those windows had revealed not only no servants but also furniture draped in white sheets, indicating there'd be no need for servants because the rooms were covered.

Not that that meant the Duke of Aragon had killed his staff.

Except, as much as it pained Myrtle to agree in any way with her sister, or give credence to any story she told, Myrtle could and would readily admit—at least to herself—that the frosty, rude duke she'd met that morn was certainly a reasonable suspect.

He'd been determined to terrify her.

Or perhaps that was just his natural way?

But was he a killer . . . ?

He'd likely want her to believe that.

But he kept a pup, and the dog had been devoted . . .

Such weren't the actions of a murderer.

Unless he fed his victims to his dog, as her sister had suggested . . .

"Stop," she muttered to herself.

Alas, seated and partaking in dessert, she could have stood amidst the pastries and puddings and cakes and danced a jig before her family, and still gone unseen for the activity at the enormous, lace-covered rectangular table.

The McQuoids, from her cousins to her siblings to her parents and her aunt and uncle, were all engrossed in their discourse.

Each one of them excitedly discussing the journey they'd make to Scotland on the morrow.

Dropping her elbow on the table, Myrtle rested her chin atop her palm and stared morosely off into the distance.

At what point had the family who so loved London in the wintertime ceased wishing to make their holiday memories here?

At what point had she become the sole McQuoid bent on maintaining their memories of this place?

Seated beside her, Dallin, her eldest brother and the future Earl of Abingdon, leaned in. "Why so glum? Missing Mrs. Belden's? Or envying Arran for his travels?"

"Oh, hush," she muttered, giving him a light kick under the table. It was easy enough for him, a man with full freedom to make light of her circumstances these past years. "The only way I'd envy Arran is if he were journeying to this very townhouse for Christmas."

Dallin ruffled the top of her head much the way he had when she was a small girl, fluffing those ridiculous curls that her mother and Mrs. Belden had tried in vain to tame.

In an attempt at nonchalance, she dipped the edge of her spoon into her fluted crystal bowl and took a bite of vanilla pudding. "What do you know of our neighbor?"

Dallin puzzled his brow.

"The Duke of Aragon," she clarified, clearing a second bite of pudding.

Suddenly, her brother widened his eyes. "Ahh."

Do not indulge him. Do not . . . do not . . .

Alas, she'd always been hopeless at hiding her curiosity, and her eldest brother, along with her eldest sister, knew it.

"'Ahh,' what?"

Dallin leaned in. "I take it Cassia has gotten in your ear?"

Her shoulders sagged, and she leaned in. "I knew it was rubbish," she spoke in a loud enough whisper to be heard over the commotion of her family's lively discussion.

"Oh, no," Dallin said in grave tones.

Her smile quavered. "N-no?"

Because Dallin might delight in making her mad, but he wasn't the storyteller Cassia had always been.

"I've never met the fellow personally, but Aragon's wife died some years ago."

Her heart stuttered. "He is a widower?" she whispered. And a very young one at that. He couldn't be more than thirty years old. If that. No wonder he was so very miserable.

Dallin nodded. "No one really knows the details. Only that it was sudden. They left London, and only the duke returned. They say he went half-mad, killing his servants."

"If he went half-mad, it would mean he loved his wife very deeply," she said softly.

Her brother snorted. "Or that he carries guilt for whatever fate she met . . ." Dallin let that linger there before picking up his claret and turning his attention to their cousin Brone, seated at his left shoulder.

And once more, Myrtle found herself forgotten. Only this time, she was grateful for it. For the remainder of the gathering, and then alone, all the way to her chambers, she was allowed to replay in her mind everything her siblings had shared about the duke.

Surely they were outlandish, outrageous rumors and tales concocted by people who actually had no idea what fate had befallen the Duchess of Aragon. And in the absence of facts, there were invariably gossips, happy to fill the void with salacious rumors and tall tales.

A short while later, changed into her nightgown, Myrtle slipped under the heavy coverlet and stared overhead.

No matter how much she burrowed into the blanket, the cold gripped her.

Sleep eluded her.

Memories throughout the day persisted.

Plink.

She blinked back the sharp sting of pain of water striking her eye.

What in blazes?

She opened her eyes and noted those details that, in the light of day, had escaped her notice: the enormous—nearly three feet across—wet stain . . . directly overhead.

Myrtle cursed.

The same moisture falling slowly from the ceiling had turned her fresh pillow and sheets wet.

This was why they were leaving, after all.

This right here.

It didn't do anything to make her feel any better.

Because they were leaving.

Neither her family nor the staff had bothered to suggest Myrtle seek out more comfortable chambers. But then, that would have required those same people to *care* enough.

Suddenly besieged by the urge to cry, she swung her legs over the side of her bed and jumped down.

The cold of the floor immediately met her.

A cold made all the worse by the fact that she was soaking wet.

Shivering, her teeth chattering, Myrtle headed for her armoire.

Her largely empty armoire.

Shedding the damp garment, she let it fall to the floor and traded it for a simple, white cotton nightdress.

Her teeth still chattering, Myrtle fished past the remaining garments hanging from neat little hooks within, most of the dresses and items better suited for spring and summer than the unrelenting winter cold that would meet them in Scotland, bypassing gown after gown before reaching the fur-lined cloak that had been left behind.

A gift from her parents, who, in Myrtle's absence, had seemed to forget that above all else, she despised fur-trimmed garments, a luxuriant comfort of man that animals had to give their lives for.

Myrtle stared a long while at the garment, recalling the very day she'd been given the gift.

Her siblings had laughed and rolled their eyes at such a response last Christmas when she'd unwrapped the package.

Her parents had only half listened.

They'd already resumed talk about some piece of gossip or another, or the holiday fare they'd have that day. Or really, anything and everything that didn't have a jot to do with Myrtle or what she felt or cared about.

Just like everything else about her they'd forgotten, too: what made her laugh. What made her sigh, and those things that filled her with fury—activities like hunting and the senseless slaughter of animals for her garments. That, when there were plenty enough of garment choices that didn't require such sacrifice on those creatures' part.

Or mayhap they'd never really known anything about her.

Mayhap no one ever had.

Giving her head a shake, dislodging the useless self-pitying musings, Myrtle yanked the article out of the armoire and, sending a silent apology to the animal who'd been slaughtered in the name of style, tossed the garment around her shoulders.

Immediately enfolded in a wonderful warmth, she burrowed deep within the folds of the cloak, hating to admit, even in silence and only to herself, that there was something to be said for converting those skins to a garment, after all. That it turned out there was a benefit to lining one's clothes with that fur.

She grabbed a pair of slippers at the bottom of the armoire and pulled on the silvery, shimmery articles. They pinched her toes, and her foot strained out the side.

And yet the discomfort of the poor fit was a good deal better than the stinging ice cold of the floor under her bare feet.

Pausing only to gather up the velvet sack at her bedside that contained the precious-to-her minerals she'd collected through the years, Myrtle set off in search of an alternate chamber to seek out sleep that night.

A room with a roof that didn't leak steadily enough to soak her bed and kill her by morn from the freezing cold of it.

"Unless that hasn't been part of their plan, too," she muttered as she made her way down the hall, a corridor blanketed in quiet as her kin slept, with only the dancing flames of the long tapered candles to keep her company. Perhaps they wanted her to be absolutely miserable so that she'd cease complaining about the fact that they were leaving for the holiday and beginning the long journey to their family seat in Scotland.

Of course, all that would have required extensive thought on their part about Myrtle, and simply put, given these past four years, she didn't much see that as being a driving force in their decision to let her rest her head in bed, one bad storm away from floating off like some gilded piece of flotsam.

Nay, it was more likely they'd simply done what they did best where she was concerned: forget her.

Myrtle bypassed room after room where her siblings now rested.

At one point, she'd have absolutely sought out her elder sister's chambers and invited herself in. Cassia would have complained, as elder sisters were wont to do where younger sisters were concerned. But she'd have allowed her to remain—grudgingly . . . and ordered her quiet, and to quit squirming.

Her youngest siblings, still in the nursery as they were, would hardly have a bed for Myrtle. The lone small bed in that room not for the babes in the family was reserved for the nursemaid.

Myrtle reached the stairwell that led abovestairs to a row of guest chambers where her aunt, uncle, and cousins now slept.

That was the thing about being home . . . Everything was familiar in the household one grew up in, from which family member occupied which room at the holidays to which chambers were always vacant.

Seeking out one of those vacant ones, Myrtle let herself inside.

She blinked several times to adjust her vision to the pitch-black within. Without so much as the benefit of the intermittent candles that lined the halls, an unnatural dark blanketed the room. Myrtle hung at the entrance of the guest chambers a long while. A very long while.

She despised being alone.

And tucked away in the last room of the forgotten end of the hall, away from her McQuoid cousins and siblings, there was no doubting she'd be well and truly alone for the night. More than half tempted to return to her soaking bed, she hung there, considering her options.

Creeeeak.

Somewhere within the household a lone floorboard groaned. Her heart jumping, and she along with it, Myrtle shut the door and moved deeper into the room.

And instantly regretted it.

Stretching a hand into the inky void of night's hold, she searched around for the imagined ghosts she'd always feared as a girl to the point that her eldest brother and sister had teased, having fun at her fear of the dark.

They'd expect her to be afraid still.

Only, she wasn't a small child.

She was a grown woman on the cusp of making her Come Out.

That silent reminder came more for herself, an attempt for the logical part within to take hold and shake free of the child's fears she carried.

Drawing deeper within the folds of her cloak, she rubbed her hands together and marched over to the bed. At some point the servants had draped the furnishings in stark white sheets, and the fabric outlined the frames of the pieces about the room, lending an eerie look to those articles. They were like ghosts, reaching their arms out to her . . .

For her . . .

"Stop it," she said, loudly into the quiet.

There are no ghosts, and there are none of the bodachs, those old Scottish hobgoblins her eldest siblings had terrified her with tales of.

Childhood nightmares and legends were in the past. She'd had four years to do what her parents had sent her away to do—grow up. To stop behaving like a hoyden, and to stop being so gullible as to believe the yarns her siblings spun.

"I'm not a child. I'm not a child." She muttered that mantra as she felt the bedding, searching for a hint that the roof overhead had so failed this mattress and pillows and coverlets, too.

A cold lingered upon the fabric of the down coverlet, but only a natural chill from the night and not the wet from a leaking roof that had thoroughly soaked her own pillow and parts of her bed.

Alas, it appeared even the bones of this house were set on making her miserable: only her chambers had suffered.

More than a little regretful at finding it so, and also finding no reason to leave and swallow her pride and curl up with Cassia so she didn't have to be alone, Myrtle drew back her hand.

Her eyes still fought against the dark, and her mind still struggled with the eerie ring of silence that hung like a phantom specter in the quiet.

Shaking all the more, fear adding an extra intensity to her trembling, Myrtle made a straightaway for the windows. Tripping over her skirts in her haste and then swiftly righting herself, she continued crashing ahead and grabbed the curtains and tossed them open.

Instantly, the nearly full moon's bright glow sent light streaming into the previously black chambers, and she drew in a slow, quiet, relieved breath.

All but a sliver remained from that otherwise perfect orb, allowing for a full illumination of the rooms and also casting light out over the household directly across the street.

Unbidden, her eyes crept over to the Duke of Aragon's property.

The moon played off his townhouse, too, revealing gleaming crystal windows and heavy curtains all perfectly drawn to keep out light . . .

Or strangers? a voice whispered.

Even as she silently urged herself to not give in to the fantastical, to not feed the irrational thoughts that at night, when the world slept, took on an even greater life and vividness.

Alas, she was helpless to stop the thoughts from rolling through her head: her family's whispered warnings about the duke.

"He went mad . . ."

"They say he collects one log for each of his victims . . ."

"Why, he practices his swing . . ."

Just then, out of the corner of her eye, she caught a flash of movement. Her heart racing, Myrtle followed that flicker, and she froze.

Tall and attired in the same midnight shades as when they'd met that morn, there could be no mistaking the bear of a figure strolling through his courtyard. He strode with a brisk purpose; against his shoulder rested . . .

Myrtle gasped. "Surely not," she said, her voice shaking slightly from cold but mostly from fear. She pressed the tip of her nose to the frosted windowpanes. Still unable to catch a clear glimpse of him, she rubbed her palm frantically over the glass, scraping away the ice fragments so she might see clearly.

Because then she'd have confirmation that her mind had run amok with fear this night, and irrationality had shoved out all the grand logic and reason she'd worked on honing these past years.

She froze.

Only, her eyes did not deceive.

Her gaze homed in on the gleaming metal propped against that enormous shoulder.

An axe.

"He's killed servant after servant . . ."

Stop it.

He was absolutely *not* a killer.

He had a dog.

Of all the uncertainties in the world, the one thing one could always rely on were those people who loved pups.

And the Duke of Aragon was a man who clearly loved his dog.

Albeit a wolflike dog certainly capable of tearing a person's limbs off if it so wished, and his master so commanded. But that was neither here nor there.

She'd already gone over all this in her mind.

He was a lonely fellow. Surly and brooding and angry.

But that hardly made the fantastical tales told by her sister about a man who'd killed his staff true.

And furthermore, being lonely was certainly a sentiment she could relate to all too well. Why, she could actually relate to him very—

Just then, the duke stopped, and his gaze went flying up.

Myrtle froze, her heart hammering wildly as she was held motionless by a piercing stare that, even with all the space separating them, managed to penetrate her.

That frosty, harsh, and unforgiving glare as powerful hundreds of paces away as it had been a single step from his wrath.

With a slow, methodical intent to his movements, the gentleman turned the axe over in his hands, and raised it slowly—

Gasping, Myrtle raced across the room and dived onto the bed. Wrestling her way under the white sheet, she burrowed under the covers and lay there.

Tomorrow, she'd leave. Nay, in just a few short hours, she and her family would be loaded into the carriages, and they'd make the long journey away from this household and onward for Scotland.

Only this time, unlike all the times before it, as Myrtle lay shivering under the covers, as she drifted off to sleep, she found herself cowardly eager to put some distance between herself, this place, and the enigmatic duke across the way.

Chapter 4

Through the years, Val's relationship with God had been rather complex.

As a boy, he'd attended mass with his parents, but the Lord and Savior had been more of an otherworldly, unapproachable being to whom Val had not felt a personal connection.

He'd not, however, failed to believe in the all-powerful God—until that gruesome carriage accident nearly four years to the date.

That moment with his young wife—their babe in her belly—staring sightlessly up at the dark night sky had been the instant he'd ceased to believe. With the snow falling furiously, those flakes clinging to her brows and lashes while her eyes had remained wide open in death, Val had known there was no one overhead, after all.

For how could a supreme creator capable of moving mountains and making miracles have done nothing to stop the death of a woman with the purest, kindest heart?

He'd gone through the expected motions of Polite Society, holding a funeral with a vicar speaking in solemn tones, the words of a hymn intending to bring comfort but only strengthening Val's sense of an absolute absence of any man seated atop a throne, in control of all, and deserving of prayer and praise.

Yes, Val had ceased to believe.

Until now.

Now, with winter snow already beginning to fall and his neighbors and their noisy, nosy brood, and their extended relations, equally noisy and nosy, all scrambling inside carriages, he thought he might have been wrong.

Mayhap there was a God, after all.

They were leaving.

And by the stream of servants filing into conveyances, it was all of them.

Yea, and here he'd believed nothing good remained in this world. Only, with the McQuoids on their way to wherever it was they traveled during the holiday season, it didn't really much matter to him. It didn't matter to him at all. Just that they were leaving.

There'd be no noses pressed to the window or constant stares directed his way.

Or young women peering inside his windows and chattering his ears off and attempting to steal the affections of his dog.

Despite himself, he did a search of the assembled kin, the men attired in black cloaks, the women dressed in matching shades of green as though it were a requirement expected of them as McQuoid women. With the snow beginning to fall rapidly, they had the look of a gaggle of ducks set upon by a wolf as they ran in frantic circles, confused into chaos.

He couldn't have picked her out of that lot of staff and family had he wanted to.

Which he absolutely did not.

Why, then, did he feel a sense of reluctance?

"Only because I want to ensure they're gone," he muttered to himself.

Because they were always a nuisance, but they were increasingly a bother when all their kin assembled, each clamoring for a glimpse of him, for reasons he couldn't understand. Nor cared to.

It was why even now he, who cared about absolutely nothing and no one, watched on with a feeling as close to glee and relief as he expected to ever again experience, as a ridiculous line of some twelve or so carriages were packed with people . . . and then rolled off with one following after another.

He stared until the last had left, until they were, each and every one of them, gone, and then promptly dismissed for the day the handful of servants who'd stayed on.

So that Val was well and truly, and thankfully, alone.

KnockKnockKnock.

That gratitude proved as short as had the happiness in his life.

With a curse, he dug his fingertips against his temples and pressed . . . and prayed.

KnockKnockKnockKnock.

Alas, the figure on the other side of that door proved stubborn.

KnockKnockKnock.

The interloper in his peace and quiet was decidedly not leaving.

Val marched over to the door and yanked it open hard enough that the figure on the other side was left with his hand poised midknock. A jovial smile wreathed the younger man's face.

"Answering our own doors again, which can only mean one thing . . . You've sent your servants off for the holiday season."

As much a jabberer as the new neighbor who'd cornered Val yesterday, this one always proved just as hard to shake. As such, he'd not correct his brother and inform him that he'd a butler with him still, or that he'd given the older man the mornings and afternoons off.

Opening the door had been a mistake.

Val made to close that heavy panel.

Alas—

"Whoa there, big brother." Sidney, his only sibling and the future heir to his dukedom, managed to duck under Val's arm and let himself inside.

"Aren't you traveling?" Val muttered and, giving up on all hope of Sidney taking himself off, made for his offices. Sidney always left London long before now.

Nearly of a like height, his brother, younger by two years, fell into step beside him. "In other words, why am I here?" His brother made a *tsk*ing sound with his tongue, preventing Val from answering. Not that Val had any intention of doing so. "Happily for you, I'm not due to leave for another five days, and you know I always pay a visit at the Christmastide Season."

Yes, he did know it. With his brother later than usual, Val had simply thought—hoped?—his brother had gone on his way, and that Val would be spared the jovial visit with talk of family and togetherness at the holidays.

"But what kind of brother would I be if I didn't pay my usual visit and attempt to convince you to come along for the fun?" His brother flung an arm around Val's shoulders, pulling a grunt from him.

Sidney laughed.

Because Sidney always laughed. Their family had told tales through the years of the marquess having been born with a smile and a giggle.

And Val? Well, Val had once been of a like temperament. Always ready with a smile, even more ready with a laugh.

And why shouldn't he have been? He'd been born to a happy family—granted, with a devoted father who'd died too soon.

And then, he, luckiest in life in so many ways, had found love and a like joy with his wife.

Just like that, the dark was ushered in.

With a growl, he shrugged off his brother's touch.

To his brother's credit—or mayhap it was more accurately a testament of his stubbornness—Sidney gave no outward indication that he'd noted that rejection of his brotherly affection. "I know what you are thinking," his only sibling in the world began.

"I rather doubt that," Val muttered. For if Sidney were aware of what he was thinking, he'd not have bothered with coming.

"That I should give up on the hope of you joining me," his brother went on, impressive in his ability to ignore Val's coldness. "Alas, big brother, I know one of these days that you will come, and my efforts will not have been in vain."

They reached Val's offices, and even as his brother stopped outside the room, clearly awaiting a response—nay, more specifically, clearly awaiting an indication that this was the year when his efforts would be met with a different outcome.

Val, however, continued on his course, making for his sideboard, where he fetched a bottle of fine French brandy and a single snifter. Carrying his provisions over to his desk, and without bothering to offer his younger brother a drink of his own, Val poured.

Undeterred, Sidney joined him, settling into the winged seat opposite him with his usual smile in place. "I believe you want to come."

"You also believe in gold at the end of rainbows and fairies and—"

"Ah, point taken! But what a better life it is when one believes in magic and goodness."

And what a miserable one it was to have lost the love of one's life and realized goodness was fleeting and magic didn't exist.

Val stared emptily into his glass before giving his head a firm shake. He tossed back another swallow.

"I've no intention of coming to spend the Christmastide Season," he said bluntly so his brother could disabuse himself, and their mother, on whose behalf he'd no doubt come time and time again.

And with that, Sidney's usually smiling, lighthearted demeanor ceded the way to an unusual-for-him solemnity. He leaned forward in his seat and turned a hand up. "Mother wishes for you to be there."

There it was. The first his brother had ever acknowledged that in all the years since that tragic winter's night.

And Val expected she did wish for him to come.

Without fail, she arranged and threw the most lavish, the most exuberant Christmastide holiday party. The house filled with guests, distant kin and close friends alike; it was a celebration that, as a boy and young man, he'd always looked forward to enthusiastically.

It was also the affair his late wife had looked forward to as well.

It had been the place where they'd first met.

The event at which they'd fallen in love.

And then vowed to someday continue the tradition of spreading Christmastide joy to—

Feeling his brother's gaze on him, Val shook his head hard.

Sidney's eyes were still serious, his expression more than faintly knowing. "Mother regrets very much what happened, Val," he said quietly. "She feels to blame."

"Of course she's not to blame," he responded in terse tones meant to end this discourse, one that they'd never had, and one Val didn't wish to have. Because he preferred to let the hell of that day live on in his own memory. The misery and suffering of it belonged to Val, exclusively. What his mother, or anyone else, for that matter, felt was irrelevant. "So do feel free to reassure her; I do not hold her responsible." It was Val who was to blame.

Just as it was Val who'd lost everything that night.

"But she believes she is," Sidney persisted, unrelenting and refusing to let the matter go. "And she believes your failure to come 'round or leave this . . . house is because of her."

"My failure to leave this house comes from the fact that I want to be here," he said, taking another swallow of his drink.

"You should come—"

"Why?" he asked, cutting his brother off. "Why should I go?" He didn't let Sidney have a chance to answer. "Because I should somehow care more that Mother feels badly that my wife died on a carriage ride to her house party? Because I should don a grin"—and a fake one, at that—"and take part in the joyous affair so that other people might feel better?" Val sank his elbows on the edge of his desk and leaned forward.

"You did not die that day, Val."

He recoiled, his entire body jolting away from that quiet pronouncement from his brother.

Val sucked in a slow breath through his teeth. "But I did, Sidney. I did."

And someday, his brother would likely fall in love and feel the unending joy Val had known for the brief time he'd been wed . . . and would know. And, God willing, would also not know the agony that came in losing one's partner in life.

Sidney tapped the arm of the chair, drumming his fingertips along the gleaming black leather in time to the ormolu clock that ticked away the passing seconds. "There's nothing I can say to convince you to—"

"There is nothing."

Still, even with that abrupt rejection, Sidney remained affixed to his seat. Ever the eternal optimist, the fellow filled with hope, as Val had one time been.

"One of these years, you will change your mind, brother," Sidney finally said, and then with a reluctance to his movements, he stood. "And I will be ever so glad to see you there." Reaching inside his cloak, he withdrew a small, wrapped package. "Happy Christmas to you, brother," he said, setting down the gift he always arrived with this time of year.

Val inclined his head.

Happy Christmas . . .

That warm salutation hovered in the air, even as his brother took his leave and beyond, and Val sat there in silence with those two words.

Happy Christmas?

It was a salutation issued every winter by his brother. And yet, Sidney failed either to know or to care that since Dinah's passing, there was nothing, and would be nothing, worth celebrating.

With Sidney at last gone, Val opened the deep bottom right drawer and deposited that gift alongside the three others tucked away there.

Letting out a boisterous bark, Horace bounded over and nudged his head inside, nosing the packages there. Each wrapped as they'd been in a similar packaging, each decked with a gold velvet bow.

"Stop," Val muttered, and the dog immediately complied, falling back on his haunches and releasing a small, piteous whine.

Val pushed the drawer filled with his brother's gifts closed, and picking up his snifter, he downed his drink.

Setting it down with a *thunk*, Val headed to the stables to saddle his mount in search of the peace that he could find only in riding alone.

Chapter 5

One thing Myrtle had never known or experienced in life was absolute quiet.

With many talkative siblings and equally voluble parents, and even noisier aunts, uncles, and cousins, it'd been an impossibility.

And then she'd gone off to Mrs. Belden's. Though there'd been constant lessons on etiquette and the rules of propriety, all of which required ladies to learn quiet, modulated tones . . . expecting those same students, who'd numbered some fifty girls together, to be quiet had been as unlikely as teaching a stubborn sun to love the English skies.

That morning, however, Myrtle rose to find the room still dark and the house as quiet as it had been when she'd made her journey through the halls in search of dry bedding.

Yawning, she scrubbed at eyes still blurring from sleep.

Or mayhap it was that the cold had awakened her. Shivering, she burrowed under her blankets and in the folds of her cloak, searching in vain for an elusive warmth.

Alas, today was the morn they would leave.

With a sigh, she struggled onto her elbows and swung her legs over the side of the bed.

"Withers and whiskers," she cursed as she rushed for the door. "That is deuced cold." Miserably so.

Heading back for her chambers, Myrtle made her way through the halls so she could seek out the warmth of the fire that had surely been stoked through the night and change into warmer garments for the day's travel.

The house would be all abustle with the staff seeing to the final preparations for their departure this day.

The breakfast table would be filled with as much noise, as her kin all competed to be heard over one another.

Or perhaps there'd be no breakfast . . . because the staff would all depart this day, too. Unlike in the past, when some would remain on when the house was closed up, with Mr. Phippen and his building set to commence, there'd be no servants to stay.

Loving the breakfast meal as she did, inside Myrtle wept, and her stomach added a mournful grumble of sorrow at the sheer—but also very likely—possibility that they'd not break their fast until they were on their way.

Only, as she walked, more and more quiet reached her.

There were no servants racing to and fro with garments or items that had almost been left behind.

There was no parent overseeing the final preparations, calling out reminders to their eldest children the same way they would and did for the youngest McQuoids.

Myrtle's steps slowed, and she came to a complete standstill.

In fact, there was . . . nothing.

Absolutely nothing.

The candles had been doused.

At some point since she'd made the trek to a different wing of the house, white sheets had been laid over the remaining furnishings.

The quiet that had hung in the nighttime air as her only company when she'd sought out her guest chambers proved the same silent friend to greet her that morn.

Or mayhap it wasn't morn?

Reaching her rooms, Myrtle pressed the handle and let herself in.

Her bed had since been covered with those same white linens.

Frowning, she headed for her vanity, and peeling back the edge of the sheet, she consulted the gold and porcelain there. The painted couple who framed the circular timepiece connected fingers, holding hands as if they were all that held the crystal cylinder aloft.

She leaned down and peered at the numbers there.

"Nine o'clock," she said aloud, and unlike the habit she'd developed over the years of speaking to herself, this time there was a deliberateness to that pronouncement, one that came from the need to hear herself so that she might hear *something*.

"Mama?" she called out, her voice an answering echo. "Papa?"

Only more silence met her calls.

And somewhere amongst her search of the main floors and the hall where her extended family slept and then the freezing kitchens, devoid of the usual fire that blazed in the stoves, it hit her—why . . . they'd left. Her family had left for Scotland.

Surely not.

Her teeth clanking from the cold, Myrtle frantically rubbed her hands together, and heading to the nearest window, she brushed a palm over the frosted pane.

A light snow had begun to fall, coating the ground with a dusting of white.

Only . . . is it really so impossible to believe your family forgot you? You've been all but forgotten for the past four years.

Myrtle stood there, tapping the tip of her right foot on the cold earthen floor as she let the truth of her family's departure and her circumstances sink in.

They had not only left . . . They had left *her*. They'd gone on to Scotland to hold the revelries that were always reserved for London.

And here she was, with only herself for company.

No noisy cousins about.

No vexing siblings.

No always-correcting-her parents.

And Myrtle slowly ceased tapping her toes, and a slow smile turned her lips up.

She was alone here in London.

With a jubilant shout, she took off running; bypassing her own rooms, she made for Cassia's chambers. Not breaking stride, she threw the white-paneled double doors wide.

Unlike Myrtle's room, fairly littered with pots to catch the moisture dripping from the ceiling, her sister's chambers were perfectly dry. Running headlong for the four-poster bed in pink satin, Myrtle launched herself onto the top; the mattress bounced, and she rolled onto her back, flinging her arms out wide as she burrowed into the comfortable bedding, chilled from only the silky material and not the same deluge of roof water that had thoroughly soaked her own bed.

Of course they'd return.

They would realize shortly that she was here and be forced to turn the carriages back.

Depending on how long it was before they did, why, her family might have no choice except to remain in London for the holiday season.

Until then, she was alone.

On the heels of her initial giddiness came rushing in the reality of her circumstances.

She was . . . alone.

There were no siblings or servants about.

There was just her.

And suddenly she was unsure whether to find herself excited about her solitary state . . . or filled with fear.

"Do not be a ninny," she muttered into the quiet, and unlike most all the times before when she'd spoken to herself out of habit, now she did so as much to hear the sound of her own voice so there wasn't this absolute silence. "You are not a child." Myrtle popped up and headed across the room, over to her sister's armoire. "You are a grown woman, due to have your first London Season," she reminded herself as she searched the many dresses that had been left behind.

Because unlike Myrtle, who'd been sent to finishing school and lived away from home, Cassia resided here year-round.

Frowning, she grabbed a sapphire dress, opting for one cut in velvet, and hugging it close to her chest, she wandered over to the windows and stared out.

In the short time between her flight from the kitchens to Cassia's chambers, the snow had begun to fall in earnest.

The streets below proved as empty as her household.

There were no passersby.

There were no street sweepers.

Or servants.

It was as though all of London had been abandoned.

And that absolute stillness below added a whole other layer of isolation to her current circumstances.

She shivered, from the fear of being alone as much as from the wind battering relentlessly against the window.

And then she spied it.

A sliver of movement.

Nay, not "it."

Rather . . . him.

Surly and rude, and more than a bit boorish, the Duke of Aragon.

Myrtle rubbed her palm over the frosted glass to better get a look at him, not even bothering to attempt to conceal her interest or her study.

With the snow and the space between them, he'd never notice her.

He wasn't friendly. Far from it. In fact, with all his growling and grumbling, he'd been quite rude.

With everything her brother had revealed at dinner the previous evening, however, the gentleman was certainly entitled to his misery, and to being miserable.

And she tended not to opt to spend her time with people who were miserable.

However, with all of London gone but for the two of them, beggars could hardly be choosers.

As such, when the gentleman guided his horse through the two gates that hung open outside his properties and climbed astride the enormous creature, setting the mount off at a quick canter, Myrtle hurried as best as she was able through her morning ablutions, and then she grabbed some volumes off her bookshelf, headed down the stairs . . . and out the door.

❄ ❄ ❄

As much as Val despised Christmas and the company of people, that was equal to how much he loved riding his horse.

At the heart of the London Season, he took care to ride well before the sun rose, at the ungodly hours when people slept and he could be assured that he wouldn't have to suffer through anyone's company.

But the winter was different.

During the winter, he was free to ride without a worry of the hour or running into people for the simple reason that London was empty.

Which he did, and did often.

And yet, as he returned from his morning ride, dismounting outside the front of his residence, he found London wasn't so very empty, after all.

And what was worse . . . for a second time that day, he found himself . . . with company.

Unblinking, Val stared at his stables.

The young lady sat just outside them on an overturned crate that, since his absence, she appeared to have dragged over and fashioned into a makeshift seat for herself.

With a book held between her fingers and all her attention on her reading, the minx may as well have been at the Temple of the Muses bookshop rather than seated outside in the midst of a rapidly increasing snowstorm.

She licked the tip of her gloved index finger and turned the page.

Val narrowed his eyes.

"What the hell are you doing here?" he barked.

The lady emitted a little shriek; the book flew from her fingers, shooting upward before landing with a thump, muffled by the snow, on the earth.

She hopped up. "Your Grace," she greeted with a confusing amount of warmth and eagerness.

At his presence?

Most feared coming 'round him for a host of reasons.

Those who did—his butler and, on occasion, Val's brother—did so out of obligation.

"I asked what the hell you are doing here," he demanded for a second time when the lady continued to stand there with that wide, double-dimpled smile on her plump cheeks.

She rescued her book and then held it aloft, waggling the small leather volume his way. "I was reading."

His brow dipped.

Reading?

"Reading," she confirmed with a nod, silently answering the question that had existed solely in his mind.

"Not that I haven't read it before," she prattled. "I have. Several times." Skipping over with a jauntiness in her step, she turned the book his way once more and stared expectantly at him as he read the title.

He skimmed his eyes over the gold-embossed words there. "*Pride and Prejudice*," he read aloud. "By . . . a Lady?" Val looked at her.

She stole a furtive look about. Who did she think was here? Lord knew it appeared her family was not coming to his rescue anytime soon.

"May I confide something?" she whispered when she'd returned her attention to him.

"I'd rather you didn't," he muttered.

"You must not share this with anyone," she continued, "but since we are friends now—"

"We are not."

"I trust you'll honor my confidence." She paused as if for effect. "The author . . . is a woman."

"I gathered as much by the inscription."

"By the name of Miss Austen," she added over his droll interruption.

Lady Myrtle's smile widened in what he would have taken as an impossible feat; that was the sole reason he found himself focused on that grin, and not the way it lit her eyes or—he swallowed hard. What the hell were these thoughts?

"She and her family are neighbors of my aunt Leslie and uncle Francis, and it was during my summer visit with them in '09 that I learned I'd be sent off to boarding school," she shared. "Miss Austen stumbled upon me, crying at the lake between our families' properties."

Unbidden, an image entered of Myrtle as she'd been, with her cheeks stained with tears and her eyes swollen from crying, and his gut clenched, and he didn't want to think of her sad. What was this? He didn't want to think of her . . . in any way.

"And then," Myrtle went on in wondrous tones, ones that demonstrated an obliviousness to his turbulent thoughts, "she shared with me that she, too, was sent to boarding school, and that it would not be forever. She told me good came of it, because she was able to nurture her love of writing." Myrtle paused only long enough to catch a breath. "I would share my Austen collection with you. Not that she is my Miss

Austen, per se," the lady went on, and he had a sudden and familiar-around-her urge to dig his fingers into his temples. "She belongs to everyone. That is, the *gift* of her writing does," she said without even pausing for a breath between those two ridiculous statements.

The gift of her writing. What a load of ridiculousness that was.

Lady Myrtle held the book out, all but pressing it against his chest, and then when Val made no attempt to touch that title, she did.

He grunted, automatically snapping it from her fingers.

At his side, Lady neighed loudly.

"You will be most pleased, I suspect, with *Pride and Prejudice*," the young woman said, petting his mount on his nose. "Though you cannot go wrong with *either* of her titles, I assure you. This, however, is my favorite, and as such I always recommend other young women begin with this one."

His brow dipped another fraction. Other young women?

"Not that you're a young woman, per se—"

"I'm not," he said flatly.

"Just that, the extent of my interactions, aside from that with my brothers, has been reserved to discussions with other young ladies. I'd recommend Miss Austen's works to men, too. That is, other men . . . if I knew of any."

One Christmas, when Val had been a small boy, of mayhap seven or eight years, his father had gifted him a rainbow-painted top with a needle-thin handle. To this day, he remembered the very moment his father had set the child's toy a-spinning. He'd followed its circular dance upon the nursery floor until his eyes had gone crossed and he'd felt dizzy from watching.

This moment with Lady Myrtle McQuoid felt very much like that one.

"You're speechless," the lady said with that same grin in place.

In fact, he might even go out on a limb and wager his coveted privacy and solitude that wide upturn of her lips was their natural state.

"Miss Austen has that effect on women." She paused. "And men," she amended. "As I mentioned—"

"You do not know men aside from your brothers," he snapped, providing the words for her to spare himself from her cheerful chattering.

She beamed. "Precisely. Though I do know you now."

He stared dumbly at her awhile, as it took several long moments of silence for her words to register.

"*We* do not know one another," he finally exploded, shaking the book between them.

"Well, technically we *do* know one another. We've met several times."

My god, she was a headstrong, vexingly obstinate thing.

"Two," he clipped out. "We've met twice."

"Two is more than zero, thereby suggesting we *do* know one another."

Mad. He was going mad.

Or mayhap he'd already descended into full-blown insanity?

There'd been any number of times since his wife's passing when he'd believed himself mad. This proved his actual descent, and all because of a slip of a lady poised between girlhood and womanhood.

"Get out," he snarled, holding her book toward her, wanting her gone.

The lady held her palms up and drew those gloved digits close to her chest. "Oh, no, Your Grace. That is a gift."

"I don't want any gifts, and I don't need them."

"You will want it once you begin reading her." She waggled her eyebrows. "And technically you do need this *particular* gift, as you don't have any copies of Miss Austen and you haven't read her works."

"My l—"

"Please, call me Myrtle."

"I'm not calling you Myrtle."

"Because of propriety. Mrs. Belden would approve."

"Who in hell is . . . ?" He shook his head. "Never mind. Get going."

"So you can read, yes! I will leave you to it." The lady dipped a polite curtsy. "That way when we again meet, we might be able to speak about Miss Bennet and Mr. Darcy?"

"Who?" he blurted.

She gave another waggle of her dark, well-shaped eyebrows. "You'll see. Good day, Your Grace!"

He'd see?

They'd meet again and speak . . . ?

Which meant the chit intended to return.

Which also meant he would be expected to see her again.

All this, when the absolute thing he wished was to not see or be with anyone.

Determined to disabuse her of that fool notion, he stuck his face in hers. "I don't want your company, and I don't want your book. I don't want anyone here. I want to be left alone, and certainly by you. Am I *clear*?"

The only thing clear in that moment was the rapid intake of her breath, highlighted by the little clouds of white she puffed into the winter air.

The lady's smile slipped, and she cleared her throat. "I think you will thank me for that book someday, Your Grace."

"I won't."

"However, I know when I'm not wanted."

That he rather doubted. "Come along, Lady," he gritted, collecting the reins of his mount.

"Of course!" The young woman—Lady Myrtle—hastened to join Val, his horse, and Horace.

Cursing, Val abruptly stopped. "Not you," he barked. "Definitely not you."

The lady immediately came up short. "But you said . . ."

"My horse," he growled.

The young woman drew back, then looked from the horse to Val and then back again at his horse.

Don't ask. Don't indulge her. Don't encourage her.

"What?" he snapped.

"You've named your horse . . . Lady?"

He'd not. Rather, his wife had, and he would have changed his own name to Bartholomew Baldo if it had assured him just one of her smiles.

Myrtle leaned down and assessed Val's mount . . . between his legs. "Er . . . I . . . You do know that your horse is, in fact, a male." As was her way, she didn't allow him a word edgewise. "You see, there"—she straightened and pointed to the flesh dangling from between his legs—"are his male pieces. That is what makes him different from a female. Or, that is what I've heard, anyway."

And with her rambling on with a lecture on male and female horse bits, he didn't know whether to be shocked or horrified or amused.

Amused?

He silently scoffed. Certainly not that. He wasn't one who was entertained by anything. And certainly not anyone. And most decidedly not by *her*.

"I know that my horse is a blasted boy," he snapped as she went to stroke Lady's nose. "And he doesn't like to be stroked there."

Except, as she caught Lady by his snout and touched her nose to his, rubbing the enormous creature in that way, the stallion nudged Myrtle affectionately, leaning into that touch.

Myrtle winged an eyebrow up. "It seems there are two things you don't know about your horse."

"I've already told you," he gritted out. "I *know* he is a male."

He may as well have saved his breath. The lady had already turned all her attention back to the mount, nudging him with her nose, mimicking those movements as if she herself were a horse. All the while, Myrtle cooed and heaped praise upon the fickle creature, who edged ever closer to her.

Val opened his mouth to order her gone, because no one went near his horse, and certainly not strangers.

But something held him back.

The way the sun's rays played with hair so black its edges shimmered blue.

Nay, it was . . . her smile.

It held him entranced, fixed to the ground, his thoughts useless to formulate the coherent and sharp order that would send her fleeing.

Because . . . he'd not seen a smile . . . quite like hers.

There'd been another . . . close.

But this one was even more generously wide, with enormous dimples and two rows of more than slightly crooked teeth.

As if she felt his stare, Myrtle stopped midsentence to Lady. "Oh, dear," she whispered.

Oh, dear, indeed.

She'd caught him staring, gawking like an enamored schoolboy. Which he wasn't. He had been once but would never be again. Even with all that, however, he could not bring himself to look away . . . or formulate a response that would help him save face.

Then Myrtle slapped a horrified palm over her mouth. "I'ff-sumfing-in-my-teef."

It took several silent attempts at deciphering those mumblings to make anything coherent out of her words.

Spinning on her heel, Myrtle presented him with her back and proceeded to—

"Are you digging around your mouth?"

"Yeff."

And then it happened. The muscles of his mouth that had forgotten the proper movement remembered them all over again as a smile formed.

It emerged slow and painful from the effort required of muscles no longer expected to form that expression.

Suddenly, the lady turned, startling the grin from his face.

"Well?" she enjoined.

He shook his head confusedly.

She flattened her lips, revealing an uneven line of perfectly white but decidedly crooked teeth. "Did-I-get-rid-of-it?"

"You did."

She smiled. "Splendid. It isn't in form for a lady to go about with food stuck between her teeth . . ."

As she proceeded on with what he had fast learned was common-for-her prattling, he conceded that he was a deuced scoundrel for having let her believe that lie. Or a coward for having been so desperate to hide the fact he'd been staring captivatedly at her that he'd allowed her to think she'd something in her teeth.

Perhaps he was really just both a coward and a scoundrel.

"No gentleman would wish to wed a woman who is poorly groomed, according to Mrs. Belden . . ."

That name again. "Who in hell is Mrs. Belden?" he asked, having been so lost in thought he'd failed to note when the lady's one-person dialogue had gone so far off the straight and narrow.

"Mrs. Belden," she repeated with the same sense that he should know as she had about her Jane Austen. "She is headmistress of my finishing school." She paused. "My family sent me away." The lady stared expectantly at him. Her eyes, always twinkling with mischief and humor, had gone . . . dark. Like someone had snatched the stars from the night sky, and left a stretch of desolate, inky blackness in their wake.

"I . . . see," he said, because there was something he was supposed to say here, but for the life of him, he couldn't make out what those words should be.

Val of old would have.

Val of old would have erased the sadness and restored the sparkle to eyes meant to shine.

She cleared her throat. "Yes, well, Mrs. Belden is one of the most respected headmistresses in England."

"Are there that many of them in England?"

The lady, failing to detect the playful nature of that question, puzzled her brow. "I . . . do not know. I trust there are a good many."

Humor. It was something that had once come as easy as his own grin, but also a skill that had since faded.

"I've been there for four years."

Ah, so that was why he'd failed to catch sight of her at a window . . . or anywhere.

Lord knew, had she been inhabiting that household across from his, he would have noted her. She would have made a bother of herself in some way.

Why did that thought only elicit another ghost of a smile, and not the surly annoyance that had been there at their earlier meeting?

"Did you . . . enjoy your time there?" Where had that question come from?

"No!" She beamed, her smile like a thousand suns emanating a warmth that managed to penetrate the perpetual cold that gripped him. "I despised every moment."

He grunted. "That should make you smile?"

"Well, you asked a question, and did something more than grunt or"—the lady dropped her voice to a rough, deep, angry growl—"'I see' . . ."

Val frowned. "I don't sound like that."

"No," she agreed. "Your voice is always a touch angrier."

And with that, the lady turned on her heel and hurried off . . . leaving Val, book in hand, staring after her.

He'd not feel guilty. He'd not feel guilty.

She was the one who'd been looking in his windows.

And who'd made a pest of herself.

He'd nothing to feel bad about or for.

And yet, no matter how many times he silently reassured himself that he was in the right, an emotion that felt very much like guilt sat like a stone in his belly as Val came to the shocking discovery that he was capable of feeling, after all.

And he vastly preferred it when he'd felt nothing.

With a curse, Val stomped off, bringing his mount back to the stables and heading indoors . . . with a copy of Jane Austen's *Pride and Prejudice* in hand.

Chapter 6

Kneeling at the kitchen hearth—the cold kitchen hearth—Myrtle assessed the fire.

Or rather, her feeble attempts at a fire.

After all, there'd have to be an actual fire in the hearth to constitute a fire.

The bucket of coal and the lone handful of leftover logs she'd found outside lay in an untidy mess about her.

She sat back on her haunches.

How had she lived in this household, and Mrs. Belden's, and in all her seventeen years never paid attention to just how those fires were made?

It was because she'd been born a lady and never been required to know about things like fires.

And it was a terrible way to have gone through life.

A raise. When her miserable family finally got 'round to remembering they'd left her and came back to collect her, the first thing she intended to exact from them was an assurance that they'd double the wages of every last servant.

Giving up on her futile attempt at building a fire, she turned her thoughts back over to . . . the duke.

He was a surly one, her neighbor.

Even more so than she'd credited.

Yesterday's visit with him had been conducted for several reasons, however. One: she'd been alone and the quiet of the house had left her uneasy. Two: based on the rumors Cassia had shared, Myrtle had wished to verify whether he was a safe enough fellow to be around. And three: if her brother had been correct in what *he'd* shared about the duke, well, then the gentleman had to be deuced lonely, and as such, his surliness wasn't surliness, but really sadness.

And she'd never been one who could simply turn the other way where "sad people" were concerned.

For that matter, he needed a friend as much as she herself did.

It was why she'd given up her only copy of Jane Austen's works.

It was why, all afternoon and then into the evening hours, she'd sat at the window seat overlooking his residence and the streets below, waiting for her family's return, and thinking of him still.

She'd scanned her gaze over the snow-covered streets, waiting to catch a glimpse not of her returning family . . . but of him.

What had happened to the duke's wife?

Had he loved her?

If he was brooding and surly, then the obvious answer would be yes.

It would also explain why he wished to be alone.

Those questions had stayed with her until her eyes had grown heavy and she'd fallen asleep on that window seat.

This morning, after she'd washed her face and changed her garments, thoughts of her exchange with the duke lingered still.

And she could not sort out just why he occupied her thoughts.

He'd been rude.

Very, very rude.

The following morning, with the warm cloak she'd found donned, and basket in hand, she made her way outside once more.

This time not to her surly, miserable neighbor's household.

She'd certainly thought about visiting him again.

Not because she liked his company. She didn't. And not because at any number of points through the remainder of yesterday afternoon and evening, she'd been riddled with fear at being alone.

Nay, this time, something altogether different motivated her.

As if on cue, her stomach rumbled low and loud, that growling made all the louder in the winter still of London's now empty streets.

Hunger.

She was deuced hungry.

And despite her expectation that her family would return, they hadn't, and she'd been left attempting to figure out what in blazes to feed herself.

She might not be capable of lighting a fire, but securing food was something she could do.

Hungry and cold and lonely were perhaps three of the most miserable states, and she'd landed herself in all of them, with the only person who appeared to have remained in London being a man who wanted absolutely nothing to do with her.

His harsh words of yesterday played around her head, his angry snarl better suited for the wolf dog who kept him company.

I don't want your company, and I don't want your book. I don't want anyone here. I want to be left alone, and certainly by you. Am I clear*?*

"Well, that is fine; I don't want your company, either," she muttered under her breath as she traded the cold of her household for the outdoor chill.

She made her way outside and crossed the street, heading on the same walk she'd oft accompanied Cook on as a girl.

Given her position in the McQuoid household, Myrtle was well accustomed to being rejected and unwanted. Nor were those self-pitying thoughts, but rather ones steeped in a well-known and accepted-by-her-long-ago truth.

She'd been willing to go next door to meet the duke because she was alone, and after everything her brother had shared, well, she'd thought him sad, and lonely, and thereby they'd be perfect company for one another.

"I won't make that mistake again," she said, swinging her basket as she went.

Myrtle reached the familiar bakery. The smells wafting from within the establishment filled the streets, and her stomach gave another growl.

She patted her hungry belly and let herself inside.

A short while later, her basket filled with various items from pastries to fresh loaves of bread, and several apples she'd asked to purchase from the baker, all of which she'd asked the kindly fellow to charge to her family's account, Myrtle found her way back home and broke out into a quiet song.

> "Good King Wenceslas looked out
> On the Feast of Stephen
> When the snow lay round about
> Deep and crisp and even
> Brightly shone the moon that night . . ."

Except—she slowed her steps—this particular song only made her think of the gentleman who'd been adamant in his desire to have her gone.

Such appeared to be the way with everyone whose path she crossed, from her family to surly neighbors alike.

Why, her parents couldn't even be bothered to return for her. In fact, she'd wager the food she'd managed to find herself that they'd not even realized yet she was missing.

And suddenly beset by a wave of moroseness, Myrtle picked up her pace and stomped ahead, the pair of serviceable boots she'd commandeered from the servants' quarters grinding the light layering of snow and ice upon the cobblestones under her feet.

Myrtle arrived 'round the back of her family's townhouse, and stopped.

This time, it wasn't fear that froze her in her tracks, or her own self-pityings.

A pair of men, roughly dressed, stood outside her townhouse, assessing the stucco household, pointing periodically and nodding.

Two familiar gentlemen.

Mr. Phippen's builders.

Her stomach sank.

Splendid.

They intended to begin their work. Except . . .

Myrtle frowned.

That didn't quite make sense.

According to her parents, they had granted Mr. Phippen and his men the holidays, and those workers weren't set to commence until at least the day after Christmas.

Clutching her basket close, Myrtle shivered, watching. Waiting for them to leave. Thinking they intended to remain.

Except she found herself also confused as to why they should be here.

It was likely some detail the head of the project had tasked them with. The renovations weren't set to commence until after Christmas, but that didn't mean they didn't intend to begin work sooner.

She'd just have to send them away.

Inform them that she remained, and that her family was returning.

Only . . . they didn't approach the front of the townhouse.

Rather, they disappeared down the side of the impressive structure.

Dampening her lips, Myrtle set off in pursuit, but something made her keep a distance between herself and the two men.

Perhaps it was the childlike fear that came in being completely and totally alone.

Or perhaps it was something more. *Perhaps it is your intuition telling you that those men aren't to be trusted.*

"Stop this instant," she said, needing to hear her own voice, but still keeping it low so as to not alert the unlikely pair of men of her presence . . . and pursuit. She reached the corner of the townhouse and peered around the edge.

The two men continued their peculiar assessment. Pointing at the lower windows . . .

Her eyes flared.

Of her father's curiosity room.

But they'd insisted Mr. Phippen would send others; Myrtle had been told that they'd come two days earlier merely to inventory the items, and not to pack them away.

Perhaps they were . . . waiting for those people to arrive who would see to the rooms.

She shivered in the cold, clamping her teeth hard to keep them from chattering and revealing her presence to the unsuspecting men.

Except, the longer she waited, the clearer it became that either the party they waited for was very tardy or there was no one else coming.

As time marched on, the uneasy sensation in the pit of her belly grew.

If they were here to conduct work . . . why would they sneak down the side alley?

Would they not have been provided a key with which to gain entry by her family and Mr. Phippen?

Nay, something was not right here.

And she intended to find out precisely what that was.

❄ ❄ ❄

She'd gone out early. Again.

Going off on her own without the benefit of a maid or sibling or strapping footman.

They were details he shouldn't have noted.

Not as a man who didn't involve himself in the lives of anyone . . . and certainly not those of strangers.

And yet, he'd been unable to keep himself from noting that detail.

Just as he'd not been able to *not* study her as she'd been on that window seat, staring across the way at his household. Just as her kin did.

Only, there'd been something different about that nose pressed to the glass pane this time.

Her focus hadn't been reserved for just him and his household, as had been the case for her family.

Yes, her attention had periodically returned to his townhouse.

No, this time, she'd stared off into the streets, as if she were searching for someone.

And it really wasn't his business who she'd been searching for.

Or the lonely little air to her.

Or anything about her.

It was why, with the unopened volume of *Pride and Prejudice* at his side, he'd wrenched himself away from his own window seat and snapped the curtains closed, certain he wouldn't see her again.

But he did.

It had been a matter of chance. He'd absolutely not been looking for her when he'd returned from his morning ride, sought out his offices, and looked out the windows.

But she'd been there, going off with a little jauntiness in her step.

And he'd been baffled as to why a young lady should or would go off anywhere alone.

Perhaps her family granted her greater freedoms in the winter, as all had left.

But that didn't mean the lady was safe from danger.

Danger could befall her anywhere.

Surely her family had sense enough to realize *that*.

Either way, her affairs—their affairs—were their own.

He told himself that, even as he waited at the window seat, her book still resting there, untouched, unopened . . . and then he spied her.

Val straightened, unsure how to account for the way his heartbeat picked up its cadence.

Outside, with that same basket in her fingers and her back to him, she crept along the side of her family's townhouse with footsteps he expected she thought were stealthy.

She'd returned.

Good. Now he could go back to . . .

Nothing. You do absolutely nothing.

Which was certainly the only reason he'd noted that the lady had gone off on her own, or that she'd now returned and was—

She disappeared around the corner.

"Good," he mumbled. "Out of sight. Out of mind."

"What is that, Your Grace?" His butler popped his head into Val's offices.

"Nothing, Jenkins. Take the day," he instructed.

"As you wish, Your Grace." With a bow, the loyal servant shuffled off, leaving Val alone.

As he wished it.

Except . . . his gaze drifted once more to the window.

She is not my problem. She is not my problem. She is—

His mind proved anything but compliant. With a dark curse, Val spun on his heel, and gathering his cloak from the foyer, he swung it around his shoulders and headed for the door.

Horace gave an excited yelp and danced around Val's legs, his gait awkward from the limp he'd sustained years earlier, but the excited spring in those canine steps clear.

"You're not coming," he said tightly. "Stay."

His dog immediately dropped his head between his front legs and emitted a piteous whine. In the span of less than a day, guilt reared its head for a second time.

"Trust me, you do not want to come," Val said for the loyal dog's benefit. "The lady is a bother. She'll give you nothing but a megrim."

Horace whimpered his protest once more.

"She is," Val insisted. "And it's cold outside and—"

Sitting on his haunches, Horace rested a massive paw on Val's leg.

Bloody hell on Sunday. With another curse, Val wrenched the door open and patted the side of his thigh.

Horace instantly fell into step beside him.

Master and pup made their way down the snow-slicked steps as Val headed in the direction he'd last seen the lady go.

She was probably already indoors.

She was—

He caught sight of her.

Appearing completely oblivious as to his presence, she craned her head around the corner of her family's townhouse and peered off in the distance.

Val stopped, and Horace immediately followed suit.

She'd sneaked off that morning; that was what accounted for her lack of escort.

He should have expected as much from the troublesome minx.

And even as he'd reiterated in his mind again and again that she was not his problem, he still found himself striding down the length of the courtyard cobblestones.

"You do know," he began as he reached her side, "that it—"

The lady emitted a sharp shriek and spun swiftly on her heel.

She swung her wicker basket hard against his arm and then, without missing a beat, brought it down on his head.

He grunted as several apples rained down around him, followed by several flaky pastries.

Yes, he should have known better.

The lady gasped. "Your Grace, you startled me. You really shouldn't go sneaking about on a lady."

"On a lady who is sneaking about on her own?" he asked dryly.

"Especially that." She nodded, desperately hopeless when it came to detecting sarcasm. She turned and stole another peek around the corner. "They're gone," she murmured.

"Who is?" he asked, despite himself.

Muttering to herself, giving no indication she'd heard Val's question, Myrtle dropped to a knee and proceeded to gather up the gleaming red apples.

And the situation was better for it. Engaging this one in any way was a mistake. As it was, having sought her out was the pinnacle of folly.

She stuffed the fruit into her basket and then turned to the two pastries resting forlornly in the snow. "Do you think they're ruined?"

Did he . . . ?

It took a moment to process that she spoke about the pastries. But then, she had retrieved the tarts and held them up for Val's inspection.

"I'd say you'd be better off with your family's cook baking you fresh ones that hadn't hit the ground," he said dryly. "Yes."

With a forlorn, little sigh, she looked at the cherry and apple tarts. "Here you are," she said, holding them out, and Val froze briefly at that offering, reaching a hand out.

Horace bounded over, and with an enormous bite, he gobbled one of the treats whole, and then the other from the lady's gloved hand.

Val's cheeks fired hot, realizing belatedly she'd been offering those pastries to his dog. Which of course made more sense; he'd already declared them ruined. And there'd been the whole bit of him rejecting her gift yesterday.

"I'm happy one of us was able to enjoy them," she cooed, catching the dog's head between her arms and nuzzling him with her cheek.

"Don't," Val said sharply, and the lady stilled. "He doesn't like to be petted."

Horace had lived as solitary a life as Val these years and was as unaccustomed to the human touch as Val himself.

Myrtle frowned. "He seems to like it just fine."

And then wholly disregarding his warning, she placed her cheek against Horace's.

Horace, who stuck his giant pink tongue out and lapped her cheek, making an absolute liar of Val.

"Oh, yes, he seems quite the terrifying beast, he does," the lady said with laughter ringing in her bell-like tones. "Isn't that right?" she cooed once more at his pup. "You're the biggest, most terrifying beast."

Horace panted excitedly, licking Myrtle on her opposite cheek.

Val tightened his mouth. "Will you stop that?" he snapped, not really certain whether he spoke to the spirited sprite or the faithless dog.

Neither paid him any heed.

The two appeared quite content with one another's company.

Through their warm exchange, Val stood there, folding his arms at his chest and tapping his right foot impatiently, willing his blasted dog to take note.

He could have drilled a damned hole in the universe with that drumming and still not have interrupted the happy exchange.

Bright color filled the lady's cheeks, and her eyes glimmered and sparkled with the brightest light . . . and he froze, his boot grinding to a slow halt.

Surrounded by darkness, his life one of agony and sorrow, he'd forgotten what it was to see joy in real life. It had been so long since he'd experienced anything beyond misery that he'd come to believe the happiness he'd once felt, witnessed, and shared had been the stuff of dreams.

Only to find himself confronted with those sentiments in this young woman, a stranger, one who was untouched by life's cruelty, and as such, one who was capable of that wide, sincere smile that wreathed her cheeks in the joy that came from within.

At last, Myrtle seemed to note his attention. She paused and looked up.

"I think we've displeased your master, sir," she murmured to Horace.

The dog merely panted all the more.

She patted his head but otherwise made no move to stand. "What is his name?"

When presented with signs of annoyance, his staff ran in the opposite direction.

In fairness, they went out of their way to avoid him in general.

All his friends and family largely stayed clear of him, opting to give him the solitude he craved.

This woman should prove the one person who didn't.

He didn't know what to do with her or make of her.

"Horace," he said gruffly.

"Horace?" She considered the dog a moment, then patted the top of his head. "It suits you mightily, it does. You are as big as a horse."

"He is as big as a horse, Val . . . We must call him Horace . . ."

That memory intruded, and he braced for the expected rush of pain, the stabbing needles as they pierced his chest, that place where his heart had once beaten, whole and happy.

That didn't come this time.

He drew back, recoiling from the absence of the only sentiments that had been familiar to him.

"What are you doing here?" he demanded, his voice harsh, and Myrtle looked his way again.

Confusion crinkled her brow. "Petting your dog?" she ventured.

My god, was she being deliberately obtuse?

"Out here," he snapped, motioning to the area around them.

The lady's nose scrunched up, and it was as though, bright and cheerful as she always was, she wasn't capable of a complete frown. "This is my property, Your Grace," she reminded him. "I rather believe the better question is what are you doing here?"

Yes, she had him there.

That was a fair enough point.

"I caught you sneaking about."

"Well, it's not really sneaking about if I'm on my own properties," she said gently. "Is it?"

He flattened his lips.

No, she was correct on *that* score, too.

Suddenly, the lady's brown eyes brightened, and her always generous smile was firmly fixed in its usual place. "Why, you were—"

He was already shaking his head.

Val needn't have bothered wasting that negating movement.

"Worried about me, weren't you?" she finished, and somehow that impossibly wide grin grew.

"I absolutely was not. I do not worry about anyone."

She pointed down at Horace.

"He's a dog. Not a person."

"Hmph," Myrtle grunted, and then grinned again. "But you were watching because you were worried, and I thank you for your concern." She lowered her voice. "I believe two men are watching my townhouse," she said, and then stared at him as if expecting he'd be as shocked and horrified as she herself was.

He shook his head.

"Yes." Myrtle lifted two small, gloved digits. "Two. You see, I suspect they might have an interest in my father's curiosity collection."

As she rattled on, he recoiled for altogether different reasons. Good God, what had he done, engaging her?

"And his collection is quite vast . . . some of the oldest and finest, and everyone knows of his treasures . . ."

At last, what she was suggesting penetrated his fog.

"Are you saying you believe someone intends to steal from your father?"

The lady nodded. "Precisely."

One such as Lady Myrtle McQuoid would possess an overactive imagination.

"I tried to tell my father and mother, but *nooooooooo*." She stretched more syllables than he'd ever known were capable of being added to a single-syllable word, and as if that weren't exaggeration enough, she waved her palms in front of her for emphasis. "They insist Mr. Phippen has them doing his work, which I find *highly* suspect. Inventorying items," she muttered under her breath. She shook her head. "They don't even know antiquities. As such, what were they even labeling them?" She stared at Val as if expecting he'd have the answer to that very question.

He attempted desperately to follow what in blazes she was saying.

And failed.

He shook his head.

The lady jabbed a finger in the air. "Exactly. If they don't know what the historical significances of the pieces are, they can't properly inventory them."

"You believe there are men who've come to steal from you?"

"I've already said as much, have I not?"

She had.

Twice. Mayhap even three times now. It was all confused at this moment.

As was he, and everything else when it came to Myrtle McQuoid.

"Not from me, per se," she clarified. "But my father, as it is his collection . . . I don't have valuables. Not any that I've collected," she spouted on, and then her gaze suddenly grew wistful. "Unlike my older brother Arran. He has a collection of his own and has seen the world in his travels."

She'd a faraway look to her, as if equal parts entranced at the possibility of travel and envious of the brother whom she now spoke of, and he found himself intrigued in that moment by the lady before him, who herself was besotted not by bolts of fabric but by the prospect of seeing a world beyond London.

Discomfited by this unwanted awareness of the lady, he forced them back to the worrying that had brought about an already entirely too lengthy discourse.

"Your father himself has hired these men," Val said.

"Yes."

"As such, I expect he'd know those he's hired."

"Then you do not know my father," she countered. "He is very trusting." She held Val's eyes. *"Very."*

This . . . from her? Good God, what did that say about the man who'd sired her?

"If you happen to see anything amiss, Your Grace"—she leaned in and dropped her voice to a whisper—"anything at all, you must come and alert me."

He kept his features deadpan. "You've my word."

"Thank you." Myrtle flashed another one of her sunny smiles, and oddly, that flash of cheer didn't have the same grating effect it had before. Suddenly, she chewed at the tip of her glove. "I daresay if we're now working together to apprehend these fiends, we are certainly friends now."

"We're decidedly not friends." He didn't have friends anymore. And he didn't want them. The fewer people to care about, the better it was. The better he was, in not having to expose himself to the kind of pain that came in loving too deeply.

"As such," she carried on as if he'd not even spoken, "you must call me Myrtle."

"Myrtle," he muttered. Except it really wasn't so awful. It rather . . . suited her.

She frowned. "And I'll call you . . . ?"

"No."

She pursed her lips. "*Hmph.* You'll be *that* kind of duke, then."

Don't ask. Don't ask it . . .

"And what kind is *that*?"

"The one who insists on being referred to as Your Grace. Good day, *Your Grace*."

And gathering up her basket and ignoring his protestations, the stubborn minx continued on with a spritely little step, leaving him as he always was after a meeting with her—completely and totally befuddled.

Chapter 7

"What is wrong with the name Myrtle?"

The following morning that voice, both slightly annoyed and faintly curious, slashed across the morning quiet and Val's musings, startling a curse from him and knocking the burden in his arms to the snow-covered cobblestones.

A basket swinging in her hand like she was a veritable Red to his Wolf, Lady Myrtle hastened over, stopping only when she reached him.

"I . . ." Befuddled as he always was around this one, Val managed only to shake his head.

"My name," she said when she reached his side. "Yesterday when I suggested you call me by my name, you went, *Myrrrtle*." She growled in such a near dead-on impersonation of his voice that Val found himself smiling. "I'll have you know," she carried on, as she so often did in that conversation for one, "I don't blame you. In fact, I quite agree with you."

"I . . . ?" Val found himself managing nothing more than a shake of his head.

"I've always quite despised my name."

Hearing her say that bothered him for reasons he didn't understand.

"Myrrrtle," she said aloud in her best imitation of those low, gravelly tones of his.

The kind of tones that suggested he wasn't one given to talking.

In fairness, he wasn't. He didn't interact with other humans anymore.

"You do know they say I've killed my household staff," he said in a bid to end this discussion and send her running.

"I do," she said without missing a beat. "You do know if you hadn't, you would have people about to help you," she piped in as she set her basket down. Stooping over, the lady stuck between childhood and womanhood fished through snow entirely too deep for London for the logs he'd dropped.

Despite his better judgment, and despite a commitment to not engage anyone, a question left him. "I beg your pardon?"

"As you *should*, for killing your staff," the lady scolded as she handed two logs over to him, shoving them against his chest.

Val caught them reflexively.

"At the very least. Killing servants is in bad form." Lady Myrtle paused in her search and then, bending down, dug through the snow, pulling out another log.

She added it to the fast-growing stack in his arms.

And he proved as helpless to keep back a second question, this time a droll one. "And killing anyone else is in good form?"

"Well, I'd say servants are deserving of far greater respect and appreciation for the work they do. In fact, I can think of a number of unkind lords and ladies who the world would be best served if they met an accident or as quick an end as your servants did."

It didn't matter what outlandish tale she and her deuced nosy family had concocted, and yet . . . "I did not murder my servants," he said in the same frosty ducal tones his late grandfather had perfected and Val had vowed never to use.

But then, that had been before he'd met *this* one.

The lady patted the top of his gloved hand. "As all killers certainly insist."

The young woman straightened, gathered up her skirts, and he expected—prayed—she intended to leave. But only returned to her search for the remainder of his wood.

And he, Val Bancroft, the Duke of Aragon, found himself at a complete, total, and absolute loss.

As she hummed a happy little tune under her breath, it stirred the air, filling the winter sky, and wafting higher, up to the heavens—if there were, in fact, such a place in the hereafter.

> "Good King Wenceslas looked out
> On the Feast of Stephen
> When the snow lay round about
> Deep and crisp and even . . ."

Val froze.

> "Brightly shone the moon that night
> Though the frost was cruel
> When a poor man came in sight
> Gathering winter fuel . . ."

The lady paused briefly in her song, and Val gave thanks to a God he'd ceased believing in that she'd stopped. "Funny that you are a poor man gathering fuel. Not *poor-poor*," she jabbered. "But there are different *forms* of poor, and you certainly fall into one of those categories."

Uncaring of which she'd place him in, just wanting her gone, he was opening his mouth to tell her as much when she erupted into song for a second time.

> "Hither, page, and stand by me,
> If thou knowst it, telling

Yonder peasant, who is he?
Where and what his dwelling?"

And it mattered not the icy snow beneath the heels of his boots or the frigidity of the winter's day—a sweat broke out over his skin as he was transported back to another young lady, cheerfully singing.

The lyrical tones of an earth-angel.

"Bring me flesh and bring me wine
Bring me pine logs hither
Thou and I shall see him dine
When we bear them thither . . ."

Her voice had risen high above the storm wailing outside their carriage windows, and the wind battering the walls of it, with Val laughing and joining in until—

The world came whirring back. It certainly helped to shake the past that this lady's off-pitch, discordant song bore no semblance to the celestial voice of another, a ghost who haunted him still.

"Sire, the night is darker now
And the wind blows stronger
Fails my heart, I know not how
I can go no longer . . ."

"Will you stop your singing," he snapped.

The lady paused briefly, lifting her focus from the task that had occupied her, and held his gaze with a fiery, piercing intensity that bespoke a hint of hurt and even greater defiance.

In that moment, as the silence dragged on, he who'd ceased to feel bad about anything was hit by some emotion he'd long believed himself incapable of again feeling or knowing.

Guilt.

And the young, charming rogue he'd been long ago would have known how to cut the tense, awkward silence; he'd have been able to erase the sad little frown she gave him and dimple her cheeks. But neither was he that young man, nor did he even wish to be again.

In the end, it was she who broke the impasse. "Is that what they did wrong?" she asked, curiosity tingeing her query.

He puzzled his brow.

"Your servants," she went on. And not allowing him a word edgewise—not that he had a damned one in that moment—Lady Myrtle's black eyebrows shot up. "Of course it is. You killed them because you hated their singing. *Tsk. Tsk.*" She clucked like a chicken. "It's in even worse form to kill a jovial servant for singing."

And with that, she proceeded to sing louder.

Val briefly closed his eyes and emitted a black curse that would have sent most grown men bolting and might have been effective in scattering this fey lady . . . if she hadn't been belting out a damned carol at the top of her lungs.

In their brief but telling exchanges, he should have known his skill as a duke attempting to command her to silence would be met with only obstinance.

"What the hell are you doing here?"

"I am paying you a visit," she said.

"Me?"

She nodded.

So she'd rather spend her time with him, a stranger, and at that, one she took as a murderer of his servants?

"You have your family," he said gruffly. It was more than he had. At that pitiable and useless reminder, he used the moment as an opportunity to dispel her. "And you should be getting back to them. I'm sure they are wondering where you've gone off." It was a lie. Her noisy, nosy family, who were always staring out their windows at his damned household, were likely grateful for the reprieve.

Except . . . he'd watched her entire family leave. Surely, they'd not left the young lady—

"They've gone." She spoke quietly, confirming his unspoken thought.

He frowned. Val really didn't care about the lady or her circumstances, for the simple fact he didn't care about anyone. "Gone *where*?" he asked, unable to account for why, then, that follow-up question for the lady should slip past his lips. But really, what family went off and left a lady alone with their servants?

"Scotland. For the holiday."

"The holiday?"

"Christmastide." She paused. "It is Christmastide, you know."

"The English don't celebrate Christmas."

"I'm Scottish."

"*Of course* you are," he muttered.

The lady cupped a gloved hand to the shell of her ear. "What was that?"

He knew better than to further engage this one. "Noth—"

"You *said*, it's because I'm Scottish. I'll have you know there are plenty of English who celebrate the holiday."

His stomach muscles seized. He did well know that.

"*Many* lords and ladies," the gibbering creature went on over his tumult, refusing to let the talons of grief fully sink their claws into him as he'd become so accustomed.

As such, he stood in abject confusion, with more of her ramblings on about the Christmastide Season.

"And Jane Austen," she was saying.

"You with this Jane Austen again," he mumbled.

He may as well have called the honor of her family into question for the horrified look she cast his way.

"I have failed her completely," she bemoaned. "And you. I've failed you."

"This I have to hear, and by 'have to hear,' I mean I do *not*—"

Lady Myrtle threw her hands up in the air; in her exuberant gesticulation, she caught him in the arm with the log she held.

Val grunted, but so passionate in her defense of the unknown woman, Lady Myrtle didn't so much as break stride and offer an apology.

"Knowing the secret I've let you in on about Miss Jane Austen, surely you see she is the most wonderful Englishwoman of all time."

"Nay, she isn't," he said, his gaze locked beyond the lady's shoulder on his empty household.

Some unfamiliar-to-him stranger was decidedly not. There'd been just one woman who would remain the only—

"She most certainly is. Long live Miss Austen." Lady Myrtle raised her voice up to the sky.

His gut seized, as it invariably did with reminders of how precarious life was.

"Someday, the whole *world* will discover Miss Austen," the lady went on in reverent tones. "She will be known as the most famous, the most talented, the most gifted writer of all time."

"Shakespeare. Keats. Coolidge. Chaucer."

Lady Myrtle punched the air with a finger in rapid succession to each word she spoke: "Man. Man. Man. *Man.* All men."

He should have known better than to engage her.

"Miss Austen, however—"

"Is a female?" he asked dryly, immediately startled by the fact he'd managed . . . any form of humor. Even the sarcastic type.

Lady Myrtle beamed. "Precisely." Her smile dipped, and her slightly too-high-and-broad brow wrinkled. "Where was I?"

"Leaving?" he ventured hopefully.

Either ignoring or failing to hear him through her distracted thoughts, the lady tapped her chin in a contemplative little way.

"Where were we . . . where were—" Her eyes brightened. "I have it! Christmastide!"

He groaned, but once again her ramblings were loud enough to rouse neighbors at this early hour, had there been any about, and drowned out the sounds of his annoyance.

"My cousins and their parents *also* celebrate the Season—"

"Who also share your Scottish blood and customs and ways, and as such, one would expect your family all celebrates."

She lifted a finger high and waggled it under his nose. "Ah, yes, but only half of their family is Scottish, as my aunt married a *very* English gentleman. Mr. Francis Smith."

Lady Myrtle said it and stared at Val like he was supposed to have some bloody idea who in tarnation Mr. Francis Smith was.

Mayhap if he was silent, however, mayhap if he failed to indulge her in any way, she'd just cut out with her infernal telling and let him get back to his household and his damned misery and—

Apparently, the lady required no input from him.

"Leigh Hunt also spoke out in support of reviving the celebration of the Christmastide Season." She paused and gave him a long look. "I take it you know who Leigh Hunt is?"

"The essayist," he said automatically, even as he sought to sort out why in hell he remained here.

Shock and confusion. That would do it to any gent, especially one who'd been removed from society as long as Val had.

"*Hmph, of course* you do." The lady waggled insolent brows at him. "Hunt being a male writer and all."

Val growled.

"As I was saying," she continued, apparently a good deal less affected by his unintentional—though customary for him and suitable to this moment—surly response. "Queen Charlotte introduced the custom of the Christmas tree . . . which I expect you, as someone who knows absolutely nothing about the holiday, will find particularly shocking, and . . ."

As she gabbled on, a long-ago fireside discussion between him and another, a lady who'd not gone out of her way to annoy him and who'd been capable of making him smile, intruded on the present.

"They have trees inside for Christmas, Val . . . We must have one; we simply must . . . Imagine, it will be so magical."

She had been so magical.

"You want a tree inside our home? Then when we arrive at Donneborogh," he said of his Somerset estates, "we shall have one, Your Grace."

His late wife's tinkling, bell-like laughter filled the corners of his mind, melding with the droning of the lady now lecturing to him.

"Why, one would think it was just the gentry, but it was not. It was—"

"I don't want to talk about the Christmastide Season," he began, intending to bestow a lecture upon her that would send her running and silence her on the matter forever.

"We've just done so."

He spoke over her. "And why people celebrate."

"To feel and spread cheer," the lady added. "I think that should be fairly obvious and not have required further clarification."

"Or *how* they celebrate," he said, ignoring her.

"I've just covered some of that."

"Or what they eat."

"Beef and mincemeat and pudding and—"

"No more talk of Christmas," he thundered, startling several wood pigeons from the ledges they perched on, the wild flapping of their wings sending feathers floating forlornly down to the earth.

And if he were one to still be impressed by women, he'd have found himself admiring the fact that she'd not gone running off, weeping at his bellowing shout, and that she instead remained, her feet planted to the ground, meeting his gaze still.

Granted, her cheeks were paler and her eyes wider, and damned if it wasn't like he'd kicked the household mouser for the way he felt about himself, yelling at a lady who was likely so young as to not have yet seen a London Season.

He should have known better than to allow himself a moment of pity or weakness where this one was concerned.

"Is your Christian name Oliver?" she asked curiously.

At that sudden, unexpected, and out-of-nowhere question, Val cocked his head. The queue tied at the nape of his neck tipped to the right of his shoulder. "No."

"Hmm," the lady murmured to herself. "I would have thought with your aversion for Christmas, you were a regular Oliver Cromwell. He banned carols and festive get-togethers, decreeing them against the law, punishable by imprisonment." She paused, apparently wise enough to catch the horrified look he surely wore. Misunderstanding the reason for that look, she clarified all the details he didn't care to hear. "Oliver Cromwell is an English statesman. He led the armies against King Charles I during the English Civil War and—"

"I know who Cromwell was," he clipped out between clenched teeth.

"—ruled the British Isles as Lord Protector from—"

"I said I know who Lord Cromwell was," he shouted to be heard over her.

"Of course you do." Lady Myrtle batted her eyes innocently at him, and he didn't believe for a damned minute that flutter, as he didn't think there was a damned thing innocent about her. "Cromwell being a famous Englishman and all, he was no doubt covered in your Oxford days."

"Cambridge," he said between his still tensed lips.

The lady tipped her head.

"I went to Cambridge."

"Oh, that is interesting, indeed. I would expect a duke would be more of an Oxford man, given it's the oldest and all."

And if Val's hands had been free of the wood he'd been holding, he'd have jammed his fingertips into his temples and pressed hard. But she wasn't speaking about Christmas, so he took thanks where they could be had this day.

Myrtle sighed. "I should be on my way. Goodbye, Your Grace."

He should be relieved at that—both with her leaving and with her having quit attempting to get him to divulge his Christian name.

"Myrtle," he called when she started to leave.

Myrtle turned back.

"Val," he said gruffly. "My name is Val."

A slow smile formed on her mouth, that sparkle of merriment and joy . . . It transformed her into someone far from ordinary, and into a woman who really was quite captivating.

"Val," she repeated, as if testing it. She gave a nod. "It suits you." She made to go.

His curiosity, however, proved too strong. "How so?"

"I know what you're thinking," she said.

He rather doubted that.

"You're assuming the name puts me in mind of Valentine of Passau, the hermit bishop," she went on.

Wonder of wonders, Val felt his lips pull up at the corners in a rusty smile. "Actually, I've never heard of him." Against all better judgment and reason, Val found himself all the more intrigued by how this young sprite of a woman had come to be in possession of that information.

Alas, it was a question that was to remain unanswered. "But the name's Latin roots mean 'strong and healthy,' which . . . well, I've never known a duke, let alone any other nobleman, who chopped his own wood and carried armfuls of it the way you do."

And this time when she waved and left, he found himself lifting his hand in parting goodbye, and staring after her until she'd gone.

Chapter 8

When Myrtle had been a small girl, she'd oft found herself competing to be heard amongst her large, raucous Scottish family.

To make herself noticed, she'd put energy into pranks that would earn their attention.

She'd sung the loudest of all her cousins and siblings.

She'd scaled the trees outside her family members' chamber windows and hung ribbons from the branches to make the world more colorful for them when they'd stolen a glance outside, then regaled them with songs and stories . . . until one of her eldest brothers was sent to pluck her back to safety.

That safety invariably resulted in an uproar of her parents lecturing her on the dangers, and her siblings lamenting that they had a sister as precocious as she, and she'd been ultimately lost in the proverbial shuffle.

Through it all, there'd never *not* been noise.

Shivering on the window seat in her Corner Parlor, the blankets wrapped about her person, Myrtle sat with this new, dreaded, unfamiliar, and awful silence.

She stared off and out at the duke's household.

At least Val was near.

And in thinking of him in his big, lonely household, she felt less alone in *hers*.

Creeeeak.

She jumped, her heart racing as she whipped her gaze off in the direction of those eerie groans of the old house, ones she'd failed to hear when her family and their staff had been sharing these walls. But now, in her solitary state, everything was louder. And everything was more terrifying.

"Stop i-it," she whispered, her teeth clanking together, only it wasn't solely from the cold. That trembling came from the fear in being alone.

And then she heard it.

Rap-Pause-Rap-Pause-Rap.

And then absolute silence followed that last, faint knock.

Myrtle froze. She was hearing things, was all.

She was—

Then it came again.

Rap-Pause-Rap-Pause-Rap.

A patterned knocking, as if the person on the other side of that door knocked without wishing to be heard.

As if they sought to confirm no one was within the house so that they might invade and sneak their way in.

Her mouth dry and a sheen of perspiration coating her palms, Myrtle swung her legs over the side of the bench, letting her stockinged feet hit the floor.

It came again:

Rap-Pause-Rap-Pause-Rap.

Padding across the room, Myrtle grabbed the steel poker next to the cold, barren hearth and, clutching it close, crept toward the sound of that rhythmic tapping.

As she picked her way quickly through the house, she took care to avoid the noisiest, most unforgiving of the floorboards, the chill of the floors scarcely penetrating. All her attention remained locked on the direction of that tapping.

At last, she reached the foyer.

Only silence met her.

Whoever had shown up on her doorstep had ceased knocking.

Because they verified no one is here. Because they know the household is empty . . .

Terror sent Myrtle's gut into upheaval, churning and twisting as it always did when her family insisted she ride the boats at their family lake and she invariably ended up casting the contents of her stomach into that same body of water.

Raising her poker instinctively higher and holding it closer, she crept forward, avoiding the windows, keeping herself out of sight.

The moon had penetrated the side glass panels and illuminated the foyer; eerie shadows danced upon the floors and off the walls, adding to her ever-heightening fear.

Myrtle bit her lower lip hard, her ears straining.

And then she heard it.

Muttering.

Faint and barely distinguishable, but still decipherable.

Oh, God.

They were here.

And when they discovered she was still here, aware of their plans for her father's artifacts, and that there was no one else about—

Her thoughts came in panicky time to the rapid beating of her pulse in her ears.

Edging over to the doorway, she turned the lock, pressed the handle, and before her courage completely deserted her, she drew the door open.

In need of a good oiling, the hinges screamed and squealed, inordinately loud in the nighttime stillness.

Only silence met her.

Mayhap she'd merely imagined that knocking.

Perhaps it had been . . . at one of the other households.

Mayhap—

A shadow drifted forward, followed a moment later by a broad, tall, powerful form stepping inside.

Shrieking, Myrtle charged forward, brandishing her makeshift weapon.

Something went clattering, as the intruder dropped whatever burden he'd been holding.

He was too tall for her to properly get the aim she wished, so Myrtle settled for bringing the steel poker down on his shoulder. "Get out, you horrid fiend and miserable cur of a thief," she shouted, smacking him a second time.

Over the din of a dog's barking, she made out a harsh curse.

A familiar harsh curse, spoken in an even more familiar voice.

Myrtle froze midblow, her arm poised overhead. *"Vaaaaaal?"*

Val, as in her neighbor, the angry duke who'd insisted they'd never again meet.

"At your damned service," he muttered, rubbing at his arm.

She gasped, her fingers coming up to catch the slight sound of her shock, as the weapon slipped from her fingers and clattered upon the marble floor, as the implications of what she'd done—and worse, what she'd almost done—hit her.

"What are you doing here?" she demanded, charging forward. And Horace gave a happy yelp in greeting—one that, given she'd nearly gravely wounded his master, she certainly didn't deserve. "I nearly killed you."

"You wouldn't have killed me. Your aim is deuced poor, and your strikes, though annoying, are largely ineffectual."

She bristled. "I'll have you know my aim is not poor."

Horace barked, as if adding his canine support to the argument.

Val winged a dark eyebrow up. "You weren't aiming for my head?"

The duke's dog lowered his big head and whined.

Myrtle scrunched her nose. "I *may* have considered it."

Did she detect the trace of a smile on his always hard mouth and his perfectly firm lips?

Not for the first time that evening, her heart picked up a frantic cadence; this time, however, it wasn't fear that lent the organ an extra beat.

But then gone as quickly as those flights of fancy in her head that she may as well have imagined it.

Val turned his attention to the floor, and squatting down, he proceeded to gather up the collection of logs that littered the patio and foyer floor.

Joining him on the floor, she set herself to helping. All the while, Horace stepped deeper into the foyer, sniffing the walls and the edge of the stairs before settling himself against a corner. "Whatever is this?" she asked perplexedly.

"Wood," Val muttered as together they filled his arms with the logs.

"Yes, I see that. What are you doing with it?" she asked when they'd picked up the last of the wood and he'd straightened.

"I'm heating your household."

Still kneeling on the floor, she remained motionless, unable to stand.

Her heart stilled, and for the first time since her family had gone and she'd awakened to find herself in the freezing house, warmth filled her; it slipped throughout her being, touching on every corner.

He'd come with . . . fuel. Because he knew she was alone. Because he knew she was cold.

Nay, not just that. He'd *seen* her.

For the first time in mayhap the whole of her life, she'd been seen. Nor had it been her family or the ladies she'd spent years with at Mrs. Belden's.

Rather, it was him.

Val.

She'd been unseen so long—mayhap forever—that she'd not known what it was to have another person look at her and truly . . .

Val shoved the door shut with the heel of his boot, the panel thumping loud, and he turned a familiar glare on her. "Where in blazes are your rooms?"

That surly, more than slightly angry snarl broke across the dizzying romantic haze that clung to her vision.

Myrtle jumped up. "My chambers?" she squeaked, a palm coming up to her heart, which had resumed its familiar race wherever this man was concerned.

He narrowed his eyes. "Rest assured, I've no intention of taking advantage of you, Myrtle."

"I didn't think that," she said on a rush. He would have had to desire her in some small way, and yet, she didn't think he was capable of anything more than a grand annoyance where she was concerned. Nor, for that matter, did she think he was capable of taking advantage of anyone. "If you'll follow me?"

She led the way. Val followed silently.

The moment they reached the Corner Parlor, he stepped inside and came to a complete stop. "This isn't a bedchamber."

"No."

He stared at her, and Myrtle clarified, "This is where I'm sleeping."

"This is where you're sleeping?" he echoed.

She nodded. "Yes, here."

"Here?"

Unnerved by the way he repeated everything she said, she nodded once more. "Yes, *here*."

And she curled her toes into the hardwood floor, praying he did not gather that this room afforded the greatest, clearest view of his townhouse, and that it was because she felt nearer to him and less alone, being in here. Praying he'd let the matter die.

"Why?"

Alas, she should have expected Val, the Duke of Aragon, was entirely too contrary when it came to anything to ever do something as simple as let a matter rest.

"Because my chambers are damp, and I prefer this room."

"Your chambers . . . ?"

"That is why my family has departed for the winter. We usually remain, because Christmas in London is always our favorite time of year; however, our roof is leaking"—she pointed to the ceiling, and he followed her finger skyward—"and the floors are rotting." She gestured to her feet, and he looked down. "Many of the chambers and rooms are suffering mightily from the moisture coming in, including my rooms, and as such, I opted to make this my chambers . . . until my family returns, of course."

If they ever returned, that was. It was appearing more and more dubious with every passing moment.

Myrtle appeared to disarm Val with her explanation, and he gave his head a big shake. Heading over to the hearth, he deposited the burden in his arms on the metal rack for wood.

"The kitchens?"

She stared blankly at him.

"Where are they?" he asked exasperatedly.

"Ah." Lifting a finger, she motioned for him to follow her. As they fell into step, he remained silent, and yet, even as she expected she should be unnerved in his tense quietness, she found herself . . . at ease for his simply being here. "Are you always this laconic?"

"Yes."

"Were you always?"

"No."

And that curt, terse delivery of that declination hinted that he'd no more desire or patience for any additional questioning on her part.

She considered that lone syllable he'd uttered. And as they made their way through her family's household, she couldn't keep from wondering what he had been like before. Imagining him with that elusive grin that sometimes stole across his face, but in a perpetual smile, and with his words flowing freely.

And she'd never known him beyond these past days, but she somehow still found herself mourning the loss of who he'd been. And recalling what her brother had shared, she'd no doubt that Val's misery stemmed from the loss he'd suffered.

They reached the kitchens.

"Here we are," she said when he still did not speak, needing to hear words spoken from at least one of them.

He surveyed the kitchens, even colder than the rooms above—if that were possible.

As he entered the room, Myrtle hung back in the doorway, and drawing her cloak closer, she huddled within the velvet material.

He moved with a methodical purpose, as comfortable in the kitchen as if he'd been a servant born to his station here. But he wasn't. He was a duke, and yet he was also a duke who . . . knew how to start a fire.

And filled with awe, Myrtle stared on.

Once, when she was ten or so, her family had invited a magician to one of their summer house parties. The mustached fellow with a thick Russian accent and black cloak and heavy, snowy-white cravat had regaled the guests with illusions and magic tricks that had held Myrtle silent, captivating her.

That moment felt remarkably like this one with Val bringing fire to life in that hearth.

Fetching several wax candles, he added the tapers to the brass candleholders; lighting first one and then another, he handed them over to her.

Wordlessly, she accepted them, watching as he went and fetched two more.

"I . . . would not expect a duke to know how to start his own fires," she said when they started back toward her makeshift rooms.

"Is that a question?"

She considered that. "I . . . suppose it wasn't." But actually, upon reflection, it was. "How did you come to know how to do it?"

"Because I like to be alone," he said bluntly. "Because I like freedom from all company, including the company of my servants, and knowing how to do things for myself ensures that I'm never dependent upon others, so that I can enjoy my solitude."

"I see," she said softly, his meaning and message clear and effectively silencing her.

Only, as they continued their trek through the dark household with Val pausing periodically to light one of the sconces in the halls, she wrinkled her brow. Despite his craving the solitary state he spoke of, he'd still come here. Without her asking, without her giving any indication she either needed it or wished it, he'd arrived at her door with an armful of wood and taken it upon himself to light a fire so that she could have light and heat. Another one of those tingling warmths spread through her veins.

The moment they reached the Corner Parlor, Val headed for the fireplace. Dropping to a knee, he set to work building a fire there. As he did, he provided her with rapid instructions on how to keep it going.

It wasn't long before a healthy fire blazed within those grates and heat spilled off the high, dancing flames.

"Do you have all that?" he asked.

"I believe so." A little sigh slipped from her lips as she drifted closer; stretching her gloved palms out, she warmed them before the fire. "I do not believe in the whole of my life I properly appreciated the simple comforts for the great ones they really are," she murmured. "I daresay I'll never take for granted again having corridors that are illuminated and a fire, or the staff and servants who cook."

As if to emphasize that pronouncement, her stomach grumbled, embarrassingly loud in its groaning.

Val grunted and turned on his heel.

It took a moment for her to register . . .

"You're leaving," she blurted as he neared the front of the room.

And for a moment, she thought he intended to continue on without another word, as though she'd not spoken.

When suddenly, unexpectedly, he stopped and turned reluctantly back.

Then, slowly, he strode back over.

Wordlessly, he seated himself at the floor beside the fire, and she sank onto the ground beside him, matching his movements, drawing her knees to her chest and wrapping her arms around them.

She dropped her chin atop the makeshift shelf she'd made of her legs and stared at the dancing flames.

"Since I was a girl . . . I've never been in harmony with the rest of my family," she confided. "I was always *the most* unruly one, when they are able to moderate their temperaments. And the rare times I *did* crave quiet, they would fill every corner of our household with a deafening roar of noise." A sad smile drew her lips up in the corners. "My house was always filled with noise. I've two sisters and three brothers, and cousins who are always about, and yet for as big as my family is, I always struggled to fit in." She paused, turning her cheek onto her knee, and looked over. "Do you have any siblings?"

"One," he said, surprising her with the speed at which he replied; his answers before this one had always been reluctant, as if any admission he'd made had come as though dragged from him. "A brother."

"My siblings are quite talkative; they're always boisterous. What of your brother?"

"It sounds as though he'd get on splendidly with your family."

And just like that, an image slipped in of her and Val, surrounded by their families in a happy tableau set at Christmastime, with laughter and Val smiling and . . . Her heart hammering, she pushed back the nonsensical musings, unsure of where they came from. Or why her soul clung to the idea of it still.

Clearing her throat, she resumed speaking. "Well, they are always noisy, and I enjoy reading."

"Your Miss Austen." He touched a finger to his lips. "You have my assurance that I shall not betray your confidence."

The realization that he both knew her interests and that most special of secrets she'd shared with no one . . . and that he spoke so very matter-of-factly and not with disdain . . . filled her heart with a wonderful warmth. She nodded. "Her works are . . . relatable. She paints a world any person might feel and understand." She braced for him to dismiss those opinions, as her instructors and family had when she'd sought to discuss her new reading passion. Only he didn't, and Myrtle relaxed all the more in speaking freely with him. "So many times, I've longed for silence. I've dreamed of a household that was completely quiet and devoid of all the din that so often comes." Myrtle turned her eyes forward and back to the dancing flames. "Only to now find myself completely alone and missing the noise and hating the silence. It . . . terrifies me," she confessed, expecting him to make one of his dismissive responses.

"I used to hate the silence, too," he said quietly, stunning her with that admission and bringing her head whipping sideways.

This time, however, his gaze remained locked on the fire he'd brought to life in the grate, his eyes distant. "In the silence, I'd sit with only my regrets, and the memories of . . . the past would rage in those moments. Until one day, I made myself sit with that silence. I made myself stop and listen through my own tortured thoughts and the quiet, and I discovered there was a peace in that quiet. I came to find it wasn't something to be feared but embraced for the focus it allowed me."

How lonely he must be. And this time, she made no attempt to conceal her study of him; she couldn't. Myrtle looked on, taking in the sight of him simply watching the fire, wanting to know more about him, and the pain that lingered in every word he ever spoke. "Those memories . . . Were they of your wife?" she ventured.

❄❄❄

Were they of his wife . . . ?

His heart hammered, and his mind screamed at him to storm to his feet and make a swift march from this household and the lady's questionings.

Because he didn't talk about his wife.

Because people didn't ask about her.

Even his brother's annual attempt to gather Val for the Christmastide Season only vaguely referenced that day, but never did he ask about it or speak of it.

Even so, Val sat, unnerved, disquieted by the ease with which this woman now spoke of his loss and his past.

He slid a hard glance her way and made a *tsk*ing sound. "Listening to gossip, are you?"

"My brother mentioned that you were a widower."

"Gossip," he said icily. And this oddly soothed him. It reminded him that Myrtle McQuoid was just a stranger and nothing more to him than that.

"Not gossip as much as a statement about your circumstances. That is, if you are, in fact, a widower." She paused. "Are you?"

God, she was fearless.

He couldn't name a single person, including the woman who'd given him life or the brother whose blood he shared, who'd ever think of speaking so freely and plainly about Dinah.

Mayhap that was why he found himself answering her. "I am." Val rubbed a hand down the side of his cheek.

"Did you love her very much?"

He stilled, his gaze locked ahead. "I did," he said quietly. "I loved her with all I was." And with her passing, the parts of him that had existed had all died. The light within him had been extinguished, and all the warmth inside had gone cold. "It is a loss I will never, ever recover from."

A hand covered his, warm and soft, a touch that was delicate and unhesitant, and Val looked down.

Odd, he'd been so sure he'd only ever be cold, and yet there was only heat at this woman's gentle touch.

"I am sorry."

Sorry.

At Dinah's passing, how many notes had been sent or condolences offered, where countless people had said the very words this woman now spoke?

"I trust those words are incredibly . . . empty," she said softly. "But then, when presented with such a loss, what words are there?"

None. There were none.

"Do not let it die," he said, scrambling to his feet. "Wake periodically and stoke the flames; otherwise, it will go out."

"You're leaving," she said.

Did he imagine the regret in her voice?

Nay, he didn't.

From her every thought to every emotion, the lady was an open book.

"I am."

"Of course you are," she said on a rush, her cheeks pinkening in an endearing little blush.

She was afraid to be alone.

The person he'd been wouldn't have given a damn because she was a stranger, and even if she weren't, she certainly wasn't his problem.

So what was it, then, that held him to the floor, hesitant to leave?

He drew back.

Hesitant to leave?

What madness was this?

"Myrtle," he said, grabbing his hat and jamming it atop his head.

The young lady inclined hers. *"Val."* And he'd wager the emphasis she placed on his given name was a statement more than anything about the formality he'd resurrected between them.

With that he left, all but racing back to his household, fearing that if he did not get some distance between them, then he'd never manage the feat.

He shut the door to his townhouse and leaned against the panel.

Seated beside him, Horace cocked his head.

"This is for the best," Val said tightly.

Only, as he remained there alone with his dog and the silence of the house, why did it not feel that way? Why did he find himself wishing he were still across the way with a lady who smiled too much and sang even more?

Chapter 9

I loved her with all I was . . .

Now it made sense.

Now *he* made sense.

With his wife's passing, he'd had his heart shattered.

How could a man, or any person, for that matter, recover from the pain of that loss?

To have found the love of your life, to have known the greatest of happiness, only to have it all wrenched away.

And what had he been left with?

Nosy members of the *ton*, people like her family, with their noses pressed to the windows, looking for a glimpse of the man . . . treating him like some sort of circus oddity. Was it a wonder he was cold and distant and brooding? What reasons did he have to smile?

Staring at the flames he'd kindled and she'd stoked since last evening, Myrtle absently added another log. Then, picking up the poker, she jabbed at the log, stirring the ashes.

And she watched absently as flames licked at the edges of the wood, turning them black before ultimately consuming it, swallowing it up in a grand blaze that cast the most wonderful heat.

And yet . . . she didn't feel it. She couldn't feel it.

Not fully, and not truly.

Not with everything she'd learned about Val last evening.

All she knew was that despite his misery and insistence on wanting to be alone—which she didn't doubt for a moment—he'd still arrived at her door to start a fire because he'd known she'd be without light and that she'd be cold.

And the generosity of that spirit, Val's chivalry, offered a glimpse into the man he'd been before. How lucky his wife would have been.

And it was surely a black mark upon Myrtle's miserable soul that she found herself envying a ghost for having had a man like Val in her life, and for having been so completely and thoroughly loved by him that in her death, he'd ceased to be a man who smiled.

But he deserved that.

Oh, how he did.

Contemplatively setting down the steel rod, Myrtle straightened and headed over to the window overlooking the four corners of the London streets outside her windows.

Her gaze, however, locked on just one place.

Nor was it nosiness or curiosity that compelled her this time. It wasn't wonderings about her peculiar neighbor.

It was him.

Val Bancroft, the Duke of Aragon—the man.

She hugged her arms around her middle.

What must it be like to have loved so completely, or in the case of his late wife, to have had the love of such a man?

A man who wanted nothing to do with any other woman, or the world on the whole, because his heart had belonged fully to her?

Again, the green-eyed monster took a bite out of Myrtle's conscience and the corner of her mind now fixed on the man occupying that townhouse.

He—

A shadow flickered down below, and her heart raced as she looked for a glimpse of him.

And then she froze.

It was . . . them, once more.

The lion and the badger, as she'd taken to thinking of the two.

All her musings about Val were instantly forgotten as fear slipped in.

Eventually, the day was coming when Mr. Phippen's entire team arrived on the doorstep, intent on beginning work. She'd already resolved that if they were to do so, she'd simply greet them and explain that there had been a change in her family's scheduling, and she would ask them to leave.

Except there was no steady stream of workers.

There was no arrival of equipment.

It was just they two: the lion and the badger.

And just like the previous two times she'd caught sight of them, they perused her home the way a beggar child might the crystal windows outside Gunter's.

Her fingers quaking, and her teeth trembling along with them, she reached for the window's clasp; fiddling with the metal hook, she managed to free it and throw it open.

Several birds perched on the ledge right outside took noisy flight, squawking their shock at the interruption.

A rush of cold blew into the room to greet her, slapping at Myrtle with the ferocity of this particular winter's morn.

The two men below glanced quickly up.

"G-good day, sirs," she called down, praying they attributed that quavering to the cold and not to the fear that licked away all logic. "M-my family has been delayed in our travels and will remain through Christmas." She added a dramatic pause. "Though they've sent word to Mr. Phippen," she announced, crossing her fingers at her back. "And I'm sure you're aware about the delay in the construction project."

The lion scratched his forehead, or rather at the place where his brow surely was. The thick red curls hanging about his face made it nearly impossible for him to do anything but touch the hair there. "No one said anything to us about a change in schedule."

"Isn't that the way." She made a *tsk*ing sound with her tongue. "I am very sorry that your employer failed to inform you. I—" Myrtle stopped midsentence and looked over her shoulder in an exaggerated way. "What was thaaaat, Mother?" she called in the direction of a pretend parent. "Yes, I . . . know . . . I will shut them. I'll be along shortly."

Turning her attention back, she glanced down at the two men below.

Myrtle started in feigned surprise at seeing them still there waiting. "Forgive me. I've been summoned to help with Christmastide decorations to be hung."

"Yar staying through Christmas?" It was the lion who asked, and she was beginning to suspect that the other fellow beside him—the squat, stocky one—was a mute, incapable of sound and capable of only staring. "Yar *entire* family?"

"Indeed," she exclaimed, fixing a wide smile on her cheeks. "All eight of us. My mother and father, and my big, *very* big, brothers, and my two sisters. And did I mention my brothers are very big? My cousins, too, are here. Along with my aunt and uncle," she added. "It promises to be a joyous holiday." *Enough, Myrtle. Bring it to a stop now.* She cast another look back toward the doorway. "I'm cooooming," she called, adding several syllables to create a sense of sincerity and annoyance. Turning once more to the silent pair peering boldly up, she gave a little wave. "A happy Christmas to you, sirs."

With that, Myrtle drew the windows firmly shut, clasped them, and rushed off.

Or rather, she rushed headlong over to the gold velvet curtains.

Her heart hammering erratically against her rib cage, Myrtle remained motionless, scarcely daring to move or breathe.

Had they bought it?

She had been very convincing. If she could say so herself.

But thanks to Val, there was now fire coming from a chimney, and at night there'd been the flicker of light from the candles he'd lit and fireplaces he'd brought to life.

Biting the inside of her cheek, Myrtle gripped the curtain and edged the material back a fraction, allowing a slight sliver by which she might stare freely out.

The pair remained, both wearing matching looks of skepticism on their pockmarked faces, both scratching at their brows with opposite hands, twins in actions but polar opposites in appearance. She would have normally been amused by the sight they made.

Leave, she silently pleaded. *Just leave . . .*

It was several moments that seemed to stretch for an eternity before the pair hastened off, a quickness to their steps that hinted at not two men determinedly leaving, but men rushing to avoid notice.

And no matter how many times she assured herself her mind was merely overactive, and that she was imagining danger in places where none existed, the fear remained low in her belly, churning and twisting.

Just then, the lion looked back.

Myrtle jumped away from the window, setting the curtains into a damning flutter that she prayed he didn't notice, just as she prayed he'd failed to see her standing there, staring after them . . .

With the clock ticking, she remained, counting the beats on that ormolu piece atop the mantel, *one-two-three-four-five—*

She counted all the way to two hundred, and nothing happened. Absolutely nothing, that was, beyond the howling of the forlorn winter's wind and the crackling of the fire in the hearth.

Surely if the pair of strangers hadn't believed her and intended to storm her household, they would have done so already?

She backed away, heading in the reverse toward her fire, all the while her gaze remaining fixed on the windows.

Or mayhap they wouldn't. Mayhap they are even now looking through windows as you attempted to do at Val's.

And if they did? God help her, it wouldn't take much for them to deduce that the rooms were empty and her family was missing, and that Myrtle was the only one who remained.

Swallowing hard, Myrtle stretched her wobbling fingers about, searching for the metal poker. Her fingers met cold steel, and she stirred the embers there and added a log to ensure the fire continued to blaze . . . before setting the poker aside.

With fear fueling her steps, she hurried off in search of the one person aside from that pair of strangers who remained in London.

Val.

His name was a whispered litany in her head, a reminder that she wasn't alone. Not really. He was here.

And yes, he didn't want her about. In fact, he didn't want anything to do with her, but he'd also proven gracious enough as to not turn her away.

And taking hope and faith in that, she quickened her steps and headed down to the kitchens. After she'd added several logs to that fire, she fetched the wax candles and their stands; lighting two at a time, she carried them slowly to the main floor, and placed them upon the windowsills.

She made a dozen trips in all, carrying two dozen candles.

Her work complete, Myrtle hummed a Christmas carol under her breath.

Now, she had a trip to make.

After all, there was only one sure way to ensure a man's cooperation.

With that fueling her, Myrtle grabbed the largest wicker basket and took a quick detour.

Chapter 10

After leaving Myrtle last evening, Val had resolved that exchange between them would be their final one. He'd revealed more to her, a mere stranger, than he had to anyone these past years about his life. About Dinah.

Alas, it appeared fate was determined to muck up those efforts.

Or rather, *she* was.

RapRapRapRapRapRap . . . RapRap.

Horace barked, scrambled to the front of the room, and jumped up so that his paws were planted on the door.

The dog proceeded to whine and scratch.

RapRapRapRapRapRap . . . RapRap.

And Val knew.

If he hadn't known because of his dog's eager reaction, he'd have known by the spirited little rhythm of that tapping at his door the identity of the person on the other side.

He knew that it wasn't his brother returning, intent on convincing him to join their mother for the holiday season.

Knew it wasn't a beggar child or person, desperately knocking on doors.

Or anyone else . . . for one simple reason: people didn't knock on his door.

It was one of the reasons he'd been so very comfortable relieving Jenkins of that responsibility during this interlude when the servants were gone.

Val slid his fingertips into his temple and jabbed himself several times.

Oh, how he wished he'd not granted that reprieve.

For he didn't want to see her again.

He didn't want to see the pitying look that had been there in her revealing eyes after his telling.

He wanted peace and quiet and for her damned family to come and collect her and—

RapRapRapRapRapRap . . . RapRap.

"Christ," he hissed, his words a prayer and not a mere exclamation.

She wasn't leaving because she was a stubborn minx.

Stomping his way from the library to the foyer, Val steeled his heart as he went, determined to keep those walls around himself firmly in place.

He wrenched the door open, and by the way Myrtle stood with her fist poised, raised as if to strike, he'd interrupted a fourth of those grating knocks.

"Val," she greeted, her deep hood and enormous cloak giving her the look of a child playing at dress-up in her mother's wardrobe.

"I am busy," he said crisply, and made to shut the door.

The minx slipped under his arm and stepped inside. She paused only long enough to favor Horace with a long stroke of his enormous head. "I won't take up much of your time," she announced, pushing the fur-lined hood back and revealing that riot of curls, which at every new day since he'd met her had grown increasingly wild, as the lady herself.

He'd always had a preference for blonde, and yet, those midnight-black strands gleaming at the ends, hopeless to be constrained or tamed, perfectly suited her. She was a fey fairy always up to mischief. A mermaid who'd found her way to shore and retained an ability to cast her net out to unsuspecting captains and land men and—

"I know what you are thinking," Myrtle piped in, freeing him of that maddening path his thoughts had been waltzing down.

Giving his head a slight but hard shake, he pushed the door shut. "I rather doubt you do," he muttered.

Around her feet, Horace danced, his limp making his movements uneasy and awkward. Unlike Val, the dog made no attempt to conceal his excitement at their morning visitor.

Egad, what madness had that been, those pathetic, poetic thoughts about this woman—any woman, no less. But especially this garrulous one with a tendency of making a nuisance of herself.

Myrtle smiled widely and then displayed a basket he'd failed to note until this moment. Lifting it high, she waggled it before him.

And Val searched for a hint of the pity he'd expected to be greeted by that morn. Instead, only a smile met him.

He stared at her crooked smile, with two rows of teeth that, even with the generosity of her mouth, seemed to be in competition for space. Yet that smile, with two big dimples . . . entranced.

She gave her basket another little shake. "I've come with baked goods."

At her side, Horace whined and whimpered, lifting a paw up toward that wicker article.

And another detail which had previously escaped him cut through the cacophony of his chaotic thoughts.

The sweet hint of apple and sugar hung in the air, and he sniffed once.

"Here, it is unfair to make you wait," she cooed in those high-pitched tones she reserved for his dog, and then with Val briefly forgotten, she fished out a small tart and held it over to the dog.

Horace consumed that confectionary treat in one gulp, lapping her fingers.

The lady laughed and favored the dog with another pat.

And . . . everyone feared his dog.

Leave it to this woman to be the one who treated Horace like an enormous puppy.

Everything about her . . . unsteadied him. And he didn't want to be unsteadied, damn it.

Val wanted his feet on a firm ground, where he was free to be the man he'd been since Dinah's passing—a lonely one.

And she was getting in the way of his solitude.

"You need to leave," he said frostily, infusing as much ice as he could into that statement to get her to go.

"Yes," she agreed. The young lady paused and cast a glance over her shoulder, as if she were searching for something. Or someone? "But I do need you to come with me." Myrtle leaned in and dropped her voice to a ridiculously loud whisper. "It's why I've arrived with treats. To bribe you."

"To bribe me?" he echoed.

"I'm teasing." Her smile grew even bigger. "Well, sort of, I am. I do need your assistance, and I thought it would be polite to reward you with baked goods for helping me."

He stared dumbly at her for a long while, that smile still firmly in place. She spoke to him without the pity he'd expected to be greeted by that morn, but rather with all the warmth of two people who'd been friends for a lifetime. Val, who no longer had friends. "You're out of your damned mind," he finally said.

"Hardly," she scoffed. "I was going anyway and merely added to my order." Myrtle glanced at Horace. "And I added some for you, too, dear boy!"

Dear boy?

The *dear boy* barked happily, his giant tail thumping the marble floor hard in a quick staccato beat.

The lady rewarded his canine joy with another baked good.

"Enough," Val said tightly, and Myrtle's smile instantly quavered and his dog went silent, staring at him with giant, accusatory eyes—sad ones.

I will not feel guilty . . . I will not feel guilty . . .

The mantra didn't help. He was reminded once more in this lady's presence, and in his curt response to her, that he was still capable of feeling remorse. Nay, of feeling anything.

It was why when he again spoke, he gentled his voice—as much as he was able—though the gruff quality still coated his tone. "You cannot be here."

"Because we might be seen together?"

"Precise—"

"Because no one is here."

"I have three servants here." A fact which would send any proper lady running from fear of having her reputation ruined.

She blinked. "You do?"

"I do."

"Oh." She paused, wringing her hands. "My family, Val? They aren't coming back."

It was his turn to scoff. "Of course they are." After all, they couldn't simply . . . leave her here. A young lady, alone in London. "You think they'd just forget you."

"I do," she said quietly, giving a solemn little nod. "Because they did, Val. They sent me away to Mrs. Belden's, and I've been gone so long that they just . . . forgot me."

He shook his head, attempting to process that last statement from the lady.

"I was at a finishing school," she explained, mistaking the reason for his stunned silence. "My parents sent me away there so that I could become a proper lady."

It'd been a waste of funds and prayers and hopes on her family's part. He bit the inside of his cheek to keep from saying as much, discovering to some surprise he was still capable in some part of not offending.

The lady had not been tamed; in fact, he'd wager the solitude he coveted that not even God himself could have managed.

Myrtle stared at the tips of her toes, studying them intently, as if they contained answers as to where her family was. She was quieter than he'd ever recalled, quieter than he'd believed the noisy chit was even capable of.

He had a sudden inclination to pulverize her elder brothers and the father who'd failed to protect her.

"Of course they're going to return," he said gruffly a second time, offering up that reassurance. In the past, he'd have managed something more charming and reassuring. This was the best, however, he could manage after years out of practice. "They'll return, and you'll leave and join them for the Christmastide Season . . ."

And I'll be alone . . .

Funny. It was precisely what he wanted and had been praying for since she'd darkened his windows several days earlier. And yet, somehow that reminder that echoed in his mind didn't have the same . . . eagerness it'd had. It left him oddly . . . regretful.

"Oh, yes," she said matter-of-factly, lifting her head. "I know . . . *eventually* they'll recall I'm not around, and then they'll return, but until they do, I'm here on my own and in need of help." Myrtle stared pointedly at him, and it was a moment before he realized—

"My help?"

She nodded.

He scrubbed a hand down his face. *Do not ask . . . Remind her that she should go and—*

"What kind of help?"

And then immediately he wished he'd never asked, after all.

"I need a bath."

He choked on the saliva in his mouth.

Myrtle rolled her eyes. "I'm not asking you to bathe me—"

He strangled all the more, bending down and doubling over.

Myrtle thwacked him hard between the shoulder blades. "Or to help me dress."

She was going to kill him.

She was going to suffocate him with his own spit.

"No." He finally managed to get out that emphatic rejection.

She stared at him with forlorn eyes, her smile gone and her expression sad, and it was then he knew he was lost. Because he was becoming increasingly aware of the fact that he wasn't so immune to feeling, after all. Nay, he wasn't so very immune to *her*.

Cursing, he took her basket, and yanking the lid up, he reached inside and grabbed the first pastry his fingers touched. Val took an enormous bite of the Queen's Cake.

"Alriff," he said around the large mouthful.

Myrtle smiled, and damned if it wasn't like when the sun found its way amidst the perpetually grey, cheerless English skies.

"Splendid." Thrusting the basket against his chest, Myrtle drew her hood up and led the way.

Val stared after her retreating frame, watched as she let herself out and headed across the courtyard, so trusting with her expectation that he'd follow as he'd said.

And for a moment, he was tempted to push the door shut behind her, turn the lock, and keep her out . . . because every day he let her in more and more, and it left him unsettled.

Myrtle turned and peered back; with her hood up as it was, he felt her probing stare anyway. "Are you coming?"

He cursed. Yes, he was coming. Ignoring her question, he grabbed a hat, jammed it atop his head. "Stay here," he commanded his dog.

Horace glared in return.

They remained locked in a battle, master and dog.

"Oh, fine," he bit out, and Horace immediately barreled past him, bounding down the steps after Myrtle.

Val continued at a distance behind the pair.

The young lady spoke to his dog with the same comfort and ease she did Val . . . and what he suspected was an ease with which she spoke to anyone.

He didn't know what to make of her.

Perhaps that was why at every turn he found himself agreeing to . . . things he'd never in a lifetime believe he'd agree to, like helping her prepare a bath.

They approached her family's home, where he noted the windows were filled—

He stopped midstep. "What are those?"

Myrtle glanced about. "What is what?"

He jabbed a finger at the windows.

"Candles," she said, and resumed walking.

Val found his feet once more and moved into step beside her. "Candles?"

"Well, they are for—"

"Never tell me, the Christmastide decor?" he interrupted.

"Yes, that, but also to give the appearance of light so that those thieves think there are more people home than just me."

"Of course, how could I have forgotten the pair of thieves?" he drawled.

"I know, really, Val," she chided, endearingly oblivious to his sarcasm. She reached the servants' entrance first. "Here we are!"

Myrtle let Horace in.

Instead of rushing in behind to get out of the winter cold, she waited for Val. "I cannot thank you enough," she said as he entered and she shut the door behind them.

With that slight click of the panel closing, he saw the two of them . . . alone.

Yet again.

Tension hung in the chilly air; the quiet rang heavily, so loud in silence that he detected every breath Myrtle drew.

And his own. It came slightly rough and ragged.

Get in, get out.

That became the new mantra.

The sooner he readied her bath, the sooner he could get the hell out of here.

With that motivating thought compelling him, Val did a sweep of her family's kitchens.

Locating a wooden bath, he dragged the piece out.

As he did, she stoked the fire.

Despite his best efforts, Val felt his eyes drawn to her.

The fire raged still, indicating she'd tended it through the night, meaning she would have had to leave that makeshift bedchamber she'd made for herself, come down here, and then head back abovestairs. "You banked the fire," he said quietly.

Myrtle shrugged. "If I didn't, the fire would die, and then where would I be?" She smiled.

He couldn't think of a single lady of the peerage who'd recall the lesson and then see through those efforts. But she had.

Val proceeded to gather up buckets, and after filling them in the well outside, he returned, placing those pans upon the stove, heating them, and then adding them to the bath. Over and over. Until at last, the tub was full, and steam poured from the top.

He made to leave.

"Please, don't go," she said on a rush, and he froze. "Not that you should remain in here, per se . . . but rather, stay here in the—"

"No."

"Corridor, just until I finish bathi—"

"No." As in, absolutely, bloody not.

And against all better judgment, born of thoughts purely beyond his control, an image slipped in of Myrtle shedding her garments and climbing into that steaming bath. The heat of that water would leave a crimson flush about her skin, skin he'd wager was cream white, or did the same freckles he spotted on the bridge of her nose cover the rest of her? Desire consumed him. An unfamiliar response for him toward any woman since his wife's death, but also a physical response as old as time.

His shaft grew hard and throbbed uncomfortably at the images his traitorous mind had called forth.

"Val?" Myrtle's voice, with its slightly high-pitched elfin quality, as he'd come to think of it, contained a trace of hesitancy.

"I'm not staying here while you bathe, Myrtle," he said impatiently, finding his way once more. "As it is, me being here with you now, like this"—in any way—"would see you ruined." He should find a servant. Send word for his brother, indicating he needed a pair of maids.

So why didn't you . . . ? a voice taunted.

Because he'd wanted to be here with her.

He grunted. "I have to go, Myrtle."

"But I'm scared . . ."

Her voice came small and desperate, and they were such sentiments he'd not expected this bold woman to be capable of. And he'd hand it to her—she'd proven braver than most women at having found herself in the circumstances she did, for as long as she had.

Closing his eyes, Val balled his fists. *She isn't your problem. She isn't your problem.*

That mantra proved as useless this time as it had all the previous ones.

And as he failed to convince himself, he did the next best thing: he attempted to convince her.

"There is nothing to be worried about, Myrtle," he said, infusing a touch of exasperation in his voice in an attempt to break through her irrational—but still understandable—fears at being alone. "No one is here."

"That is it exactly," she said, and then rushed forward. "No one is here but me." She lowered her voice to a whisper. "And they know it, too . . ."

When he'd been a boy, and he and his brother had both been in the nursery, they'd stayed up late while their nursemaid had snored. And over her snorting breaths of exhaustion, he and Sidney had regaled one another with familiar and made-up tales of pirates whose ghosts had returned. The eerie tones Myrtle now spoke in recalled those same ones he and his brother had used.

Annoyance brought Myrtle's brow dipping low. "Did you hear me, Val? I said—"

"I heard you just fine. There are no ghosts—"

"I didn't say I'm afraid of ghosts," she interrupted. "Why would I be afraid of a ghost? They seem fine enough."

Any other time he'd have pressed her on that particularly ridiculous avowal. "Then who are you—"

"Them," she exclaimed, tossing her palms up in exasperation. "The men."

She spoke as if he knew, or as if he should know precisely who in hell she was speaking of.

"The men."

"Why are you repeating everything I say?"

Because she'd turned him upside down. As she always did. As she had since he'd found her peering inside his windows.

He tried again. "Which men are you afraid of?"

"My family hired Mr. Phippen to oversee the construction of our property, and he sent two men who I'm highly suspicious of."

"Highly susp—" He stopped himself from repeating back what she'd said just as she gave him a pointed look. Val sighed. "This again."

"Anyway," she went on, "Mr. Phippen has supposedly assigned them the role of inventorying my father's collection."

"I take by your choice of the word 'supposedly' you don't believe they are actually employed by Mr. Phippen."

The lady chewed at the tip of an index finger. "I cannot say for certain. I do not know whether they are employees of Mr. Phippen's who saw the wealth in my father's artifacts and have gone rogue . . . or whether . . ." She let her voice drift off and her gaze linger with his.

She nodded once.

She expected something of him again.

She nodded again, this time more emphatically.

But for the life of him, he didn't have a deuced idea of what that was.

Myrtle threw her hands up in what he'd come to find was her telling way of communicating her frustration. "Or whether they do not work for Mr. Phippen at all. That they are, in fact, pretending and have learned of my father's collection and are here to rob from us." When she finished, she folded her arms and nudged her chin his way.

He was silent a moment. "That is what you think?"

She bristled, and let her arms fall. "And you find it so hard to believe?"

"Well, let us see . . . One of the possibilities is that two men who were actually inventorying those items when your parents were still here are, in fact, not who they said they were, and that your parents had no idea of who was in their house, and that they were somehow men who had nothing to do with this Mr. Phippen? Do I have all of that?"

"Yes." She jabbed a finger in the air as she spoke. "Yes. Yes. And yes."

Val closed his eyes.

Val of two days ago would have left.

But not before he pointed out just how ridiculous, how fear-based the irrational conclusions she'd drawn, in fact, were.

Only, as he opened his eyes and found Myrtle staring earnestly back through the largest, brownest eyes he'd ever seen, the words froze on his tongue.

He couldn't—this time, anyway—bring himself to hurt or offend her.

Instead, he did the only thing he could think of, the one thing he'd believed himself incapable of anymore: he sought to assuage those irrational fears.

"I understand that it must be daunting for you to find yourself alone, Myrtle," he said softly, attempting to inject a gentle quality into his voice, which even to his own ears emerged as gravelly and harsh. "But imagining two men who are out to steal from your father's collection is as unlikely as ghosts haunting your house."

"You don't believe in ghosts?" she asked.

That was her takeaway? That was the one particular detail she'd fix on? Val slammed the heel of his palm against his forehead and dragged his fingers down his face. "I *believe* your parents surely have sense enough to not hire someone so untrustworthy."

"Oh, yes," she said, her features a perfect mask of wryness. "The same parents who forgot me here in London."

Valid point. He tried again. "Very well. Then these men wouldn't be so unwise as to come to Mayfair and steal from an earl. They'd risk a hanging."

"But why—"

"There are no strange men. There are no thieves, Myrtle," he said, this time with a harsh bluntness meant to penetrate her irrationality. "There is just you and me and a pair of men who work for your family who have specific tasks to see to."

"But then why creep about my family's house? *Hmm?*" she probed. "Because I saw them walking around outside just today."

God, she was as tenacious as ivy clinging to a building. Before he realized what he did, Val tossed his arms up as she did when she was annoyed. "I don't know, Myrtle," he said, exasperated. "Mayhap Mr.

Phippen employed them for tasks other than inventorying your family's property. Mayhap they also specialize in assessing windows and are conducting measurements or counting the panes or determining whether any of the glass might again be used."

The lady chewed at her lower lip, and despite himself, Val's gaze followed that innocent and unexpectedly arousing effort of her teeth worrying that narrow flesh.

His breath hitched peculiarly in his chest as another swell of desire slipped through him.

Suddenly, she stopped, and he wrenched his eyes up to meet her direct stare.

"That sounds unlikely, Val."

Through the haze of hungering, his mind was slow to process . . . and then it did.

Val's eyebrows shot up. "*My* suggestions are the ones that sound unlikely?" His voice echoed around the stone walls of the kitchen and off the low ceiling.

She shrugged.

That was it, nothing more than a little lift of those narrow shoulders in answer to his question.

Val growled and turned once more to go.

And this time, as he reached for the door handle, she didn't call out. She didn't attempt to stop him.

There wasn't that small voice, and that pitiable "please" begging for him to stay.

Val stopped so suddenly he rocked on his heels. He stared at the oak panel, willing himself to step through, to keep on going.

But for all those silent urgings, he remained unable to leave.

He turned.

Myrtle stood, and with her diminutive height, the slender slip of a young lady was swallowed by that velvet cloak. She looked impossibly small.

But her shoulders remained proudly erect and thrown back. Her chin lifted, and in her bearing, she may as well have been a warrior queen refusing to bow down to invading forces.

He pointed a finger at her. "Fine. I'll remain outside the kitchens, while you . . . while you . . ." Only he couldn't get the word out, because not for the first or even the second or third time that day, a mental image was called forth of her body divested of clothes and on display before him, naked.

His breathing grew shallow and ragged in his own ears.

"Bathe?" she supplied, her brow creased.

"Y-yes," he croaked, pointing her way again. "That. When you're done bathing, and . . . and . . ."

"Dressed?"

"Yes, that, too. I'm leaving."

And when he left this time, it was done between them. This would be the last he saw of her, and soon he'd forget her.

Because there would be no reason for him to continue to be around, and no good could come of it.

Nay, she'd be relegated to a distant corner of his mind . . . forgotten.

Only, as he quickly let himself out of the kitchens and stood in the hall, Val couldn't shake the terrifying thought that it was going to be nigh impossible to forget a woman like Myrtle McQuoid.

Chapter 11

With her first London Season approaching, Myrtle had given much thought to the man she'd one day wed.

She'd not let herself think much about what that still nameless and faceless stranger looked like.

Oh, based on both her banishment from the family and her lessons at Mrs. Belden's, she knew what was expected of her: she'd marry well and swiftly so that her parents could be free of her a second time—a final time. They, along with the rest of the world, expected her—like all ladies—to behave and be proper and dull and lifeless.

What she had often considered was what *he'd* be like.

He'd be charming, and ready with a jest.

He'd be given to an easy smile and would laugh big and heartily, as her father and brothers did.

And, of course, he'd read Jane Austen—both of her works.

And yet—considering the man on the other side of the door as Myrtle settled back into the water, slipping farther under the hot surface—Val was *none* of those things.

He was surly and brooding.

His smile came as reluctantly as the English sun.

And she couldn't imagine there was anyone who jested and laughed less.

And he certainly didn't appreciate or respect Miss Jane Austen.

He'd also accused her of having an overactive imagination—which, well, she could concede him that point—possibly. *Possibly.*

But now, she wondered if she'd had it all wrong.

What if she'd merely dreamed herself a paragon and not allowed herself to think about what it would be to wed a real man? One so fully dimensional who, with his gruff demeanor, didn't fit with the heroes of the romance tales she'd read, but who, in his every way and in his every action, was a true hero in every sense of the word.

For he could have let her to her own fears. He hadn't.

He could have left her in the cold and dark. He hadn't.

He could have simply ignored her knocking and said to hell with her worrying. And he hadn't done that, either.

For despite the rough exterior, the walls he'd built up about himself, he was also the manner of man who, with his every action, challenged her heart's natural rhythm.

He was a man whom she could imagine herself spending her entire life with.

And for a moment, an imagining slipped forward: the two of them alone, reading Miss Austen together, with Horace at their feet, and Myrtle teasing and challenging Val and—

She froze. "And what are you thinking?" she croaked, and then terror clogged her senses, and in a rush to be free of those terrifying musings, she quickly submerged herself underwater.

"Myrtle . . . are you all right?"

The water filled her ears, muting Val's voice. His concerned one.

Proving yet again that he was not the rough, unfeeling figure he presented to the world.

And she damned herself for noticing, because now she couldn't un-notice, and she couldn't slow the flow of these new thoughts of him.

"Myrtle?"

She exploded from under the depths, blinking back the sting of soapy moisture in her eyes. "Fine," she squawked. "I'm fine."

Except her heart raced, and the last thing she was sure of was that she was fine. Because she didn't feel fine. She felt confused and panicked and—

"You don't sound fine," he called back.

And she'd learned enough from Mrs. Belden to know that a proper gentleman would never dare speak such words to a lady. That a gentleman would have accepted the lie and certainly wouldn't have challenged her on her assurances.

"Well, I am. I'm bathing and thinking, and . . . bathing," she added weakly.

"It sounds like you're drowning."

"If I were drowning, would I be talking?" she shot back.

And fortunately, he let the matter rest.

For a moment.

"Are there intruders in there?"

Are there . . . ?

It took a moment, and then it hit her.

Why, he was . . . teasing her.

Squeezing the washcloth into a wet, soapy ball, she hurled it at the door, catching the panel. Water droplets sprayed as it hit with a thump and sailed to the floor with a *thwack*.

A laugh sounded on the other side of that oak panel, a deep, booming, and roughened sound of amusement.

And she stilled.

Why . . .

"Valentine . . . are you . . . laughing?"

The rumbling instantly stopped.

There was a pause as only silence filled the air. "No."

A smile deepened on her lips, and Myrtle sat upright, sloshing water on the other side of the tub onto the floor. "And now . . . lying?"

"I'm not lying. Don't you have a bath to take?"

"I do." She paused, eyeing the cloth she'd hurled his way. "Except I dropped my washcloth."

"You threw it," he corrected.

She stuck her tongue out. "Very well. I threw it, but can you fetch—"

"No."

Myrtle sighed.

Climbing out of the bath, she padded quickly across the kitchen floor. Gathering up a new cloth, she hurried over and climbed back in.

The water, still hot but less steamy, closed over her shoulders, and she sighed. And this time as she soaped her body, scrubbing away the dirt, she spoke to Val. "Do you really believe those men work for Mr. Phippen?"

"I do."

"And that I'm being ridiculous?"

"I didn't say you were ridiculous," he said in gruff protest. He paused. "But I do believe it's fanciful imagining thieves attempting to break in, particularly as they would have just done so by this point, no?"

She hesitated, considering that. "I'd not thought of that."

"Fear doesn't always allow us to be rational in our thought process." He spoke as one who knew.

"Do you have things you fear?" she asked, and she expected him to deliver either a scathing rebuke of her question or another mocking response.

"Yes," he said quietly. That was it.

She waited for him to say more.

But he didn't.

And this time, Myrtle sensed his need for an end to that particular questioning, and the woman whom she'd always been would not have hesitated to press him for more.

But she didn't.

She continued her bath in silence.

Reaching for the cake of soap, she lathered her hair, and once properly scrubbed, she submerged herself once more, and then stopped.

Blast and tarnation.

"Val, I have a problem," she said.

A quiet curse met her ears, and she found herself smiling once more at the freedom with which he responded.

"What now?"

"I forgot garments to change into. Will you fetch them for me?"

She braced for an immediate declination.

"Where am I going?"

Myrtle called out directions, and no sooner had the last word left her lips did she detect the rapid shuffle of his feet as he rushed off.

❄ ❄ ❄

The moment Val reached Myrtle's chambers, he didn't hesitate, making a path straight for the armoire and wrenching the doors open. He yanked out the first dress his fingers met . . . and then he stopped, his eyes locked on the undergarments, modest, white. There was nothing seductive or sexy about those articles.

There was no lace or frill.

Nor embellishment.

That was, with the exception of a pink bow at the center of the neckline—a bow better suited for a small child. Or an innocent.

Which was decidedly what Myrtle McQuoid was. He could now acknowledge that there was, in fact, *everything* innocent about her.

So why, even with all that, did he find himself pulling forth images of her naked in her bath, soaping her body, and—

Cursing, he crushed the garment in his fist, along with a pair of modest white stockings.

This time, fighting new imaginings of her, drawing the silk articles slowly up over trim ankles, higher, ever higher, over her calves and knees.

"You are pathetic," he muttered to himself as he turned swiftly and headed back belowstairs to the kitchens. As he approached, the distant strains of a boisterously sung Christmas carol reached him.

"Joy to the world!
Joy to the world! Oh, woah
Joy to the world!"

Joy to the world . . . It was another song he'd once sung, lending his voice to the other members of his family, and then years later, to his wife as they'd belted out the joy-filled tune.

For the memories alone that accompanied that carol and those lyrics, he should have been filled with bitterness for how his life had turned out, at everything he'd lost and all he'd missed.

Only . . . as he reached the door, that thick oak slab that did little to conceal the sounds of Myrtle's song, he could not.

"Joy to the world!
Joy to the world! Oh
Joy to the world! The Savior reigns
Let men their songs employ
While fields and floods
Rocks, hills, and plains
Repeat the sounding joy . . ."

He could not even attempt to muster the angry resentment that was always with him, because of her. Myrtle, who with her exuberance and uneven, pitchy rendition, made it impossible to feel those sentiments.

Instead, Val found himself in an unlikely way: he silently joined in, his lips moving in time to the words but still not giving that song sound. Closing his eyes, he turned himself over to feelings other than the ones of pain and sorrow and the loss that had so consumed him these past years.

> "Joy to the world then we sing
> Let the earth receive her King!
> Joy to the world then we sing
> Let the angel voices ring . . ."

He didn't feel the misery of what had been, and what now was.

> "Joy to the world then we sing
> Let the men their songs employ . . ."

He didn't find himself thinking about what had almost been.

> "Joy to the world then we sing
> And repeat the sounding joy . . ."

He didn't find himself playing in his mind the alternative ending he'd tortured himself with through the years: if they'd waited and not left in the midst of snow that had turned into a violent storm. If he'd stayed behind with his wife, and they two had celebrated Christmas alone that year . . .

> "He rules the world with truth and grace
> And makes the nations prove
> (And makes the nations prove) . . ."

Nay, he found himself filled with the same joyous lightness that had always infused his soul when that song had played. A lightness made even more so by the pitchy singer belting out her lyrics.

"And wonders of His love
And wonders of His looo—"

"Val?"

Her voice cut in, screeching across his thoughts, the broken lyrics substituted with his name jolting him to and startling him into dropping the garments he'd collected for her.

"Is that you?" The water sloshed, creating more of those naughty visuals of her sitting upright, baring her breasts to the cool night air.

Sweat dotted his brow. "Yes," he said, unable to keep the gruffness out of a reply that emerged sharper than even he intended. This time, however, it wasn't annoyance that harshened his response, but rather . . . desire.

"Oh." There came more sloshing, as if she'd sat back, slipping farther under those waters, once more. "I feared it was the men."

"There are no—"

She interrupted his exasperated reassurances. "Did you get my garments?"

Val glanced down at the floor. "Yes." Bending down, he scooped them up.

"Will you set them inside?"

Would he . . . ?

He broke out in another sweat.

She was asking him to open that door.

Had she been another woman, a more experienced one who didn't wear white garments decked with pretty pink bows, he'd have believed her request was an attempt at seduction.

It did not, however, prevent him from conjuring more of those naughty images of her completely bare of anything more than the flush on her skin left by the heated waters she soaked in.

"Val?"

"I'm not opening the door, Myrtle," he called out, his voice strained and laced with a new kind of pain.

"But I can't come out there when I'm done with my bath."

Which in speaking . . . when in hell would she be done with those waters? When, so he didn't have to think of her in them any more than he already had?

"Fine," he gritted between tightly clenched teeth. And squeezing his eyes shut, he opened the door a fraction and threw the garments inside.

They landed with a light *whoosh*.

"Thank you."

He grunted in return, and his work being truly done here, he turned once more to go.

"Please, don't leave until I'm done, Val," she called out again, her voice small and fear-tinged.

Damn it all to hell and back.

"I'm quite vulnerable, you know. If those men come by and I'm stuck in here defenseless, unable to protect myself."

If those imagined bad guys—or for that matter, any man—came upon her, the lady would be unable to protect herself.

He opened his mouth to say as much . . . but . . . stopped himself.

"Fine," he said brusquely. "Will you hurry?"

"Of course!" she exclaimed, the natural joy that seemed to always infuse her voice fully restored, and she resumed belting out her merry song.

> "Joy to the world then we sing
> Let the earth receive her King!
> Joy to the world then we sing
> Let the angel voices ring . . ."

And when it seemed her bath would never end, that he would be forced to endure the sounds of water sluicing over her naked skin, flushed red from the heat, and imagining her in all her naked splendor, at last, the Lord took mercy.

"Done!" she called out. "But I still need to change my garments, so if you can wait a moment more?"

Val swallowed painfully, struggling to get his throat to move.

Oh, God.

Think of anything other than the lady on the other side of that kitchen door, completely naked and toweling herself off.

It didn't help.

The thoughts to replace were of him pushing her hands gently aside and dragging that towel over her naked form himself. Wiping away the moisture that clung to the small of her back, running the towel along her spine, and then his lips kissing each place he touched.

He broke out in a sweat. Pressing his forehead against the heavy oak panel, Val knocked his head slowly and silently against it, his gaze locked on several initials all nicked upon the door. He passed a cursory look over the *CM*, and *QM*, to land on the *MM*.

Myrtle McQuoid.

Yes, think of her as a small girl carving her name into the wood door.

Better yet, think of the older brother who'd surely—and rightfully so—beat Val bloody and unconscious, and only then call him out for lusting after the lady as he now did.

It didn't help.

His wicked mind still only dragged forth imaginings of—

The door opened, and a black curse slipped out as he pitched forward. He hurriedly righted himself, retaining his feet . . . but just barely.

He glared.

"My apologies," Myrtle said in her cheer-filled way.

"Fine," he grunted. "Now I can . . ." *Leave.*

It was a silent directive issued by his conscience, that white angel on his shoulder who knew him to be a devil, and who sought to influence him in the ways of the right.

Only, Lord help him—and it was a prayer he sent to the heavens—he was hopeless to leave.

"I need help," she murmured, a pretty blush filling her face, already suffused with color from her bath, and leaving those full cheeks the crimson hue of a bright summer berry.

And damned if he didn't have a taste suddenly for sweet fruit.

He swallowed hard.

"Myrtle," he said, her name a desperate entreaty, roughened and hoarse.

She presented him her back.

It didn't help.

Val closed his eyes.

She'd said she'd not ask him to help her dress, and yet she stood before Val, with her back presented to him, and a swath of silken skin, pink from the heat of her bath, on display.

A feast for the eyes he'd no right indulging in.

And yet—he swallowed another hard swallow—Val was helpless to look away.

Helpless to do anything but stare. And perhaps it was because he'd been so long without a woman—it had been years since he'd bedded one, and even then, it had been his wife, and then no one after her—but desire coursed through him, heating his veins, and his body went hard.

"Will you?" she asked, a slight quiver contained with her voice that was normally steady and cheerful, hinting at the fact that Myrtle was as unsettled as Val himself.

Touching her would be folly; touching her while she remained in a state of undress would be an even greater one. And yet, to leave her partially naked would be the greatest one of all.

Wordlessly, he closed the distance between them and reached out with methodical intent to help with the fastenings on her dress.

"Don't you have any other gowns?" he asked, his voice emerging harsh from the desire he fought, his fingers shaking slightly, and he gave thanks that she could not see their tremble.

"Most were packed, and the ones that are here do not fit as well as this. This is my sister's."

"Have you considered how impossible it is going to be for you to get yourself out of this without the assistance of a maid?" *Or me.*

Except it was the wrong question to ask. It had been the absolute worst suggestion he could have made. For a whole host of reasons.

One being the image that his question immediately conjured in his own mind: Myrtle arriving on his doorstep, presenting her back to him once more, and him slowly, ever so slowly, undoing pearl button after pearl button, exposing inch after inch of her silken skin.

He tamped down a groan.

Myrtle turned. "You are right. This doesn't make sense as far as a dress selection." And then, as she stepped away from him, the fabric she held against her chest sagged in the back, falling about her bare shoulders.

Val closed his eyes and gave silent thanks as she sprinted off, heading for the door, when suddenly Myrtle stopped.

She cast a hesitant glance his way. "Will you come with . . . ?"

"No."

"But—"

"Myrtle, we are alone together; you are a young woman and I'm a man, and you'd be ruined . . ." And he'd be trapped. "If we were discovered"—he waved a hand between them—"as we are, your brother would call me out." And strangely, these days, death didn't hold the same appeal it once had.

"We won't be discovered because no one is here," she pointed out, dogged in her determination. "And . . . I'm afraid of being alone."

And there it was.

The reason she continued to seek him out.

In fairness, any young woman would have been daunted at simply the prospect of being alone.

Do not . . . Do not . . .

Bloody hell.

"Fine," he gritted out. "I'll stand outside the corridor and that is—"

"Thank you," she said quickly, and then as if she feared he'd change his mind—which he absolutely should—the lady sprinted off.

Val continued after her, keeping a sizable and safer distance between them.

That way it wasn't as easy to note the pink flush that still clung to her skin from the warm waters she'd recently climbed from.

Chapter 12

He'd stayed.

He'd stayed when he'd clearly not wanted to.

When he clearly didn't wish to be with her.

Such, she'd learned, was the way of all people where Myrtle was concerned: Her parents had sent her away. Her elder siblings treated her as though she were a small underfoot child. Her younger siblings were content with one another's company and didn't have need of their older sister. Her cousins rarely acknowledged her anymore.

And at every turn, Val sought to leave or was asking her to leave.

Even with all that, he continued to keep her company still.

"Are you done?" he called from the other side of Cassia's door, his voice tinged with impatience.

Granted, he proved reluctant in her company. "No," she said, letting her dress fall, and reaching for another gown. Her fingers caught a modest white muslin article . . . and she stopped, considering the material a long moment, before sliding her gaze sideways. Assessing the other gowns with greater care, and with less of a perfunctory nature.

Unlike her largely white and pink wardrobe, Cassia's contained silks and satins of deeper, darker hues. Bolder looks, with even bolder bodices.

That was, bolder than the high-necked, lace-stuffed ones that had been selected for Myrtle, just a few months shy of making her Come Out.

Dampening her mouth, she collected a silk gown in deep sapphire, the bodice and hemline both trimmed with crystals, and with reverent fingers, she drew the article forth.

Never before had she worn such a dress.

Eventually, she would.

But her sister, having already known two London Seasons and not wed, had been afforded a greater freedom with her wardrobe.

Perhaps in an effort to entice?

Whatever it was, Myrtle envied her elder sister the luxuriance of such a dress. What would Myrtle look like in a gown so fine?

Nay, ask the question you really wish . . . a voice silently taunted. *What would Val think of you in such a dress?*

He'd likely—

"Myrtle?" More annoyance than usual underlined his query.

"I'm almost done," she called, startled back to the moment and into drawing the garment on. "He'd likely be as unmoved as he always is around you," she muttered to herself.

"What was that?"

"I said 'don't move as they might be around here,'" she called back, not missing a beat, her tendency through the years of speaking to herself having provided her with the skill to prevaricate whatever it was she'd said aloud.

"The men."

"Yesss, the men," she repeated, a healthier, safer annoyance taking the place of any regret at Val not seeing her as he might a woman.

She balked, her entire mind, body, and soul recoiling from that.

Not that she cared if he saw her as a woman. She didn't.

With those girlish musings about him dissolving, and any and all romantic sentiments that had crept in dying, she stomped barefoot across the room.

She yanked the panel open. "I'm done."

He flicked a cursory glance over her. "I see that."

That was it . . .

She'd said she didn't care about whether he viewed her as a desirable woman, and she didn't.

But she still expected . . . some reaction from him at her being . . . in a fine sapphire gown.

"That's it?" she blurted, before she could call the words back.

"I . . ." He shook his head, looking so truly hopeless and lost that she found herself battling . . . tears. He drew back. "What is it?" His question came as a harsh command from a man who clearly didn't wish to ask it but felt compelled to do so anyway.

"I don't want to have a London Season," she found herself whispering.

He cocked his head. "I . . . don't follow."

"No man is going to want me."

"They will," he said gruffly, wrestling with the collar of his jacket.

"No, they won't. No one ever does, Val. And I'm going to find myself stuck with the next best thing: companionship."

"And companionship is so bad?" he asked with a gentleness she'd never before heard from him, and one she would have expected he was incapable of.

But then, she should have already learned at every turn there was always more where this man was concerned.

"Did you have companionship?" she returned as gently as she could, already knowing the answer. "Or did you have a grand love?"

"I had a grand love," he murmured quietly, his gaze growing sad and wistful.

"Precisely," she said, hating herself for being so petty as to resent the woman he'd had who'd known such love and devotion. "And I won't. I'm passable at best."

"Roads are passable."

"Precisely." She pounced, pointing a finger at him. "And men don't fall in love with roads." They fell in love with glorious, interesting women. "I don't have golden curls." She yanked at a sopping tress that, even soaked as it had been by the bath, had resumed a frizzy curl.

"I . . . Myrtle, you're . . . perfectly desirable."

Except, when he said it in that garbled, reluctant way, as if the admission had been dragged from him, a lady found herself hard-pressed to believe there was any sincerity to it.

She hugged her arms around her middle. "I'm not desirable, Val. People don't want me about. I'm entirely forgettable." A half laugh, half sob climbed from her throat and lent a warble to the next words she spoke. "As you can probably tell from my entirely enormous family having forgotten me." The same family had sent her away to Mrs. Belden and continued on perfectly, as if they'd always been a family of seven and the one missing eighth member had truly never belonged.

Knuckles brushed her chin, as a touch equal parts firm and gentle guided Myrtle's face over.

"I can't attest to your family's failure," he murmured, his fingers stroking back and forth from her chin to cheek in a tender touch that stole her breath, in a caress she wasn't even sure he was aware he conducted.

But she was aware.

God help her, she was aware of it, and warmth spiraled in her belly. And butterflies danced.

"Do you know what I do know, Myrtle?" he murmured, and she was capable of nothing more than shaking her head.

"I know that when you have your debut, you'll be surrounded by a sea of ordinary. Of women who were told to not smile too widely, or laugh too loudly, and who perfectly followed those terrible dictates from cold instructors. And amongst them all, there will be you, with a smile like sunshine and a spirit not crushed by the constraints society placed upon every other woman, whose light will be so very dim in the bright rays that emanate from you."

Her breath caught, and her heart along with it, and words failed.

As in this moment, with his murmured, silken words leaving her heady, she fell more than a bit in love with Val Bancroft, the Duke of Aragon.

He stilled his touch; his eyes, previously locked with hers, shifted lower, his gaze dipping to her mouth.

And she knew with the intuition of Eve that he was thinking of kissing her, and knew even as his head tipped only a fraction that he intended to.

And she closed her eyes just as his mouth met hers.

There was a gentleness to that meeting, a hesitancy that dissolved in an instant as his lips covered hers again and again.

A little sigh slipped out, and her knees sagged, and the floor shifted under her bare feet. But he was there to catch her. Gripping her firmly by the hips, he sank his fingertips gently into that skin, wrinkling the fabric, and she didn't care. She moaned, grateful as he guided her against the wall, anchoring her between the solid surface at her back and the powerful muscles of his chest, as strong and broad as any wall.

He reached a hand between them, and his thumb teased the corner of her mouth, and instinctively she parted her lips and let him inside.

He swept his tongue within that cavern, tasting her with slow, bold strokes, and Myrtle froze.

She had often thought about what her first kiss would be like.

It had been a popular discussion amongst all the young ladies at Mrs. Belden's when the school was quiet and they'd taken to their rooms for the night.

That was, not Myrtle's kiss . . . but the "first kiss" in general.

Suzanne Trelawney had been the only one amongst their ranks who'd had one. And she'd delighted in regaling the other young ladies with tales of her first kiss.

To Myrtle, the whole thing had sounded vile: wet and embarrassing and awkward. Some man sticking his tongue in her mouth?

Why, the human tongue on the whole was a rather disgusting bit of flesh.

Or that was what Myrtle had thought.

How wrong she'd been.

Oh, how very wrong.

Held in Val's broad, strong arms, his mouth on hers, there was nothing gross or distasteful.

His lips were hard and as powerful as the limbs she gripped.

He tasted faintly of apple and mint, and she sighed and conceded that Suzanne had been correct. There was nothing unpleasant about the feel or taste of him.

She touched the tip of her own tongue to his, exploring him and surrendering fully to her first kiss.

His breathing came ragged and raspy as her own as he moved his hands lower; catching her once more by the hips, he drew her close.

So close she felt the length of him, his flesh hard against her lower belly.

His "spear," as her mother had called it, in the most horrifying, most uncomfortable discussion a daughter could never wish to have with one's mother. The mention of the male anatomy, a man's member, had left Myrtle riddled with fear and disgust.

What a fool she'd been.

Val was hopelessly fascinating, and her hips moved in a rhythmic way against him, in a way that she should be embarrassed by.

And even as she broke their kiss and buried her face in the crook of his shoulder, she found herself unable to stop that gyration of her hips.

He growled, nuzzling her neck. The rough growth of a day's beard scraped her sensitive flesh, and her pulse picked up an even more frantic beat.

A little whimper escaped her, and she let her head fall back, opening herself to a different kind of kiss.

"Val," she moaned, pushing her hips against his, her hungering for this man and this moan edging out any and all embarrassment at her body's wanton response.

He stilled, and then wrenched away; his breath came as ragged as her own, his chest rising and falling in the same quick way hers did.

He stared at her blankly, his eyes containing the same haze of passion that surely clung to hers.

And then he blinked . . .

And with that up-and-down fluttering of his dark lashes—beginning slowly and then growing more frantic—a different emotion slipped in.

Horror.

He wrenched his hands up and back, drawing them close to his frame and far from hers, like she contained the head of Medusa and he feared the venomous bite of one of the serpents stretching from her hair.

Shame brought Myrtle's feet curling sharply into the hardwood floors.

"That should not have happened," he said, his voice harsh and sharp.

She nodded dumbly. "I . . . know?"

Except hers emerged as a question.

Because how could something that had been so wondrous have been . . . wrong?

He blanched, his harshly beautiful features twisting in a grimace which was somehow more painful than his earlier rejection.

She waited for him to say anything more, because anything would surely be better than those last words he'd uttered.

But then Val backed slowly away, and when he'd put some ten paces between them, he turned quickly on his heel and raced off.

As he fled, she watched him go. How was it possible to go from the most magical, most beautiful moment of one's life to the sad emptiness that came at Val's flight?

Chapter 13

The following afternoon, settled into her place at her window seat, Myrtle stared across the way at Val's household.

The curtains to that room she so often caught sight of him in had been drawn tight, but for a slight crack in thick fabric. Myrtle occasionally caught a glimpse and glimmer of movement within. She touched a finger to the cold windowpane, scratching at the slight sheen of ice, and then dusted the remnants away with her palm so that she might better see.

Yes, the facts that he'd no servants about and that no visitors entered that household spoke of a man who found solace in his solitary presence, and as such, that disdain was not reserved solely for Myrtle.

She let her hand fall to her lap. Or mayhap that was merely what she told herself in that moment.

For how else was she to account for thinking about inviting him to join her? How, after he'd fled from her home like a man whose heels had caught fire?

But then, what was the alternative? That she spend her eighteenth birthday alone and forgotten? And as pathetic as it might be to seek out the company of someone who so clearly did not wish to be with her, it was preferable to sitting alone, wallowing in the reminder that her family had forgotten her.

With a sigh, Myrtle swung her legs over the side of the bench and stood. Heading over to the hearth, she stopped to stoke the fire, adding a log and then waiting until the flames had licked at the edges and embroiled the kindling in a conflagration before returning the poker to its stand.

And before her courage deserted her, Myrtle started from the parlor and, pulling the hood of her cloak up into place, made her way to the front door and then outside.

A blast of cold air rushed to greet her, slapping her in her cheeks and stealing her breath so sharply that she gasped; the frigid air froze the insides of her nostrils.

Burrowing deeper into her cloak, Myrtle descended the handful of steps and started for Val's residence. An eerie quiet hung over the London streets, so thick and heavy and absolute, the kind that made a young woman recall she was alone and that her family had gone off and that she was at the complete and total mercy of possible thieves planning a heist.

Stop it.

It's surely your overactive imagination that has you conjuring up that threat.

After all, wasn't that why nightmares came to children when the house slept and the world went quiet?

And she was certainly not a child. She was a grown woman. Why, even one year older today. A woman who'd spent the better part of four years away from her family, learning how to survive and make a life on her own without them. How many young women could say that?

"At least two dozen or so each year that you've been gone," she muttered aloud, just so she might hear herself speak again. "You weren't the only woman at Mrs. Belden's."

Those assurances didn't help.

Quickening her steps, Myrtle hastened across the street and bounded swiftly up his steps. She already had a hand out and was knocking.

Hard.

Rocking back on her heels, she waited for several beats of silence before pounding away, louder and harder.

All the while her nape prickled, and shivers traipsed down her spine. Ones that had absolutely nothing to do with the cold or her impending meeting with Val, and everything to do with the sense that she was being watched.

A sense that danger was imminent and coming to her. For her.

"Will you answer the door?" she whispered, her breath leaving a cloud of white as she spoke. Myrtle increased her knocking, pounding as hard as she could.

Suddenly, the door was wrenched open so that her fist, deprived of the drum surface, hovered in midair.

She blinked, registering the duke's visage etched in its familiar scowl. "What?" he demanded . . . in his familiar growl.

And a wave of relief so strong at no longer being alone swept through her, and she smiled for the first time that day. "Good afternoon to you, Val!" she greeted him jovially, the joy that lightened her frame real. "May I?" she asked when he continued to stand there, a mountain of a man blocking the entrance.

"May you what?" he grunted.

"Join you?" And without waiting for him to reply, she ducked around him and saw herself inside.

"What in blazes do you think you are doing, Myrtle?" Val demanded in a furious whisper. He swept his gaze frantically over the streets outside before slamming the door shut so hard she jumped. "You cannot be here."

She frowned. "And whyever not?"

"Whyever not?" he echoed. "Whyever not?" he repeated, his voice climbing. "Because you are a lady, and I am a gentleman."

Myrtle blinked innocently up at him. "Yes?"

"And if we're discovered so, you'll be ruined, and I'll be trapped."

Trapped. Hmph. "You aren't a bear, Val," she said, unable to keep the indignation from her tone.

"A bear? A *bear*?" he said for a second time.

She nodded.

Leaning down and shrinking the great space between his taller and her smaller frame, he stuck his face in hers. "I'm not a bear."

She rolled her eyes. "I know—"

"Because if I was, you'd have sense enough to go running, and we'd both be better off, safer for it."

Was it really so hideous, the prospect of marriage to her?

If that was the reaction she was destined to garner during her London Season, then her fate and future proved grim indeed.

"You should leave now, Myrtle. Now."

He repeated himself when he was upset.

It was something she'd come to learn about him in the short time they'd known one another. And there was also . . . an intimacy to that discovery. She had come to learn the nuances of this person—this man.

Perhaps that was why his booming shouts and scowls didn't send her running in terror, as he so clearly wished for her to do.

Myrtle smiled. "I will go," she promised.

"Good." He took several swift, relieved steps toward the door. "That is wi—"

"*If* you join me," she interrupted him as he clasped the handle, freezing him in his tracks.

❄❄❄

She was mad.

It was why she wasn't going away.

It was why she remained one of the only people wholly unmoved by him and his shows of anger.

And certainly the only one who smiled in that sincere way, with a glimmer and light that dimpled her cheeks and met her eyes.

But he wasn't the only one who was going mad. Or perhaps it was his hearing that was failing him. Because those were the only two reasons that accounted for what he'd heard.

Val turned slowly back. "I beg your pardon."

"Join me," she said with another one of those sun-filled smiles. Holding up two fingers and pointing them toward the floor in an upside-down V, she made a motion of walking.

"Is your fire out?" he asked bluntly.

Myrtle shook her head. "No. You will be very pleased to know I've done a *very* good job of making sure that the fire doesn't go—"

"Are you hurt?"

This time, Myrtle's smile dipped, and she proceeded to touch her arms and stomach, as if searching for some injury. "Why, no."

"Have those brigands attempted to sneak in and steal off with your father's collectibles?"

Myrtle stopped the automatic search of her frame and held an index finger aloft. "No." She paused. "That is, not ye—"

He cut her off for a second time. "Are you without food?"

"No, quite the opposite. That is—"

"Then, Myrtle, there is absolutely no reason for me to accompany—"

"One of the reasons I've come."

"—you to your household." Val finished his sentence over her speaking.

"It is my birthday," she blurted.

He cocked his head.

And this time, there was a hesitation to her, an unsureness the likes of which he'd never before seen from her. She wrapped her arms around her middle, giving herself a solitary little hug. "I have turned eighteen today." She repeated the admission in a different way. "And I'd . . ."

"Rather not spend it alone?" he asked gruffly, and she gave a little nod, dropping her eyes to the floor.

Now the reason for her presence and request this day made sense. Even so, it was too dangerous . . . for both of them. And for so many reasons.

God rot her family. Val resisted the urge to unleash a stream of black curses about the mother and father and siblings who'd left her behind. What manner of parent forgot a child? And at that, this woman? A woman so vibrant as to light an entire room, and whose bright smile challenged even the darkest day. And it was why, against all better judgment, he wanted to say yes. He yanked a hand through his hair.

"Perhaps you'd like to join me?" Her bell-like, clear voice emerged with its usual cheer, and relief filled him at finding her restored to her natural way. The way it was most right for her to be. And it also restored him to reason, and propriety.

Val opened his mouth to issue a gentler declination. That was, as gentle as he was able anymore. "I can—"

Myrtle sank to the floor and threw her arms around Horace's enormous head, hugging the creature.

And it occurred to him. "You are inviting my dog?"

Myrtle briefly lifted her eyes up to Val's. "Well, I've purchased myself a splendid cake and would rather not eat it alone," she explained. "And we can't have that, can we?" she asked more rhetorically in a singsong way as she angled Horace's head back and forth. "Plus, I do so adore your company."

The dog's panting grew more frantic, more eager, and he gave a happy yelp, as if he understood precisely what the minx was saying.

Val rocked back on his heels. She adored his company.

As in . . . his dog's.

Whereas Val's she sought because he was the next best thing to no one.

"I'll leave you two to celebrate," he said, as for the first time in all the years he'd had Horace, he found himself resenting the magnificently loyal creature.

Or rather, once loyal.

Laughing, Myrtle looked up. "You are so funny, Val."

She believed he'd been jesting. He used to be the charming fellow capable of making people laugh. But that skill now eluded him. And yet, he could not bring himself to admit that he'd not been making a joke, not when her eyes sparkled as they did.

Myrtle gave Horace one more affectionate pat on the head, before hopping up. "We must all celebrate."

They must all celebrate.

She'd confounded him.

She'd confounded both of them, him and Horace.

It was why, a short while later, with Myrtle singing a merry tune as she went, he found himself crossing the street, accompanying her to her family's household.

> "Christians, awake, salute the happy morn,
> whereon the Savior of the world was born . . .
> rise to adore the mystery of love,
> which hosts of angels chanted from above,
> with them the joyful tidings were begun . . ."

And oddly, hearing her sing lyrics about "happy morns" and the mystery of love, and "joyful tidings" . . . did not stir his bitter cynicism or crush him with the weight of sorrow and loss. Rather, there was more of that . . . overwhelming lightness within, a lightness that found its spark from her joy that flickered like a flame inside Val.

Suddenly, Myrtle stopped walking and singing, and that flame went out. "Are you all right?" she asked. "You've gone quiet."

"I'm always quiet."

"But it's different from your *usual* quiet," she said, unnerving him with the level of intimacy that had grown between them, and the ways in which she'd come to identify variations between his silences. "This is more like you're distracted and—"

"And I'm just looking to get us out of sight and indoors so we can get on with this celebration," he snapped, instantly hating himself for turning his impatience on her.

Horace whined and rested a paw on Myrtle's knee.

She caught the enormous foot in her hands and gently shook it. "Oh, you needn't make apologies for your master's rudeness. He's just hungry for the cake."

Val's lips twitched up in a smile.

Myrtle waggled a finger at his mouth. "Aha! I knew it." She looked back at Horace. "And I'm not one for I-told-you-sos, but if I were, I'd mention that I knew your master was just pretending at being annoyed." With the usual enthusiasm restored to her peppy steps and Horace at her side, Myrtle headed onward for her home; the lyrics to her Christmas carol rang out clearly as off she went.

"He spake, and straightway the celestial choir
in hymns of joy, unknown before, conspire,
the praises of redeeming love they sang,
and heav'n's whole orb with alleluias rang."

Giving his head a shake, Val started to follow along after her. And stopped.

His nape prickled as the sense that he was being watched—that they were being watched—froze him in his tracks.

Frowning, he did a quick sweep of the surroundings, searching out the source of that unease.

A light snow had begun to fall, adding to the heavy quiet which hung upon the winter air. But for the occasional gust of howling air, however, there was nothing.

Still, unable to shake the feeling of danger—

"Val?" Myrtle called out, a question contained in his name.

Several yards away, she stared back.

"Coming," he said, and giving his head a hard shake, hurried to join her.

The lady's fancifulness had begun to rub off on him. There was nothing else for it. There was no other explaining why he'd begun to look for foes in the shadows and sense danger amidst the stillness.

Even so, as they bypassed the front doors and headed around the back to the servants' entrance, he couldn't keep from taking one last look behind him.

Myrtle opened the door, letting Horace enter first, and then followed in after the dog.

Val joined the pair, closing the door behind them.

Loosening the ties of her cloak, she removed the garment and hung it upon the hook, and headed with purposeful steps for the fire.

Myrtle dropped to a knee and reached for several logs, filling her arms with them, then extended one.

Frowning, Val rushed over. "I'll do that," he said, reaching for that burden.

She drew back slightly, retaining her hold. "I can do—"

"I know," he said, making another attempt to take them. "You're quite capable."

"You're being sarcastic," she muttered.

Another smile formed on his lips, that curve of the muscles growing increasingly familiar and common in her presence. "Actually, this is the one time I'm not." He discovered a new appreciation for Myrtle at every turn. *It is only because she is unconventional, not because of anything . . . more.* "I've never known a lady capable of starting and keeping a fire going."

"I didn't start it," she pointed out.

"No, but you've kept it going, which is no small feat." He crooked his fingers. "Must you always be this obstinate?"

"Yes."

They remained with their gazes locked, neither speaking. One thing he would always win out on where this one was concerned was silence.

But not stubbornness.

Not this time, however. "Please," he said quietly. He'd not have her tending fires on her birthday, and certainly not on the birthday when her family had left her alone.

A curl tumbled over her brow. And he had the overwhelming urge to brush the strand back. To take that curl in his fingers and feel the silken softness. "Very well," she said grudgingly, and relinquished her hold.

Setting down the pile, he collected the poker and added a log.

As he worked, she knelt beside him, warming one hand beside the fire, while the other she used to pet Horace.

"There," Val said when he'd finished and stood. He reached a hand down, that gesture coming effortlessly, as if he were once again a polite gentleman given to assisting young ladies and not the surly, mournful, empty man he'd become.

And Myrtle placed her fingers in his with a similar ease, the level of which both confounded him and terrified him out of his mind, and allowed him to help her to her feet.

He should release her. It was the proper thing to do. He'd no place touching her in any way. Even so, he couldn't break that connection; he couldn't stop himself from reversing the lay of their grip so that his fingers covered hers, or from stroking that curve between her right thumb and index finger.

"Your hands are hard," she murmured. His fingers curled reflexively, and he made to pull it back, reminded by her innocent admission that he wasn't that man.

But Myrtle brought her other palm up, keeping him there.

"No, it isn't a bad thing," she said matter-of-factly, retaining her hold upon him. She turned his hand up and raised it close for a deeper inspection. "My father's are soft. And I've never noted my brothers' hands before, and that is the extent of my knowledge of them."

She was innocent. So very innocent.

Too innocent to be with a cynical, unsmiling bastard like himself.

"I do prefer yours," she said, as capable as she always was to keep a discussion between them going with only herself doing the contributing. "They are . . . interesting. They are real." She looked up. "Do you think other gentlemen's hands are like yours?" she asked curiously.

"I . . . don't know. I'd wager not." Those he'd kept company with had played cards, sipped brandies, with the largest extent of their physical activity being the rounds they'd gone against Gentleman Jackson and riding their mounts. "I would say most respectable gentlemen aren't chopping their own wood or setting their own fires or doing anything that would leave their hands callused." Like his.

"That is . . . unfortunate." Her eyes grew sad, and at that pitying glimmer, Val stiffened. His whole body tensed as he was hit with an onslaught of . . . regret that he wasn't the same man of his past. "I'm to have my Season," she said, confounding him with that unexpected shift. "And it is of course expected that I'll make a match, and I'll likely find myself married to a man with soft hands who knows absolutely nothing about starting fires or doing anything with them."

Images paraded through his mind, a great kaleidoscope of scenes all playing out one by one in his head in rapid succession: a glowing Myrtle making her debut. A team of suitors converging upon her to sign a dance card. Those same nameless, faceless strangers dancing with her.

"Val?" Her voice emerged haltingly, and there was a question there that snapped him back from insidious musings of Myrtle with another.

He drew his hands back, and this time she did not resist him. "You want a gentleman with hardened hands?" he asked incredulously as the meaning of her regret slammed into him.

A wry grin danced on the edges of her mouth. "Well, I certainly don't want one with lily-white, soft ones," she said dryly.

She'd not been pitying him before, but rather lamenting the gentlemen whose paths she'd eventually cross.

"Shall we?" she asked, even as she all but skipped over to the table.

A small iced white cake sat in the middle of the wooden servants' dining table. Yet the confectionary treat was sizable enough to feed a family of at least five.

"You carried that by yourself?" he asked roughly as he joined her at the table.

"No." She didn't stop, flitting about the kitchen, and he followed her with his gaze, her quick, darting movements putting him in mind of a butterfly hopping from bud to bud in the summertime. "I summoned the servants back so that they might fetch it for me."

Val stiffened and whipped his gaze about.

Myrtle laughed. "I'm jesting, Val. I fetched it myself, of course." With that she headed over to a cabinet and fished around, muttering to herself as she searched cabinet after cabinet. "Where are they? Where are they?"

Of course.

As if it were the most common thing in the world for a young lady to dash about London, without so much as the benefit of a servant, to fetch her own baked goods.

She was . . . a marvel.

"Aha!" Myrtle exclaimed happily. "I found them." Spinning around, she held aloft a collection of thin sticks.

"We're playing . . . spillikins?"

Her laughter filled the kitchens once more, an effervescent sound as clear as the brightest London bells tinkling, filling corners of his soul that had been devoid of all joy for so long, sparking a light within those shuttered parts of him.

"No," she said when her amusement had faded, and with her matter-of-fact tone, she gave no indication that she was aware of the profound effect her laugh and smile had upon him. "They are candles, Val," she explained, returning with that bounty to join Val.

He did a sweep of the kitchens. "I think there's sufficient light."

Furthermore, there was no one about to look after those flames. It was a danger he'd not considered . . . until now. It was one of the reasons servants were always awake through the nighttime hours, to roam the halls and ensure candles remained lit.

"Not for light. For the cake, silly."

He looked from her face to the bounty of tapered candles she waved in his direction, before bringing his gaze back to her sparkling one. "You're going to stick candles in a cake, and I'm the silly one?"

"It is a tradition," she explained. "My brother came back from a tour of Germany and shared the story of a man he met in his travels . . . He'd been hosting a party to celebrate his birthday and had a cake he lit with candles. Arran was fascinated, and when he asked, the man regaled him with a story of a different man named Count Ludwig von Zinzendorf. He once held a grand party to celebrate his birthday and had a gigantic"—she let her arms sweep wide—"cake, and stuck within it were candles, enough to correspond with his age."

She was so wistful, her gaze so faraway it may as well have been in that room in Germany she now spoke of, and he suspected that was where her mind dwelled. In the place her brother had been that she clearly wished to go to. Or perhaps it was merely the memory of that time she'd had with her family. And he hated that she'd gone sad-eyed . . . Val ached to chase that gloom away. "If you stick enough candles to commemorate your age, the thing will be consumed in fire."

"Are you calling me old?" she asked. Dropping her hands upon her hips and scowling, she was adorable in her indignation. "Because I'll have you know . . . I'm only eighteen. Hardly an old maid."

"I'm calling your cake small."

She smiled. "Oh." Only that smile fell as swiftly as it had formed. "Now I am offended that you have insulted my cake."

"Your cake *is* small," he felt inclined to point out.

"But you still needn't speak poorly of it," she chastised, and leaning down, she dropped her elbows upon the table, her body curved like a frame around that treat she so ardently defended.

"I'm not speaking poorly of it. I'm speaking *factually* about it."

She narrowed her eyes, then straightened in a huff. "Oh, fine." Humming to herself, she carefully stuck candle after candle within the cake, and he watched her as she worked.

How long it had been since he'd bantered. He'd not even believed himself, until this moment, capable of the feat.

When Myrtle had finished placing all the candles but for one, she picked that lone taper up and turned.

"Where are you going?" he asked, freezing her in her tracks.

She turned back, giving her eyes a slight roll. "I have to light it."

And risk burning her fingers?

"Give me that," he muttered, slipping it from her grasp. He proceeded over to one of the pair of sconces still lit.

"I'm quite capable, you know," she said.

"I do not doubt it." After all, she had survived this long without the benefit of a family or staff about. He lit the taper, then held his palm up around it to protect the flame as he made the short walk back to her side. "But I'm certain there are some rules about not lighting your own candles on your birthday."

"There aren't," she informed him as he joined her at the table. "I asked my brother"—of course she had—"who asked his friend in Germany"—Curiosity appeared to run, then, in Myrtle McQuoid's family—"and *he* said that he rather enjoys lighting his own candles."

Val made quick work of lighting each candle so that a bright glow emanated from the cake, and he added the last one to the now crowded birthday treat she'd purchased herself.

Myrtle hopped onto one of the benches, and Val followed suit, positioning himself directly across from her.

They sat there . . . in silence, with Myrtle staring intently at the candles, those candles which cast a soft glow over her heart-shaped face, her tangle of dark curls having the look of a halo and giving her an ethereal look.

"Well?" he asked quietly. "Are you going to put them out?"

"You don't put them out," she said softly. "One blows them out . . . and only after one has made a wish."

"And what do you intend to wish for?" he asked quietly, thoroughly and hopelessly entranced by her.

"That is why I am taking so long," she explained, her gaze not upon the objects in question, but rather upon Val. "A person only has one wish each year, and it is best to not make it in haste . . . And it is an important year," she murmured, tacking that latter part on as an afterthought of sorts. When he saw the way her mouth tightened in the corners, and the troubled glint that dimmed the brightness in her eyes, he knew her words were anything but an afterthought.

That the talk of her Season and the future awaiting her haunted this moment.

Val held her eyes with his. "Take your time then, Myrtle," he said softly, willing her to understand what he was really saying to her in this moment. "You do not rush it." She deserved to find someone who would treat her like the treasure she was. "And if you don't," he murmured, "then eventually you will find"—*who*—"what you have been searching for."

Myrtle's lips trembled, and for a moment he tensed, fearing she was about to cry, and just the thought of it sent a shooting pain straight through his heart.

"Do you think?" she asked, her voice filled with hope the likes of which he couldn't remember feeling.

"I do." The lie came easily. She could travel the globe as the brother she spoke of did and never find a mortal man deserving of her.

"Thank you," she whispered, and then sitting more upright on her bench, Myrtle drew a breath in, composing herself. Closing her eyes, she leaned forward and blew out the flames, leaving a cloud of smoke and the tinge of sulfur upon the air, and ultimately snuffing out the intimate moment they'd shared.

For which Val was grateful.

He didn't want to think about her having her first London Season, or about her having her spirit crushed by the discovery that those men in London were even less than she expected them to be.

Or worse—his thoughts darkened—marrying one of those lesser-than-her men.

"Well?" he growled, his tone sharper than he intended, but as much as he could help it. "Get on with it."

Myrtle reached over and rapped him lightly on the top of his hand. "Be patient. You can have the first slice," she said like soothing a child.

Which was undoubtedly how he was acting in that moment. And he was grateful a moment later when she shot a finger up and said, "Plates and forks," before racing off. For the thought of her marrying and going off to some other household different from this one, away from his, so that he'd never again see her, left him . . . strangely bereft. And it left him wanting to gnash his teeth like an angry dragon eager to burn down the man who came and scooped her up and carried her away.

He froze. His mind balked, and his chest lurched along with it. Where had that thought come from?

As Myrtle returned and set down her latest bounty, Val attempted to regroup his riotous thoughts.

The sole reason he cared was because she was the first person he'd interacted with in years. It had nothing to do with . . . with . . . *anything* beyond that.

Myrtle held up the knife and then froze with the blade poised over the top. Closing her eyes, she cut into the cake. She proceeded to dish out two pieces, giving the first to him and taking the next one for herself.

They ate in silence.

Silence was something he'd become so very accustomed to over the years.

It was something he was never without.

"You never did say what is wrong with the name Myrtle," she said quietly.

"No, I didn't."

"My brothers got good strong names. Lovely ones. Arran and Dallin and Quillon. My sisters Cassia and Fleur . . . and I was saddled with Myrtle."

It was an unfortunate one.

"It's not the prettiest," he allowed, and the lady was stricken before she dropped an elbow onto the table and turned her attention to her plate, pushing the confectionary treat around the dish.

Val tightened his hand upon his fork, the metal biting into his palm, and he preferred a world in which he'd been incapable of feeling anything, especially not this hurt at causing someone pain. "But it is the most interesting."

The lady's head popped up.

And he found, though dusty and rusty and rough, he was capable of some of that charm from long ago.

Apparently he was not as charming as he'd just credited himself.

"It is a fine name," he finally said.

She stared confusedly at him.

"Myrtle," he said gruffly. "Your name is fine enough."

"No, it's not. It sounds like 'turtle' and is a name one would expect of an old spinster with two pugs on bright leashes, with bows in their ears. Garish ones, too. Not even fine, elegant ribbons."

"Are you always this contrary?"

"I'm always this truthful." She lifted a forkful of cake, punctuating her point. "There is a difference," she said, taking a bite. Suddenly, she stopped midchew and froze. "Oh, my goodness," she said around a mouthful, and then frantically proceeded to swallow.

Myrtle jumped up and raced across the room.

He frowned, following her with his gaze as she fetched another plate. "What is it?"

Ignoring him, she made a beeline for the table. "I am the worst," she lamented, and heaping the plate with a slice of cake as large as his and hers combined, she jumped up.

Confounded, Val did a sweep, searching for the company.

Myrtle dropped to a knee.

Horace instantly gave his spot up at the hearth and trotted over.

Myrtle tossed her arms around the dog's thick neck and gave him a hug.

And Val sank back in his seat. It wasn't every day that a man found himself envying a dog.

"Can you ever forgive me?" she asked in a singsong voice as she scratched Horace between his ears and nose, going back and forth, until he, so clearly in heaven from that attention, let his tongue fall sideways from his mouth, and panted happily. "You are kinder than I deserve," Myrtle murmured, touching the tip of her nose to Horace's in that endearing way she'd done so many times before. She gave the dog one last affectionate pat before hopping up and rejoining Val.

"You're good with him," he couldn't keep from remarking, when she'd resumed eating her cake.

She gave him a questioning look.

"Horace," he clarified, his lips twitching. Had she thought there was another he'd been speaking of?

"I quite adore him," she said after she'd taken a bite and dabbed at her lips with the napkin she'd fetched for herself. "We've never had a dog. I've always wanted one, or a cat, or a bird, but my mother and father said they'd agreed that they have six children, and as such, the household was quite crowded as it was, and they knew their limits." She spoke in the rote way of one who'd heard those words spoken often. Myrtle didn't take another bite. Instead, she used the tip of her fork to push a large crumb around the perimeter of her plate. "I daresay I'd prefer the company of a dog to a husband. It's terrible. I've spent all these past years at Mrs. Belden's, attempting to be someone I'm not, striving to be the perfectly respectable lady just so that I could be free of that school, only to find myself poised to present that same charade for the remainder of my days."

He stilled.

This was more dangerous territory. More of that intimate, personal talk about . . . very intimate, personal matters.

Even knowing that, he couldn't keep back the question. "Was that your wish?" he asked gruffly. "For a certain . . . gentleman?"

Myrtle smiled, and it was another one of those sad smiles that he so despised, because her lips were meant to form only those truest, purest expressions of her inner joy. "You're determined I should speak it and have it not come true? Well, I may as well because it will not come true anyway," she said, her voice catching slightly. Her cheeks pink with embarrassment, Myrtle cleared her throat and went back to eating.

And for the first time, he'd seen a true fracture in her optimism, and he ached all over again inside.

Not for the first time, however, he remained incapable of asking any further questions of her, or more, giving her assurances. Because he knew they'd be false, and also because he didn't know how to ease that upset. "Myrtle?"

She glanced up.

"There is nothing wrong with it," he said gruffly.

The lady cocked her head.

"Your name. It . . . suits you. It suits you perfectly. That's why I repeated it that day."

Her eyes went soft. "Oh." Unlike all the times before, she didn't prattle or say anything further on the matter, for which he was grateful. Because all this, easing another person's upset and sadness and working to make them smile, was so foreign, and he was so rusty and it was so uncomfortable.

Too soon they'd both finished their cake, signaling what could only be the end of her celebration and their time together.

He should be relieved, and yet it was reluctance that brought him to his feet. "I should go," he said needlessly anyway.

Myrtle stood. "Yes."

Val came around the table and headed for the door.

Myrtle joined him, and they may as well have been any respectable couple, her a lady seeing him to the parlor door after he'd come to call. And it hit him square in the gut, with how . . . appealing that imagining in fact was.

He reached for his hat, and stuffed it hard on his head, hoping the force of that movement would dislodge what were only mad thoughts.

"I should go," he said.

She dampened her lips. "Yes. You've . . . said that already."

"Have I?" he asked gruffly. When he was around this woman, it was all jumbled—what was in his mind and what was real anymore.

"You did."

"Because I should, you know. Leave."

Myrtle lifted three fingers. "Three times, now."

And something snapped inside him; something thin and tenuous broke under the weight of everything that had become confused. "Because I should leave," he barked. "I . . . I . . . shouldn't even be here. We shouldn't be together, and I wouldn't, you know," he said, taking a step toward her, hating when she backed away because he'd frightened her, and because she was afraid of him. "I wouldn't be here if your family was here, and they should be here."

Her lower lip trembled. "I know."

And tears filled her eyes, and with a groan, Val was lost.

He lowered his head to hers, even as she tilted her head back, and he kissed her.

Kissed her as he'd been aching to do. Taking her mouth with a gentleness at first, exploring the softness of that flesh, and then driven by this inexorable need, Val slanted his mouth over hers again and again, until she was moaning, and it was his name.

"Val," she pleaded, and he was lost all over again.

He swept her in his arms, drawing her higher and closer so he could better avail himself of her mouth.

Coaxing her lips open, he swept inside, tasting of that moist cavern, delving in, deeper and deeper, over and over again, until his body trembled against hers with the force of his need for her, this woman.

With a hungering to explore more of her, all of her.

It was only because he'd been without a woman for years.

And yet, even those assurances felt hollow.

Myrtle's legs went weak, and he caught her about the waist, anchoring her to him.

And Myrtle, bold in every way, and even in this, touched her tongue to his in impatient little strokes and slashes.

That boldness was part of who she was in life, and it was a part of who she would be when making love.

Only, that is a right that doesn't belong to you, a voice jeered, and he sought to slay his conscience.

Val's fingers curled sharply into the small of her back, and he immediately relaxed his grip and gentled the kiss, tamping down the tide of passion threatening to overwhelm him and begging to be slaked. And then he dropped a final, tender kiss upon her lips.

Her body still soft and pliant in his arms, Myrtle's thick, dark lashes fluttered slowly, and then with a seeming effort, she opened her eyes. Passion had left those brown depths hazy, her gaze unfocused. She blinked several times.

He released his hold upon her, and she instantly sank a fraction. "Good night, Myrtle," he said. How was his voice so steady? How, when his pulse still pounded in his ears and his heart thumped against his chest and his body still burned for her.

"Good night, Val." She moved her eyes over his face, and some of that sadness of before had returned. Did she want him to stay? Why should she? He was miserable company.

His gaze slipped over to the dog, who hovered just beyond Myrtle's shoulder, glaring at Val with canine disapproval, of which Val was decidedly deserving. "He should stay with you."

As soon as the offer left him, Val went motionless. Surely he hadn't said that aloud. Surely he hadn't made the offer he had.

Myrtle shook her head, confused. "I don't . . . ?"

"Horace."

Myrtle fluttered a hand about her chest before her fingers found purchase at that place her heart beat. "You are . . . giving me your dog?" she whispered.

"Not forever," he said gruffly. "Just . . . until your family returns." If those miserable blighters ever returned.

It would be the first time he'd ever been apart from the dog, and the thought of doing so left him queasy and unnerved . . . And yet, those sentiments were somehow preferable to even thinking of Myrtle alone as she was this night and these past nights.

Myrtle's features softened. "I cannot accept that, Val."

He grunted. "Of course you can."

"He is your companion and friend."

She understood that relationship he shared, had pegged the dog to be more than a canine to Val, and he found himself disquieted at realizing she'd gathered that in their short time together.

Unable to meet eyes that saw entirely too much for her tender years, Val rubbed the top of the dog's head. "And he will remain so. Until you return him to me." The time when these stolen intimate moments together came to an end, when London was bustling, and when she was back under the protective wing of her family and servants, preparing for her first Season, and Val would remain as he'd been for so long behind his curtained windows . . . recalling all the times they'd spent together, alone.

And he'd miss them.

It was a realization that hit him square in the chest.

Myrtle slipped her palms in his. "Thank you," she said softly.

He grunted. "It is nothing at all."

"You and I both know that is not true." She folded her fingers over the tops of his and lightly squeezed.

Now he should go. Now he *could* go.

Still, they remained there.

He remained there.

I should leave. I should leave . . .

And this time, after he touched the brim of his hat, he did.

As the door shut behind him, there was a finality to that light click that resonated like thunder in the winter quiet.

He trudged ahead, onward to his household, his now even lonelier household, everything within him crying out with the desire to return and to just . . . be with her. It was a foreign feeling that raised holy terror inside him.

This was why he needed to avoid her. This was why he needed her blasted family to come back and claim her. Because with every moment spent together, the walls he'd built to protect himself and to keep all other people out were crumbling, and he feared what would remain of him when she ultimately left.

Chapter 14

He'd celebrated her birthday with her. Nay, not only that, but he'd talked with her about her wishes.

And he kissed you. Do not forget that. For a second time.

With a groan, she rolled onto her back. "As if I could."

There'd been a heat the likes of which she'd never known before. Nay, not heat; heat would have been the candles upon her cake. This had been an all-out burning within, one that had started like the slow kindling of a fire and had grown, overtaking her, and she'd been content to burn.

"It was perfect," she whispered, needing to tell herself because the urge to share with someone just how profound that moment with Val had been was so great. "His kiss . . . our kiss . . . was perfect."

Horace released a happy bark into the night, and she turned her head. With a groan, Myrtle slapped a hand over her eyes. "Do *not* go telling your father," she ordered. Softening the rebuke, she stretched her hand over the side of the sofa she'd turned into her bed these past nights.

Horace promptly sent his tongue unfurling and licked her fingers.

"No, I know. You are a loyal friend to me, too, and I appreciate your keeping my confidences." Rolling onto her side so that she was face-to-face with Val's dog, Myrtle considered him. "It is just . . . I don't know what to make of him, Horace." She articulated this quietly, that introspective admission spoken as much for her benefit as the dog's. "Some moments, it is as though he cannot stand the sight of me."

Horace barked.

"No, I know. He's like that with everyone, surely. But other times, he's smiling and kind and"—Myrtle's cheeks warmed, and she dropped her voice to a whisper—"kissing me."

Unable to meet the dog's enormous brown eyes, she pulled a pillow over her head. "I cannot believe we are speaking of this."

The pillow shifted and then was gone.

The lacy edge caught between his white teeth, Horace looked at her from over the top of that frilly piece that had been her nighttime headrest.

Myrtle edged closer. "We are friends and can speak of anything, you say?"

With a little whine, he cocked his head.

She scratched him between the ears and then on the nose, alternating those pets that she'd come to learn he preferred. "Well, I thank you for that. I . . . have not had a friend in a very long while," she whispered. The girls at Mrs. Belden's had been more acquaintances, never the manner of friends to whom one poured all the secrets within one's soul.

Horace gave her cheek a lick, his tongue rough, before ambling over to the fire. She watched distractedly as he paced back and forth, as if attempting to find the most comfortable spot, and then sank onto the floor.

Releasing a noisy little huff, he dropped his head between his paws and stared at the flames.

Restless, giving up any and all hope of finding sleep that night, Myrtle came to her feet. Belting her robe and then adding a blanket around her shoulders for additional warmth on this frigid night, she padded over to the window.

She drew the curtains aside and peered out at the residence opposite her family's.

How funny; her family and Val had lived across from one another all these years, and yet with Myrtle having been gone at Mrs. Belden's, until these past days, she and Val may as well have been strangers in a crowd.

Holding her blanket with one hand, she raised the other and dusted her palm along the glass, attempting to scrape away the ice that blurred his household so that she might better see it, so that she could feel closer to him.

So that she could hopefully catch a glimpse of him.

Because in these past few days, she'd grown close with Val. In fact, she felt closer to him than anyone she'd known at Mrs. Belden's, or even than her own family, for that matter. Her family, whom she no longer felt comfortable being herself around.

Her eldest siblings had been friends until Myrtle had been sent away, and they'd become more strangers.

And there'd been plenty of girls at Mrs. Belden's . . . but she'd been so busy trying to be the perfect student just so that she could get herself out of that miserable place that the woman she'd been before those ladies had been make-believe. She'd been so busy pretending that none of them had seen the real her.

Val was the first person whom she'd been herself with. She'd not sought to pass herself off as anything other than . . . Myrtle.

She closed her eyes.

She didn't want to pretend anymore.

Mrs. Belden's had crushed her spirit, but it hadn't destroyed it.

She wanted to laugh freely and speak freely and see the world and live within it as she'd done with Val these past days. Val had helped her to realize that.

Their time together, however, was nearing an end. For she wouldn't be forgotten here by her family forever. They'd come for Myrtle and take her away with them to Scotland, where they would remain as the long-overdue repairs were at last done on their London townhouse. And when they arrived, it would be time for her London Season, where she'd be put on display and paraded before potential husbands until she ultimately found the one with whom she'd spend the remainder of her days.

Her heart pounded hard against her breast, and she squeezed her eyes shut.

A man who would decidedly not be Val, the Duke of Aragon. Which was fine. Because he really only tolerated her, and barely liked her.

Only, that felt very much like a lie, she told herself.

Because he did like her. A solitary man who'd closed himself away from the world, with no one but his dog for company, would never give that loyal creature whom he so clearly loved, a dog that followed him everywhere, to Myrtle.

It was simply easier to think that he didn't like her, because then it made it easier to face a future without him—a man unlike any other gentleman she'd known or would ever know.

He was gruff but direct. Honest, and yet there was a hardness to him that she'd easily recognized as a veneer he'd used to protect himself. And she wanted to pull it back. She wanted to witness and help bring about more of those grins of his, which had first looked pained and strained, but with every day they'd spent together had become more relaxed. More real.

Alas, she may be an innocent young woman. Her understanding of the world may be limited, but she was also mature enough, wise enough, to recognize in Val a man who'd loved so very deeply and who could never, and would never, love again.

And Myrtle's soul proved rotten and dark and black, for in that moment she found herself not only envious of a dead woman but also resentful of the hold she still had over Val, a hold so strong that it prevented him from truly being happy again.

Or from falling in love again.

Myrtle drew in a shaky, solitary breath and forced her eyes open.

It was as though with her thoughts of Val, she'd conjured him of thin air.

At some point he'd slipped the curtains open.

The full moon bathed the street between them in a bright luminescent glow that shone upon his residence and painted him in a full light.

And she was grateful for it.

He'd also changed his garments, trading out his familiar black trousers and black coat for a new pair of trousers. Only, he'd discarded his jacket and stood there in his white lawn shirt, a stark flag. So relaxed. So casual that her chest clenched and unclenched as she imagined him dressed so at this late hour with him and her together.

He lifted his hand in a distant greeting, and Myrtle followed suit, holding her palm aloft.

"Hello," she mouthed silently, knowing it was unlikely from this distance that he'd see that faint movement of her lips.

Only . . .

As she squinted, peering intently at him, wanting to commit him to memory, she detected it: a slight inclination of his head, an acknowledgment that he'd seen and now returned the greeting.

And he proved so very taciturn even in a soundless exchange that she couldn't keep from smiling.

They lingered there.

And for a moment she thought he'd remain there forever.

But then he lifted his hand again in a final wave and drew the curtains closed once more, so perfunctory as he shut them the fabric didn't so much as dance or flutter.

Myrtle stood motionless. Waiting for him to return. Hoping he'd push the fabric open again . . . or better yet, that he'd closed the curtains but had done so only because he intended to fetch his cloak and cross the courtyard between them and join Myrtle.

The clock at her back, however, ticked away.

As the seconds melted into moments and minutes, and beyond.

And he did not come.

A loneliness so strong gripped her heart that Myrtle found her legs unable to support her weight, and she sank onto the edge of the window seat.

He—

From the corner of her eye, she caught a flash of movement, and happiness and hope brought her heart rising as she searched over the grounds below for him.

And then she froze.

Her maudlin and mournful thoughts about Val forgotten in an instant, she tunneled all her focus on the figure below. A man who was decidedly not Val.

But rather two men. Two men who, even from where she sat inside, and where they dashed about below, she recognized in a moment.

They were dressed in garments as black as Val's, from the black bowler caps to their breeches; the lanky figure sneaked with a surprising furtiveness, matching the movements of the smaller fellow beside him.

At last, she managed to get her legs unstuck from their immobile state and dived onto the floor.

With a little whine, Horace, still seated at the fireplace, popped his head up.

Myrtle lay flat on her belly with her left cheek pressed to the cool hardwood floor and her face turned toward the window.

They were here.

I knew it. I knewwwww *it.*

She'd suspected they had nefarious intentions from the moment she'd found them inventorying her father's collection.

Being right about them, however, proved not so very satisfying. She'd have vastly preferred to have been wrong on this one and to possess the overactive imagination her parents, and Val, had ultimately suggested she had.

Myrtle silently ordered herself to gather her wits about her.

Think.

Think . . .

Calling out to her mother or father or another fictionally present family member would hardly be believable to them this time.

Forcing herself up from the floor, Myrtle darted along the row of curtains, pulling them back as she went and following the purposeful steps of the two strangers outside.

At last, they stopped, and Myrtle raised her voice. "Aliiiiiice," she called, raising her voice loud enough to be heard outside. "Will you fetch my copy of *Pride and Prejudice*? I'm afraid I'm unable to sleep."

Horace cocked his head and groaned a canine whine of confusion.

"I have company," she whispered for the dog's benefit, even as she stole another peek outside.

And then, Myrtle went absolutely motionless.

Fear snaked through her, freezing her where she stood.

A low growl emanated from behind her, and it was as if Horace at last understood the threat. For he bounded over and jumped up so that his front paws rested upon the window seat. Sniffing at the air, he moved his head about, and then his gaze locked on the two men outside. The dog's lips drew back, revealing a terrifying display of teeth.

Then he released a loud, angry bark.

Hope danced in her breast, making her feel light inside as the two raced off.

Horace continued to bark and growl long after they'd gone from sight.

The moment the threat was gone, Myrtle flung her arms around his head and hugged him hard. "You were magnificent," she praised, cooing.

Myrtle stopped. Her stomach dropping and her terror ratcheting inside.

They'd returned.

It had been naive to think they'd give up so very easily when they'd gone to such lengths to steal from her father, the earl.

"We know yar in there, gel. We know yar in there, alone."

"I'm not alone," she shouted back.

"Not another servant in this place but ya."

"I'm not a servant," she called loudly, and then raised her voice, infusing it with all the stiff, regal tones Mrs. Belden had drilled into her and the rest of the students. "I am Lady Myrtle McQuoid, daughter of the Earl and Countess of Abington, and I command you to leave."

Her pronouncement was met with a deep silence.

And then . . .

Both men burst out laughing, roaring with their hilarity.

Hmph. So much for having mastered that skill.

"Yea, sure," one of the men rejoined between his bout of amusement. "And I am the Duke of Cornwall."

"That hardly makes sense," she said. "The Duke of Cornwall is dead." She briefly recalled her lessons during her Titles and Ranks class at Mrs. Belden's. "And though it is possible for a nobleman to obtain that particular title, it has not been in use since—"

"Enough with yar damned history lesson. I'm being facetious, you stupid chit."

Myrtle folded her arms. *"Well, I never . . ."*

Horace barked his canine support of her.

She patted his head, finding comfort in his presence. Feeling less alone with him near her.

"Never been treated so poorly, my lady?" the other bounder taunted, and his overexaggerated emphasis of those syllables combined with their laughter indicated they believed her anything but.

"Actually, I haven't," she informed them tartly. "Because—"

"Never tell us, ya're the Earl and Countess of Abingdon's *precious* daughter."

Before Val, she'd believed herself adept at detecting sarcasm. She'd come to find she'd not known as much as she'd thought about spotting droll retorts, and credited Val with her edification. "I'll have you know I am one of them." Hardly precious, though. After all, devoted parents didn't go about forgetting children that were precious to them.

"And they just forgot you, leaving an innocent, virtuous lady on her own?"

They had done just that. Only, even as she opened her mouth to continue her insistence, she stopped. Because she heard their disbelief, and she knew precisely how it sounded and saw how it looked. Who in a thousand years would ever trust she was who she claimed to be? What lord and lady went about forgetting an unmarried daughter and leaving her for days on end?

"Enough of yar yammering. Open this door now!"

"Or we'll kick it in." The other thief added that threat to his partner's command.

Her skin sweating, Myrtle scrambled into motion, rushing to gather the fire poker.

Horace erupted into an all-out barking fit, his lips drawn in a terrifying sneer as he jumped feet first at the door, pounding against the panel and scratching in an attempt to get to the invaders who'd overtaken her home.

And just like that, the cocksure arrogance of the pair was gone as only their silence reigned.

"I suggest you leave," she called loudly enough to be sure she was heard between Horace's frenzied yapping. "Horace does not take kindly to unwanted visitors, and he is quite protective of me."

"Horace?"

She nodded before recalling they couldn't see her. "Yes. Horace. He is part wolf, you know, and would like nothing better than to . . . to . . . open up your necks."

She winced and looked down at the dog. "I know you are not a killer," she mouthed.

Only, he remained unaware of those assurances; instead, he continued to throw himself against the door.

"Well, open this door, and we'll put a bullet in that filthy animal."

"No!" she cried out. And just like that, Myrtle's heart stuttered as fear clipped away the brief moment of confidence she'd felt. She could not, would not, let anything ever happen to the creature. Val would be lost without the pup.

"Now, quiet that beast, and come out here before we come in there and slit his throat open."

Myrtle felt the blood drain from her cheeks.

"Horace," she said quietly, praying her voice would penetrate the bloodlust that had him in a frenzy. "Horace, *please*," she begged, and the entreaty in her tones appeared to reach him. "Sit."

With a little whine and whimper, he scrambled from his standing position, his nails scraping the floor as he went, and then he complied.

"You have to go," she whispered, giving him a hug.

He barked.

"No, stop. I . . . need you to go." She needed him to be safe. She needed him to go to Val. "I will be just fine."

Springing into movement, Myrtle flew across the room, making a dash for the connecting door. Horace followed, his nails clicking upon the hardwood floors.

"You got thirty seconds . . ." That order from her nighttime foes emerged muted and more muffled as she retreated into the connecting parlor.

Not breaking stride, Myrtle raced ahead, slipping from room to room, parlor to parlor, weaving herself a path to a doorway leading out.

And as she reached the kitchens, a sense of triumph filled her, and with an almost giddy relief, she reached for the door handle.

Then she registered the tread of heavy footfalls outside.

All those dizzyingly wonderful sentiments of before proved short-lived.

"Stop there, yar ladyship."

The click of that hammer on the other side of the door froze her in place.

Horace growled.

"This time, I am going to kill that damned dog," the fiend promised, an icy relish contained within that sent dread tripping along her spine. "If you don't cooperate. Now, let him out back, and get yarself back in here," he ordered, his voice moving between proper King's English and a street-roughened Cockney.

"Go," Myrtle whispered, yanking the door open, and Horace took flight. His legs slid periodically as he hit icy patches of earth, though he all but flew, his strides still graceful despite his periodic slip.

She eyed his retreat a moment, considering escape of her own, knowing if she did, she'd be no match for them, that Val's dog would return for her and pay the price with his life.

Drawing the door shut, Myrtle shifted course and took off running for the servants' stairs.

Chapter 15

Val was lonely.

Only, this was a different loneliness.

This wasn't the familiar state he'd found himself dwelling in these past years.

This was a new kind.

The likes of which he'd never expected to know or feel again.

Loneliness for another person—a living person, that was.

He'd been aware of her in that room she'd made her chambers.

He'd felt her there, even before she'd shown herself at the windows, waving at him.

And he'd wanted to go to Myrtle.

He'd wanted to be with her.

Every day of his life since his wife's passing had been difficult; this particular time of year, the anniversary of when she'd died, however, was especially hard. The memories stronger. The grief starker. The pain harsher.

Yet these past days, that hadn't been the case.

These past days, he'd smiled and laughed, and perhaps he was just growing melancholy. Perhaps in being around Myrtle with her zest for life and her always sunny optimism, he'd found himself remembering how life used to be. She brought to mind feelings other than grief and loss, and that was a powerful aphrodisiac.

With a curse, he grabbed the book he'd been gifted and turned the well-read volume over in his hands.

When was the last time he'd read . . . anything?

Absently, he fanned the pages, taking note of those that were bent.

A wistful smile danced on his lips. She folded the corners of her books.

It fit with the lady, impatient and not bothering with the proper marking for the book.

As he flipped through the pages, his gaze snagged upon a note in the passages. It flew by so fast, and he stopped upon another she'd made in the book. Quickly reversing course, he licked the tip of his finger and turned back, searching for that earlier spot.

He found it.

"A lady's imagination is very rapid, it jumps from admiration to love, from love to matrimony in a moment."

Myrtle would be a romantic. She'd be the kind of lady who wished for more than a title and dreamed of falling in love, and being in love, and she deserved it. She deserved a man whose spirit was as romantic as hers, and capable of . . . of . . . what Val had once been.

His throat went dry, and his mouth along with it, making it difficult to swallow.

Not that he wanted to be the man she loved.

He didn't.

He was just . . . noting that he wasn't that man.

Which meant there would be some other gentleman.

And something, something dark and insidious, sank its fangs within him, unleashing a poisonous jealousy for the one who'd possess her.

The eventual suitor and husband who'd make love to her mouth and to all of her and—

With a growl, Val angrily turned the page, finding his place, fighting the urge to look at those little marks that proved a window of sorts into her soul and thinking, and which only further deepened his knowledge of Myrtle McQuoid—and this bond he'd formed with her.

"But if a woman is partial to a man, and does not endeavor to conceal it, he must find it out."

"Perhaps he must, if he sees enough of her. But though Bingley and Jane meet tolerably often, it is never for many hours together, and as they always see each other in large mixed parties, it is impossible that every moment should be employed in conversing together. Jane should therefore make the most of every half hour in which she can command his attention. When she is secure of him, there will be leisure for falling in love as much as she chooses . . ."

He lingered on the passage.

This was it. That was all there was to this growing awareness of Myrtle. It was written right here. As a rule, outside of formal meetings, well attended by chaperones and servants, gentlemen and ladies did not share of each other's company. Val shared even less. It was only because he'd been in close quarters with her without the benefit of anyone present that there'd been this . . . intimacy. This bond forged.

Why, it would have been the case were it . . . anyone else he'd found himself suddenly keeping such intimate company with. And when thinking of it in that light, well, it wasn't quite as terror-inducing or mouth-drying. It was . . . normal.

He'd simply come to learn about her as a person, and an interesting, clever person at that.

As such, it was only natural that he would admire her and think about her and want to spend more time with her and—

Gritting his teeth, Val fanned the pages once more, starting at the beginning. This time, he turned them more slowly, and as he did, he ran his gaze over the passing paragraphs, no longer resisting that urge to search out the markings she'd made.

"To be fond of dancing was a certain step toward falling in love . . ."

In this little area, she'd made a single note, a lone word: "Sigh."

Despite himself, Val's lips tipped up again in a smile.

That was very much Myrtle. She would dream of being held and holding someone in—

Val turned the page, on to the next, and then stopped. He quickly flipped back.

"It is a truth universally acknowledged, that a single man in possession of a good fortune, must be in want of a wife . . ."

Beside the passage, she'd left a little circle with eyes drawn on, and a frowning mouth.

He paused.

Was it that she disapproved of the author's sentiment? Or did she recognize the truth the author had written and regret that this was the way of their world?

And he wished she were here. He wished she were here now so that he could ask her specifically and find out what she'd been thinking as she'd drawn that tiny mark upon the pages of this particular passage. And all the passages.

Cursing, Val snapped the book closed and slammed it down with a *thunk* upon the side table.

Dropping his elbows atop his knees, he buried his head in his hands and dug his fingertips into his temples.

What was this hold she had over his thoughts?

Why could he not stop thinking of her?

He would.

Eventually.

As soon as she left and he was free to wallow in his misery, then he could find peace once more.

Because that was a certainty. There was no peace in losing himself completely to a woman as he'd done before. For when one lost that person, the grief of that loss was a far greater, far more vicious pain, and as such, loneliness was more palatable.

A lone bark echoed outside, slashing into his frustrated musings and bringing his head whipping up.

A familiar bark that was followed moments later by a barrage of frantic yipping.

With a frown, Val came to his feet. Striding over to the window, he drew the curtains back and looked below.

His black coat brightly visible upon the snowy-white earth, Horace was instantly recognizable, and Val sighed, searching out the troublesome sprite who'd be accompanying his dog.

Only, a quick scour of the streets revealed . . . no one. That was, no one but Horace.

Why would she send his dog out without accompanying him? She wouldn't. Unless . . .

"I believe two men are watching my townhouse," she said, and then stared at him as if expecting he'd be as shocked and horrified as she herself was.

He shook his head.

"Yes." Myrtle lifted two small, gloved digits. "Two. You see, I suspect they might have an interest in my father's curiosity collection . . . And his collection is quite vast . . . some of the oldest and finest, and everyone knows of his treasures . . ."

"Are you saying you believe someone intends to steal from your father?"

The lady nodded. "Precisely."

She'd been so adamant that there'd been a threat lurking at her door, and he'd been insistent that there hadn't. He'd been so hell-bent on convincing her that her concerns were the product of a lady with an overactive imagination.

With a curse, Val went racing. Reaching the front door, he yanked one of the panels open.

Horace instantly came bounding inside, panting and barking, and they were panicked, whiny sounds heralding doom.

"Where is she?" Val demanded, even as he knew the creature couldn't answer, yet needing to ask anyway.

Nudging Val's hand with his nose, Horace did a circle about his legs.

Turning on his heel, Val raced back to his office with Horace keeping close to him.

Fear and desperation made Val's breath come noisy and hard. He reached his desk and fished out the pistols from his case. After loading the powder, he tucked one of the pistols into the waistband of his trousers and drew on his dark jacket, immediately covering up the stark white fabric of his lawn shirt.

Grabbing the other pistol, he set out, sprinting back to Myrtle's household.

Bypassing the front doors in favor of the servants' entrance, Val paused when he reached the residence.

Silence filled the air.

A silence so thick it rang in his ears as the only otherwise sound in the dead of night, that silence punctuated by Horace's slight panting.

Val looked down at his dog and touched a finger to his lips, urging him to keep quiet.

Holding his pistol close to his chest, Val did a search of the courtyard, sweeping his eyes over the shadows and sharpening his ears, listening for the hint of . . . something.

He reached behind him and pressed the door handle. It gave in an instant; the hinges squeaked noisily as he shoved it open, hinting at servants who'd proven neglectful in their duties of greasing them.

Val frowned.

He motioned with his left hand, and reading that unspoken command, Horace trotted inside, his nails clicking damningly loud upon the rough hardwood floors.

Val followed his dog in and drew the door closed behind them.

He blinked several times to adjust his gaze to the inky darkness, looking about the room.

At some point, Myrtle had banked the fire, leaving the kitchens nearly black.

As he walked, he passed the same wooden table where they had sat and eaten her birthday cake, speaking about her wishes and her future. And he attempted to tamp down the fast-growing dread for her.

It was an emotion he'd expected to never again feel for a person. It was why he'd kept to himself and not forged any meaningful connections with anyone.

And he was reminded all over again why. Because this? This was bloody awful, this worrying about Myrtle and fearing for her as he did now.

Reaching the back of the kitchen door, he gave his head a shake, dislodging the unhelpful thoughts parading through his mind.

Regardless, he had come to . . . worry about the lady. As such, he simply needed to get in, verify she was safe, and then get himself out.

With that thought fueling him, Val let himself through another door, Horace following closely at his side, releasing a little whine.

Val lifted the two fingers closest his thumb, issuing that silent directive which immediately quieted the dog.

Side by side, they walked the halls of Myrtle's family's home, and as they did, Val's gaze moved over the shadows, and once again he strained to hear . . . anything. Any hint of sound indicating the lady had found herself in harm's way, some sign that she even now faced down a pair of robbers who'd intended to go after her father's curiosity collection.

Only . . . with each corridor he passed and each door he opened, the quiet remained heavy.

At last, he reached the parlor she'd fashioned as her bedroom.

Horace promptly sank onto his haunches and stared eagerly at the paneled door.

And the sheer lunacy of what he did . . . hit him, nearly knocking him back on his heels.

My god, she'd gotten to him. Her overactive imagination had proven contagious, stealing all logic, and now had Val seeing monsters in shadows.

Why, it was entirely possible she'd been walking Horace outside for the evening, or letting him out, and the dog had simply bounded off, back to Val's.

Still, he'd come this way and should at the very least . . . announce himself, verify with his own eyes that she was tucked under those heavy coverlets and peacefully resting.

Feeling entirely foolish, he opened the door.

His eyes immediately went to the sofa.

The blanket lay in a tangle upon the floor, as if the person who'd occupied that makeshift bed had jumped up in a hurry.

His pulse picking up its nervous rhythm once more, he looked to the window seat where he'd found her so many times these past days, that other spot that, as long as he looked out across the courtyard, he'd forever see her standing at.

Empty.

Terror licked at his senses all over again, and he hastened inside . . . shutting the door behind himself and Horace.

Even having seen with his own eyes that her bed was empty, Val made his way over there, praying he'd find her in that mass of blankets.

He reached for them, catching them in his fingers, when suddenly a flash of metal caught the corner of his eye.

Val dived out of the way—

Too late. But still swiftly enough that the poker for the hearth glanced off the side of his thigh.

He grunted, releasing a curse, turning his pistol on—

"Myrtle. Christ," he hissed, the latter name a prayer to the God he'd not spoken with in years. "You nearly—"

"Val," she whispered, cutting off his words.

And then, with no regard for the gun he still held in his hands, she launched herself into his arms.

Val immediately closed them around her, holding her close, running his hand over the small of her back, taking comfort in her small weight pressed reassuringly against his.

She was well.

She was safe.

"My god, I could have shot you," he whispered furiously against her temple, the metal of the gun still clenched in his hand, reminding him of how very close he'd come to harming her.

"I thought you were them," she said, her voice nearly inaudible, and then slipping out of his arms, leaving him cold and bereft, she darted across the room and pressed her ear against the panel.

"Them?"

"They are here. Those men are here to steal my father's collection. I was right, you know." She brought the fireplace poker shooting up, highlighting her point, and nearly knocking him for a second time. He ducked out of the way, avoiding that blow. "And I'll have you know," she went on, giving no indication that she was aware she'd almost hit him, "it gives me no satisfaction that I was right. But—"

"Myrtle, will you be silent?" he whispered. "Unless you want them to discover us."

She blinked slowly several times. "Yes, I suppose you are correct. We should be quiet."

"I am quiet," he pointed out between gritted teeth. "If I may point out, you are the one talking?"

There was a beat of silence. And then—

"Yes, but you were speaking just now, and—"

"Myrtle," he said, exasperated, alternately wanting to shake her and kiss her, and thoroughly confounded by the latter.

And this time, mercifully and blessedly, she complied.

With Myrtle at last quiet, Val picked his way back over to the door, turned the lock, and proceeded over to the two connecting doorways in the corner, seeing those ones were secured, as well.

When he turned back, he found Myrtle on her knees, with her arms flung around Horace, and the sight of the pair of them caused his lungs to constrict.

Even his brother, in the times he came to visit, eyed the dog warily.

Never had Val seen anyone bond as she had with the wolflike dog—that was, anyone other than his late wife and himself.

Even then, even when his wife had been alive, the dog had been a mere pup, not yet full grown.

And this, Myrtle's clear love and adoration for the dog who'd become like the son Val had almost had, deepened the bond he'd forged with her these past days. For better or for worse. Whether he liked it or not.

Which he didn't.

Because of that level of intimacy between them.

As if she felt his eyes upon her, Myrtle looked up. "What?" she mouthed from over the top of Horace's head. And then fear lit her eyes. "Are they here?" she asked, her voice still soundless but her gaze conveying all the terror contained within that question.

He shook his head. "No." He made his lips move slowly so that assurance could penetrate.

Some of the tension seemed to leave her narrow shoulders, and Myrtle returned her attention to petting Horace.

Adjusting his hold on his pistol, Val joined the pair.

Myrtle looked up.

He raised his palms and did a pointed search of the rooms.

"I don't know where they are," she said, and he touched a finger to his lips, reminding her to be silent, but his attempts proved futile. "I am *hoping* they've stopped giving me chase, and that they will just get on with stealing my father's artifacts, but—"

"Will you be quiet?" he clipped out. "They will hear you."

"It's impossible not to."

That booming voice on the other side of the panel brought his and Myrtle's and Horace's attention flying to the door.

"Damned magpie, she is."

Val silently cursed, even as Horace jumped up and growled at the panel standing between him and the street thieves.

He held his left palm up, and the dog immediately took that signal, going silent and lying on the floor at his feet.

Her cheeks pale, Myrtle looked at Val with stricken eyes, and his heart—which he'd only just learned hadn't been as dead or as insulated as he'd once believed—ached at that fear she knew.

"You shouldn't have brought him back. I sent him to safety," she said.

And then it registered. She was speaking about Horace. She feared not for herself, but for the dog. She'd sent him out to be free from danger, while all the while she'd stayed to face down two dangerous foes, and Val didn't know whether to shake her or kiss her.

"I said, open this damned door, and this time, if you don't comply, I will put a bullet in that dog's throat."

"You won't," Myrtle cried. "You addlepated blunderbuss!"

"Myrtle." Val caught her firmly but gently around her left arm, but she surged against him, shaking a fist at the door.

"Because you'll have to put one in me first—"

"Myrtle—"

"We'll be 'appy to do it, too. Finally get ourselves some peace and quiet this night."

Myrtle gasped. "Why, I never—"

"Myrtle, will you, please?" Val whispered against her temple, and miracle of miracles, this time she complied. "I need you to listen, and I need to say this quickly. I want you to keep the panel between them and yourself at all times, but I want you to let them in—only when I raise my hand, giving the signal. Can you do that?"

Her enormous, saucer-size eyes met his, radiating such trust, more trust than he was deserving of. She nodded.

"Do not worry about Horace," he said for her ears alone, needing her to know that she mattered even more than his dog, and that he'd not sacrifice her for the animal.

"How can I not?" she entreated.

"Because he will be fine if you listen to me." It was a lie. It was a lie he gave freely, because he knew if he weren't to do so, her attention would be on the dog rather than the charge he'd tasked her with. "Here." He pressed one pistol into her hand, even as he reached for the other. "You pull the hammer—"

"I know how to shoot, Val," she said with a roll of her eyes, her tone as offended as if he'd questioned her ladylike skills on embroidering, and for the first time since they'd shared cake together that night, he smiled.

And then leaning down, he kissed her hard on the mouth. Because if there was even a remote chance he might die this night in the impending exchange, he wanted to know the feel of her lips once more.

"Open the damned door this instant." That low growl from one of those thieves broke them apart.

"Now, go," he whispered.

Her lashes fluttered, and with a dreamy little smile, she flitted over to the doorway, positioning herself precisely as he'd directed.

Refocusing all his energy and attention on the upcoming meeting, Val carefully picked his way across the flooring, joining her on the other side of the doorway, positioning himself several paces back.

Myrtle stared intently at Val with so much trust it slicked his palms with fear. Another woman had once looked at him with that expression. A woman he'd failed. As such, he wasn't deserving of her faith, and for an instant, his confidence flagged.

"Val?" she mouthed, and he forced the distracting voices in his head to the far-flung corners where he'd face them some time that was not now.

Drawing his pistol up and extending it, he raised a hand.

Without hesitation, Myrtle unlocked the door and drew it open.

One of the men immediately charged inside, slamming the panel hard, knocking it into Myrtle and pulling a gasp from her.

She lost both her footing and her hold on the pistol; coming down hard, the weapon discharged noisily in the room, a stray bullet hit the ceiling, and an explosion of plaster rained down.

"Ya gonna shoot us, are ya, gel?" the hulking figure taunted, raising his pistol. "Well, next time—"

The stinging fire of rage coursed through Val's veins, and he fired.

The report of his pistol thundered in the quiet, cutting off the remainder of that threat.

The man wailed as the bullet struck his palm, and he dropped his weapon and sank to the floor, howling and holding his injured hand close.

His partner came charging for Val.

Dropping his now useless gun, Val rushed forward. A flash of metal caught his eye.

The smaller thief jerked in his tracks, his bulging eyes stunned, and then they rolled to the top of his head and he crumpled to the floor.

Momentarily stunned, Val stood motionless and stared with shocked eyes at Myrtle.

Myrtle, who remained equally frozen with the fireplace poker raised above her head, that metal weapon she'd brought down on the smaller thief's head.

His partner commenced a different howling. "Ya killed him." He stood. "Now, Oi'm gonna kill ya, ya—"

That warning faded to a whimper as Myrtle clubbed him. He dropped to his knees and then pitched forward.

"I was going to say a pistol isn't such a good idea," she said, conversing as casually over the two men she'd succeeded in felling as she might across a dining table. "They are wholly unreliable, and noisy, and you have only one shot. As such, the poker"—she brought that article in question up, brandishing her weapon of choice—"is a far preferable option when confronting—"

Val had her in his arms in an instant, crushing her to him, holding her slender body close to his, squeezing her tightly to assure himself that she was unharmed. That she was still here.

Myrtle angled her head back, but this time made no attempt to slip from his arms. "I am fine, Val," she said softly. "Truly."

Truly.

And she was.

This time.

"Did I?" she asked, her voice hesitant, and he drew back slightly but still kept his hold upon her. He ran his hands over her arms, needing to verify for himself that she was unharmed.

"Did you what?" he asked distractedly as he made his search.

"Kill them?" She bit her lower lip. "B-because that wasn't my intention. I didn't want to kill them," she said on a rush. "Even if they did want to hurt me. I don't even like to hunt or fish. Well, I do like to fish," she rambled in her adorable way. "But I always release them after I catch them . . . unless it is for a meal. Then I apologize and explain to them that I have to eat as much as they do, and"—her fear-filled eyes went to the men sprawled facedown on the floor—"I decidedly did not want to eat them or hurt them."

Val angled her head away and drew her close once more so that her cheek rested against his chest. "You did what you had to do in that moment, Myrtle," he murmured. "You saved yourself . . . and me."

Horace barked.

"And Horace," Val added, as much for the dog's benefit as for the truth that Myrtle needed to hear in this instant.

Still, he relinquished his hold and then fell to a knee, checking for a pulse first of one man—and finding it, strong and very much there. And then he checked the other. "They both live."

Myrtle clapped, and closing her eyes, she jumped up and down as excitedly as if she were cheering on a mount at Ascot Racecourse, and not as though she'd just taken down two ruthless thieves.

Whereas Val? His hands shook. How close she'd come to . . . He forced his thoughts away from the path they were traveling.

Val came to his feet. "Come," he said gruffly, taking her by the hand. "Let us get you out of here."

"Me?" she asked as she let him pull her along. "Because we really should get *you* out of here as well, Val. And Horace."

At hearing her speak his name, the dutifully silent-through-the-action dog bounded over. Without breaking stride, he bypassed Val and jumped, his front paws finding purchase on Myrtle's shoulders.

She staggered under the dog's enormous weight—Horace, on his hind legs, outsized her by several inches.

Any other lady or gentleman would have been horrified.

Myrtle, however, laughed, and proceeded to go through slight steps as if she were dancing with Val's dog, and in that moment, his relief was so great that Val erupted with laughter, joining his amusement with hers.

"We will leave," she promised Val.

He held his arm out.

"But just"—she held a finger up and wagged it about—"one more thing!"

Val groaned. "Yes, why don't we stay and wait for them to awaken so we might join them for tea," he called after her as she rushed from the room.

"Now, why would we ever do that?" she rejoined from the hall, her voice carrying but muffled slightly. "Having tea with the men who tried to . . ."

As her voice drifted farther away, despite himself, despite the sheer terror that had gripped him and threatened to swallow him whole, he found himself grinning.

Against all attempts to be indifferent toward the lady, she enthralled him at every turn.

A moment later, Myrtle returned. "Ta-da!" she exclaimed, and the metal in her hands clinked together.

His brow shot up. "What . . . are those?"

"They are manacles," she said as she approached the downed brute nearest the fire.

"Wherever did you get . . . ?" Recalling her penchant for prattling, he thought better of it. "Never mind. I don't want to kn—"

"My brother brought them back from his travels."

"Of course he did," he mumbled.

"He said I was to use them on brutes but not family members . . . unless they were behaving like brutes, in which case I was free to use them on—"

"Myrtle," he warned.

"Oh, right! We should hurry. Will you drag that one over here?"

Puzzling his brow, he looked about.

Myrtle rolled her eyes. "The thief, Val. The thief," she repeated back as if it were every day she politely requested he bring her a felled ruffian.

Catching the bounder under his arms, Val dragged the man over; a small groan escaped the other man, but he continued to sleep. "We should have left," he mumbled as he set him down beside the other still slumbering fellow.

"I promised we will. But first . . ." Dropping to a knee, Myrtle wrapped one of the loops about the burlier thief's wrist, locking the clasp, and then locked the right hand of the smaller thief's so that the two of them were connected by those metal bonds. She assessed her handiwork a moment, and then gave a pleased little nod. "*Now* we can go."

With Myrtle's hand tucked in his, and Horace following close behind, they hurried from the room.

"Wait!" she exclaimed.

Val released an exasperated groan. "What now?"

"Can you drag that"—Myrtle pointed to a nearby table in the hall covered with a blanket—"and put it in front of the door? I'd suggest a key," she ran on. "But it would likely take too long—"

"Myrtle," he said warningly.

"Oh, yes. We should hurry." She gave a little clap of her hands. "If you will?"

And he did. Because he found himself increasingly unable to say no to her or deny her . . . anything.

"Now, can we go?" he repeated for a second time.

She beamed. "This time, we may."

And this time, they did.

There would be time enough for a different sort of terror this night, a fear he'd been battling over his feelings for this woman.

But for now, there was just this joyous relief—and he was selfish enough to take it.

Chapter 16

Myrtle sat in the window seat, wearing a warm blanket about her shoulders.

This time, however, she occupied a different window seat, staring out across the way to her own, that same spot she'd occupied these past days.

Her knees drawn up to her chest and her chin resting atop them, she considered her family's townhouse.

How much time had she spent staring at Val's residence, seeing him at the window, imagining him there, wanting to be with him?

And now she was.

She was in this house—his house—a place she'd thought she'd never be. But she was here now, with him.

And it felt . . . so very right.

And she at last admitted the truth to herself, allowed herself to see that which she'd fought.

She wanted to be here. She wanted to be here with him. Not just for this night, but for all her nights.

When she'd set Horace free and raced about her family's townhouse, with two thieves in pursuit, she'd accepted that she was going to die this night. She'd known that the end was waiting to meet her. She'd felt it. She'd seen it. Nor had those been the panicky imaginings of a young woman with an overactive imagination, as she'd been accused by so many. She'd truly seen it.

And as she'd raced around, evading the two brutes who'd searched for her, she'd thought . . . of Val. It had been his face she'd seen, and his presence she'd yearned for . . . And the future, her future she'd wanted for herself had flashed before her eyes, and in it, Val had been the man beside her.

Val, whose heart and soul and whole self belonged to a ghost. A man who had loved so very deeply and was so committed to his wife's memory that he'd all but become a recluse.

As such, he could never, and would never, belong to Myrtle. And that was what had hurt most of all this night. As she'd confronted her own end, that had been the greatest regret she'd carried. Val belonged so wholly to another, and in those moments, even dreaming of a future with him hadn't been a full possibility because she'd known even if she lived, there could not be anything more with him. Not just because of the love he still carried for his wife, but because of *Myrtle*. What were the chances Val would choose a second wife, and one given to hoydenish ways?

But you did help take down two thieves, and you have made him smile . . . a voice niggled. Even though, in the beginning, he'd clearly fought those grins . . . And that surely meant . . . something?

And he *had* come for her.

He'd charged into her home and put himself in harm's way, facing possible death . . . for her.

And that . . . that was heady stuff.

And also dangerous stuff. For it gave hope where there should likely be none. Because surely, a man who'd raced to her rescue as he had done felt . . . something for her.

Myrtle sighed. She was giving herself a hope which she so desperately wished to feed upon. "I am deluding myself."

Horace barked.

"You are being sweet. I am, Horace. I know I am. But you know your master. He is a man who would come to the aid of anyone who found themselves in harm's way."

And this time, Horace's silence bespoke his agreement.

That was the manner of man Val was, though. Oh, he might be snarling and snapping and angry, but he'd also proven himself honorable; he'd come and tended her fires and been sure she had food, even as he'd been so very clearly annoyed by her intrusion on his life.

Footfalls echoed outside his offices, and she glanced over, and a moment later, there came a brief scratching.

"Enter," she called, already knowing that the owner of that respectful rapping was not the one she truly wished to see.

The door opened, and the greying servant entered. In his arms he carried forth a silver tray filled with a teapot and a lone cup, and there was something forlorn about that single porcelain cup, an unnecessary but loud reminder that she was alone.

"Miss," Jenkins greeted as he approached, and Myrtle sat up. "His Grace instructed I bring tea and biscuits. To fortify you." He added that latter part, clearly three words which he'd heard his master speak and in turn repeated.

"Thank you," she murmured, touched by that thoughtfulness. Her heart lifted, then promptly fell. "That was very kind of His Grace."

You are making more of it than there truly is. He sent tea. It was the most English thing a lady or gentleman could do . . .

Disappointment swirled in her breast, and she made a show of taking the cup he set down and devoted all her attention to making herself tea.

All the while, she felt Jenkins's eyes upon her.

She looked up.

"He is," the older servant murmured. "That is, very kind."

She expected him to leave, only he lingered, seeming to consider his words, and her curiosity piqued, a welcome sentiment that kept her from wallowing in self-pity at having fallen in love with the one man who could never love her in return. "Is there something you wish to say?" she asked gently, encouraging him to speak his mind.

Jenkins looked her squarely in the eyes. "There are many rumors that surround His Grace. Unkind ones, cruel stories about the duke, and—"

"I am very much aware that His Grace is a good man," she interjected gently. Her gaze slipped beyond the butler's shoulder, as in her mind she saw Val as he'd been these past days. "Yes, he is gruff and surly, but I suspect those are just facades he's donned to protect himself. He's only proven honorable and kind and—"

Aware of how much she'd revealed to his servant, and how much more she'd been about to reveal, she made herself go quiet. Clearing her throat, Myrtle took a sip of her tea. After all, she was still an unmarried lady, alone in London. Acknowledging aloud to anyone the time she'd spent alone with Val which had allowed her to learn those intimate details about him threatened her reputation before she'd even had her first official Season.

"You may be assured I would never violate His Grace's trust," the butler murmured. He paused. "Or yours."

In other words, he'd not reveal to anyone her presence here, or her relationship with Val. That allegiance spoke volumes of his bond with the duke and his respect for him.

"You have been with him long, then?" she asked, fiddling with the cup on her lap, shameful in her quest to learn more about this man whom she'd soon part ways with.

"I worked for the late Duchess of Aragon's family and joined the young lady when she wed His Grace. And your assessment of him is correct. There is no fairer, more honorable man than he."

Yes, that was precisely what Val was. It was why he'd tolerated her presence these past days, despite his longing for privacy. And it was why he'd come to save her from those fiends. "What was he like?" she asked softly. "Before."

"Before Her Grace passed?"

She nodded, even as her chest constricted with an unfair jealousy at the mention of the woman who'd been tied to Val, a woman whom he'd so deeply loved that her hold upon him remained just as strong in death. "Yes."

Jenkins smiled sadly. "A more charming man there was not. He was always ready with a smile and jest, sneaking into the kitchens to join the staff along with his brother."

The man he spoke of was so *different* from the one she knew, and she tried desperately to imagine Val, who'd come to mean so very much to her, as the carefree, lighthearted fellow the servant now spoke of.

"He must have loved her greatly."

"Desperately. Their families were dear friends, and he'd known her forever. They were friendly as children, but that relationship became romantic."

In other words, he'd loved her forever.

Whereas Myrtle . . . Myrtle was a mere stranger to him. Someone he'd known but a handful of days, and because of his love for his wife, it would never be more with her.

Sadness glimmered in the butler's eyes, eyes that sparkled with a glassy sheen of tears. "When Her Grace perished, it was as though His Grace died, too. The joy that had always existed within him . . . It was like a light that was snuffed out. He was changed. Curt. Depressed. It was as though a stranger overtook the form of a man who'd been loved by all. Most of the servants quit after that transformation."

"But you did not," she murmured, admiration and appreciation for the old butler stirring in her breast.

He straightened, bringing his shoulders back. "Because the duke was a bit brusque? I would never. His Grace was hurting, and I was disgusted that so many of the men and women who served under me should abandon him in his hour of need. Alas, they proclaimed too many hours of his snarling and stomping about had passed for them to remain on any longer. I had to set up a new staff, a smaller one, who is willing to overlook his bluster. People who do not remember him as he used to be."

"Happy," she said, gripping the stem of her cup hard, and then forcing her hand to relax so as to not crush the porcelain.

"Yes. Happy." Jenkins's eyes met hers. "But these past few days, His Grace has been different."

Her heart stirred in her breast. "Different?"

"He's never apart from his dog." Jenkins glanced pointedly at the dog slumbering at the front of Val's desk. "And that dog never wishes to be apart from him. Horace was a gift from Her Grace, and the bond between master and pup was strengthened between them when they survived that tragic accident."

Myrtle leaned down reflexively and stroked the dog's silken coat, seeing him in a new light. Seeing him as that special gift Val had received from a woman who'd meant more to him than anything . . . and then imagining the agony of her death, which had left Val and Horace alone. "I trust a person can never truly recover from that loss," she whispered. But, oh, how she wished they could.

"No." Jenkins murmured his assent. "One does not ever truly emerge from such tragedy." He paused, a pregnant stretch of silence that brought her attention back to him. "Or that was what I believed. Until now."

Until now.

"He's been more the man he used to be, and I do believe that is not coincidental," he added, giving her a meaningful look.

Myrtle touched a hand to her breast. Was he suggesting . . . ? Was he saying . . . ? Surely he did not mean that Val had appeared changed for the good . . . because of her.

Jenkins inclined his head. "That is precisely what I am saying, miss," he said, answering her unspoken question.

There came a brisk, perfunctory knock, and she shot to her feet with Horace hopping up beside her.

A knock that was so very clearly his that her heart raced.

Val entered the room. At some point, he'd changed his garments, swapping them for more of those familiar black clothes.

His gaze went between Myrtle and Jenkins before landing squarely on Myrtle.

With a murmur and a bow, the butler slipped from the room, leaving the two of them alone.

"You returned!" She couldn't contain the joy that found its way into her exclamation.

"Did you think I would not?" he asked, and had that question come from any other man, it would have been gently teasing.

Val's, however, contained his usual brusque annoyance, and she recalled the butler's words about how he used to be. It was also the gruff man she'd come to know, and it was familiar to her. Strangely comforting, even.

"Of course I did," she said, and some of the tension slipped from his shoulders. "After all, it is your townhouse."

He frowned.

"I'm teasing, Val."

He grunted. "I know." He remained framed in the doorway, making no move to enter. "Do you need anything?" he asked. "Has Jenkins seen—"

"No, no." She was swift to reassure him. "I'm quite fine." He'd the lone servant who remained on at her beck and call. The greying, older fellow had fetched her blankets and brought a plate of food. A plate that remained untouched. He'd also remained stationed outside Val's offices while Val had collected a constable and brought them to Myrtle's home. "He's provided me with everything I need."

"I am glad."

I am glad.

How very . . . formal they were.

So formal that she may as well have dreamed the closeness they'd shared these past days.

"They are gone," he said.

"Gone?" she echoed.

"I waited while the constables escorted them from your home. They do not know, Myrtle."

She stared blankly at him.

"They are unaware that you are here in London. I explained that I am a friend and close neighbor of your father's and saw two men breaking into his household."

When it came to protecting her from discovery, he'd thought of everything. She should be touched. But she proved a selfish creature once more . . . for it also revealed the great lengths he'd gone to be sure it wasn't found out that she'd been alone with him, which would ruin her name and require him to do the right thing by her.

"Myrtle?"

"I am relieved they've been captured," she said. Which wasn't untrue. She forcibly shoved the pitiable musings to the side of her mind, saving them for a later date when she was alone.

"At some point when we made our escape, they awakened and attempted to leave, but apparently in their haste, they ran headlong into the table you had me place in the hall and tumbled over it, knocking themselves out for a second time."

She should smile. She should be elated. She'd felled her family's burglars twice this night. Instead, the dread that had gripped her the moment she'd realized they'd breached her home stirred to life, and Myrtle folded her arms around her middle.

Val was immediately across the room.

He reached her, setting down a leather satchel she'd not noted . . . until now.

"They will not return, Myrtle," he said gruffly, taking her lightly by the arms and rubbing gently. "Not now that they've been discovered by both of us. And now that there are people aware of their intentions to rob from your father, they cannot return. Not without risking the constables and guards who'll be there in wait."

Guards?

"I took the liberty of hiring several men to watch the various entrances of your family's townhouse."

"You did?" she whispered.

He nodded. "You indicated your father's antiquity collection meant a good deal to you and him, and—" He coughed into his fist.

He'd thought of everything.

Touched by that kindness, she took his hands in hers. "Thank you," she said softly.

"You needn't thank me." An endearing blush filled his cheeks, and she fell in love with him all the more.

He'd known what that collection meant and had sought to protect it, spending his own monies to see her home guarded.

And then she stilled.

And her.

He'd made sure there were men stationed outside.

Going cold, and besieged by the sudden urge to cry, she slipped her hands from his and, to hide their tremble, picked up her teacup. "I thank you for seeing that I'm looked after. I trust my family will return soon, and you will be well compensated for your efforts on our behalf."

Val scowled. "I am not looking for compensation," he gritted out with a heavy amount of annoyance coating that low growl.

"I didn't mean to suggest you were," she said when he took a furious step toward her. "Just that—"

"You believe I intend to leave you in that townhouse as your family did, forgotten while the guards I hired oversee looking after you?" he demanded.

"I . . . uh . . . yes?" His eyes narrowed into thin, dangerous slits. "No?" she ventured, her voice pitching slightly up with that second question. His lashes dipped even lower. "Er . . . maybe?"

With a little whine, Horace covered his face with his paws.

Val growled. "I'm not leaving you alone," he said curtly, and she couldn't even be offended by his tone because of the reason for it.

He was offended that she'd expected he should leave her. Which meant . . . he surely cared in some way. That she was . . . more than a responsibility to him.

Her hopes were dashed in an instant with his next words. "I'm not waiting for your family to remember they've neglected you. We leave at first light," he said, picking up his bag and setting it down atop the immaculate surface of his desk.

She found her voice. "We leave at first light?" What was he saying?

"I'm personally escorting you to your family's Scottish estates." He proceeded to open the drawers, adding items to his valise as he talked. "It does not make sense for us to wait any longer." Because he'd given up on her family remembering her, and yet, he also proved too kind, too gentle to say as much, and any other time she might have felt a warmth at that concern for her feelings. "I'm seeing to the arrangements." He made to close the bag, but Horace gave a piteous whine.

I know how you feel, pup . . .

The dog proceeded to scratch at the bottom drawer.

Muttering something to himself, Val yanked that panel open and withdrew a handful of wrapped packages and threw them inside. "Are you happy?"

"Yes." She blurted out that lie. Because how could she tell him? How could she . . . ?

Val gave her an odd look. "I was talking to Horace."

She curled her toes into the floor. "Oh." And because in that moment it was entirely easier to look at Horace than at the man whom she'd fallen heels over head for, she glanced at the pup, who'd lain down on the floor and resumed snoring. "Er . . . he seems more content?"

"Yes, he does at that," he said, giving his head a wry shake.

She wanted to ask him what those packages were. She wanted Val to just remain with her here, and she yearned to talk with him about those wrapped gifts, and everything else in between. She wanted to use her dwindling time with him to discover everything there was to know about Val and Horace and . . .

"If you'll excuse me?" And dropping a deep, respectful bow, Val grabbed his bag and left her standing there.

He was taking her to her family.

She should be grateful.

And yet . . .

He was so eager to be rid of her and his sense of duty was so great that he'd pack her up immediately.

They would be alone together on the journey.

There was that small consolation—she would be able to steal these last final moments with him, and as pathetic and desperate for him as she was, she would take even those scraps.

❄❄❄

It had been years since he'd paid a visit to anyone. Not his brother. Not his mother. Not the many friends he'd had before.

He'd not gone to his former clubs.

He'd remained exclusively at his London townhouse, content to shut out the rest of the world and to live in solitude.

As such, the shocked, speechless, jaw-gaping reaction from his brother, Sidney, was to be expected.

His brother immediately found himself. "Please, sit." He motioned not to the seating at the desk where Val now stood, but to the leather button sofa near the roaring fire.

"That won't be necessary," he said sharply, more sharply than he intended, but as gently as he was capable of anymore.

He'd been speaking in those brusque tones for so long his tongue and throat were incapable of making any other sound.

Sidney gestured once more. "Val, it's just four o'clock in the morning, and you're paying me a visit for the first time in four years. Sit."

Val stiffened, and then crossing over, he claimed a spot on the lone winged chair beside the sofa.

He waited for his brother to join him, then opened his mouth to unleash the words he'd rehearsed on the way here. "I—"

"A brandy?" His brother cut him off.

"No."

Sidney, however, was already headed to his sideboard. Once there, he proceeded to make not one but two drinks that he carried back. "Here."

Val frowned. "I don't—"

"It's a good bottle of French and was always your favorite. Take the drink, Val," his brother said gently but firmly.

Val took the drink, then promptly set it down. "I require assistance," he said the moment his brother had seated himself.

"What do you need?"

"I need use of one of your carriages."

"It is yours, as well as one of my drivers."

Val opened his mouth to deliver the practiced speech and then stopped. "That's it?"

A rueful grin formed on his brother's face. "Did you think I'd deny you anything?"

"I . . ." He hadn't known what he'd expected. He'd been a miserable bastard to so many—to everyone—since Dinah's passing. His brother, once his best friend, had become a stranger, a gulf having grown between them, sown by Val's need for self-protection.

"You are my brother, Val," Sidney said simply. "I love you."

Unnerved by the freeness with which his brother now spoke of his love, Val grunted.

His brother's grin grew rueful. "Worry not, big brother—I know you love me, too."

And he did.

It was why he'd shut the other man out. It was why he'd not wanted to see him, and suddenly it seemed very important that his brother know that.

Val cradled his glass tightly, and he forced himself to lighten his grip. "It hurt so very much," he said hoarsely.

"I know, Val. I know."

Only, unless one lost one's wife and child, one could never truly know.

He stared into the amber contents of his drink. "I didn't want to lose like that again, and so . . . it was easier to just cut those whose loss could hurt me . . . in that same way again . . . from my life."

The time he'd spent with Myrtle had taught him how to use his voice again, and though he'd never move with any ease around people—his family included—he'd found a way of at least . . . functioning with other people. That would be the gift she left him.

"Thank you for sharing that," Sidney murmured.

Val inclined his head. He didn't deserve his brother's gratitude. He required his forgiveness.

"I will admit . . . to some curiosity. Dare I hope you . . . might be considering a journey to Mother's?"

"No," he said instantly.

It was still too soon for him to make that same journey to that same event, along those same roads.

Perhaps it would always be.

Regret lit his brother's eyes. "Perhaps someday."

"Yes," Val murmured. "Perhaps someday."

He lied.

But he couldn't bring himself to end this shared connection with his brother.

Sidney looped his leg over his opposite knee. "Dare I hope you'll at least share your destination?"

"No," he said flatly. He'd trust his brother with his very life, but Val did not intend to share about Myrtle. Myrtle and his time with her were memories reserved just for him.

Curiosity sparked in his brother's like-blue gaze. "Now you have me intrigued." Val felt his cheeks go warm. "Worry not. I shan't press you, dear brother. I shall remain intrigued and allow you to your privacy."

Taking that as his cue, and suddenly very eager to return to his household . . . and Myrtle, Val set his glass down and came to his feet.

His brother immediately followed suit.

Val hovered, then held out a hand across the small coffee table between them.

Ignoring that offering, Sidney stepped around the table and hugged Val. "Happy Christmas, big brother."

Val stood there, tense, stiff, unmoving, and then his arms of their own volition folded reflexively around his only sibling. "Happy Christmas, little brother," he said gruffly, and then stepped out of his brother's arms. And disquieted by that display of emotion, something still so new and raw and unfamiliar, he headed for the door.

And as he walked, his brother's tidings registered, and Val's steps slowed.

How many times at this same point in the year had Sidney offered those wishes? And each time he had, Val had met it sneeringly with the jaded cynicism of one who knew he'd never be happy again.

Only, this time . . . this year, that feeling . . . hadn't come. The felicitations had fallen just as freely from his lips.

And he knew why.

Because this was the first time in all these years that Val had not been alone. That he'd spent the days leading up to that festive holiday celebrated by his family and so many others with another person.

With Myrtle.

Myrtle, who had more cheer and more spirit and more smiles than anyone he'd ever known.

He was reaching for the door handle when his brother called out, staying him.

Val looked back.

"What you said before . . . about having kept me and Mother and the world out," he clarified when Val cast a silent question his way. "Cutting those you love and care about won't protect you from hurting when they're gone, Val," Sidney said gently. "It will simply leave you with a profound regret for the time you did not have to spend together. All you can do is take what time you have, what moments you have together, and make the most of each."

And with those words ringing in the air, Val inclined his head and left.

Chapter 17

Myrtle had been bereft when she'd realized the urgency with which Val sought to be free of her and his sense of responsibility for her.

That was, until she thought about the time they'd have together, alone.

Desperate for every crumb of his time and company, she had found not just solace but joy in the impending journey. Joy because she would be alone with Val. She would have the carriage ride to spend with him, talking with him and learning all she could before he was gone.

In the end, she wasn't even to have that.

In the end, she'd have nothing more than the occasional glimpse of him out the carriage window as he rode his mount and she made the journey to Scotland alone in the fine-rigged black carriage early that morn.

Horace nudged her hand with his wet, black nose, and she favored him with a pet. "Forgive me, friend. I did not mean to imply that your company is anything but welcome." He whined, then pressed his nose against the glass, staring out at the snow-covered grounds. "Especially as you so clearly want to be out there"—*too*—"but you are stuck in here with me."

Horace lapped her fingers with his rough tongue, and she patted his head distractedly as she stared out at the rapidly passing landscape.

Everything following the assault on her family's household, and Val's timely rescue and the events after, had proceeded in a whirlwind.

He'd escorted her home and waited outside her chamber doors while she'd filled a valise for the journey to Scotland. And all the while she had packed, she'd waited for him to join her inside.

Of course he wouldn't.

He was too honorable to accompany her inside her bedchambers.

But she wished he had.

Not for any reasons that were . . . wicked, though there had secretly been a wish to know his embrace once more.

Rather, she'd wanted him to join her so they might talk.

He hadn't.

And then they'd made the walk nearly silently back to his townhouse—a walk she'd made many times before, these past days.

Morning had dawned, and the carriage had been readied, and she'd been loaded within, but only after she'd broken a fast on bread and sausage and an apple brought to her upon a tray by his butler, Jenkins.

Restless to give her fingers something to do—to give *herself* something to do—Myrtle chipped away at the frost formed on the inside of the window, dusting the remnants away with her palm. She searched outside, looking for a hint of him.

And then she spied him.

Riding alongside but just behind the carriage.

Myrtle tossed the window open and arched her neck back so she might better see him.

Val instantly rode forward. "What is it?"

"It is cold."

"Then you should close the window."

Had those words been spoken by any other man, they would have been rude.

Val, however, was only matter-of-factly blunt in every word he spoke, and she couldn't contain a smile. "I was more remarking it for you," she called loudly enough to make her voice heard over the noisy clatter of the wheels and the thundering of his horse's hooves mixed with the rhythmic thump of the team pulling the carriage.

"I'm perfectly fine."

She pointed outside. "Your nose is red."

"I don't feel it," he said, his gaze directed on the road ahead.

"Well, it is no wonder because it is so cold."

He blinked slowly, and then his gaze landed on hers; he gave her a peculiar look. "You should close the window."

His meaning couldn't be clearer. He didn't want her company or her talking. He was content—nay, happy—with his *own* company.

Myrtle clasped the sides and leaned farther out and inhaled deeply. "I love the wint—"

"You're going to fall out," he said sharply, and she would have been touched by his concern if he hadn't sounded so deuced annoyed.

"I have quite a good grip, and I'm firmly planted on my seat." Cupping her hands around her mouth, she yelled up to him, "I thought we might talk."

"What do you need to talk about?"

He was endearingly bad with this conversation stuff.

"Not *need* to. *Want* to."

"All right," he said, speaking through gritted teeth. "What do you want to talk about?"

"If you could have any meal for the Christmastide dinner, which would you choose?"

He eyed her like she'd sprung a second head. "*That* is what you want to talk about?"

She nodded.

"Whyyyy?"

And by the several extra syllables he'd managed to squeeze into that single word, she may as well have popped another head out.

"Because I'm curious."

"About what I like to eat."

About him.

It was both the same and different, all at the same time.

"Indulge me," she called.

"I . . ." He shook his head.

"Nothing?" she asked incredulously, leaning out a fraction more. "I find that—"

"Will you get back inside?" he asked, a trace of franticness in his low baritone.

"I will," she promised, and then edged out a fraction more. "If you—"

"Mincemeat pies, a roast with potatoes, carrots, lobster bisque, and Shrewsbury cakes for dessert. Now, for the love of God, will you please just . . . sit back in your seat and leave me be."

The "for the love of God" had felt totally unnecessary. The "leave me be," however, cut to the quick.

Fighting to mask the hurt that ricocheted through her, Myrtle forced a smile and sat back on her buttocks. Very well. "Horace wishes to join you outside."

At hearing his name mentioned, and the possibility of joining his master beyond these carriage walls, the dog popped up.

"No," Val said tightly.

With a little whine, Horace sank onto the floor once more and rested his giant head on her knee.

"He would prefer it."

"I would prefer you shut the window, and yet I'm not getting that, am I?"

"You are quite surly today," she said on a huff.

"Myrtle," he said, bringing his mount even closer, so close if she stretched a hand outside, she could touch him and his magnificent black horse. "It is cold."

"I'm fine with the t-temperature." Her teeth chattered, and she thanked the noisy turn of the carriage wheels and the pounding of the horses' hooves that concealed that tremble.

He gave her a pointed look. "You're shivering," he shouted over the din.

He'd heard that?

She smiled, and to make sure he could better hear her, she leaned out a fraction more. "I am more than fine. In fact, I quite enjoy the weather and—"

"And you are hanging precariously out the window, Myrtle. So for the love of the Lord in Heaven, will you please sit back on your bench and shut the window?"

He'd used her Christian name in the presence of a servant. It was a testament to the extent of his fury that he'd allowed that lapse.

Nay, it wasn't just fury. It was . . . annoyance.

He was annoyed with her.

As eager to be rid of her as she was to remain with him.

Tears threatened, and mustering the remnants of her tattered pride, Myrtle lifted her chin. "I am fine with the cold, you know." And keeping her features as even as possible, she made a show of closing the window.

Almost immediately, Val kicked his mount ahead, putting distance between himself and the carriage, and she followed him until he'd disappeared to no more than a speck, and then not even that in the horizon ahead.

A lone tear streaked down her cheek, and no sooner had she raised her palm to dash the drop away than another was there, followed by another. And another.

"He really cannot wait to be done with me," she whispered, and then promptly burst into tears.

Horace whined, and scrambling awkwardly on the floor of the carriage, the creature put his front paws on her knees, and lapped at her face.

A laugh broke through her tears, and she hugged his head.

"You are wrong," she said. "He will be happy to never again see me."

Horace gave her cheek another lick.

"Now, you, I know, will miss me," she assured, hugging him all the tighter.

And then, as soon as the words left her lips, the reality hit her: this parting would signify the end of her time not just with Val but also with Horace.

Myrtle promptly burst out into fresh tears, besieged by an onslaught of grief and fresh suffering.

She'd miss the both of them.

She'd miss the brooding master and agreeable pup.

She'd miss their company and friendship. In a very short time, she'd come to be closer with these two than with any other soul in the world.

And instead of having a life with them, she'd set out alone on her London Season, never catching so much as a glimpse of him—it being expected by her family and all, that she would marry some other man, a man who was not Val.

Myrtle sobbed all the harder.

And she didn't want to do it.

She didn't want to do any of it. Suffer through the machinations of a Season where she was paraded before suitors and expected to hope that one of those dandies with lily-white, uncallused hands would find her amenable enough to pay call on and court and ultimately marry.

And there'd be kissing and wedding vows exchanged and a marriage bed and—

Myrtle shuddered, horror and disgust taking the place of her misery.

She couldn't do it.

"I won't do it," Myrtle said into the quiet, and with his tongue lolling sideways from his mouth, Horace bobbed his head excitedly, as if he understood her vow and, with his love of her and his master, approved.

And she didn't have to.

A calm stole through her.

All along, it'd been expected that she conduct herself a certain way; she'd been sent away and spent years crafting a facade of a perfectly flawless lady in the hopes that her parents might welcome her back, in the hopes that Mrs. Belden and the other instructors might deem Myrtle's edification complete. Ultimately, she'd . . . lost herself.

With Val and because of him, she'd found her way. She'd remembered what it was to speak freely and not stifle her words or her humor or her thoughts. She'd just . . . been herself these past days, and she didn't want to go back to who she used to be. She wanted a husband who loved her and accepted her as she was, with all her garrulousness and dry sarcasm.

And in the absence of both, she'd not settle.

She'd not do what society and her parents expected of her, any longer.

Dashing the tears from her cheeks, Myrtle drew in a surprisingly slow, steady breath, and a peaceful calm stole over her. Opening her mouth, she proceeded to sing.

> "Stille Nacht, heilige Nacht
> Alles schläft, einsam wacht
> Nur das traute hochheilige Paar.
> Holder Knabe im lockigen Haar."

❄ ❄ ❄

She was singing again.

And he should be glad.

Because as long as she was singing, then she wasn't opening that window and calling out to him to come join her in that terror-inducing contraption.

And even more importantly, she wasn't leaning out of that same terror-inducing contraption, leaning out while the coach swayed slightly back and forth, as those miserable conveyances did, and risking breaking her neck or her body.

With her safely secured, he'd ridden on ahead, determined to put distance between him and the chatty minx. He'd been so very determined to keep that space.

But his thoughts, they'd continued going back to her, refusing to relinquish the reminder that these were the last moments he'd have with Lady Myrtle McQuoid. That soon he'd deposit her at her derelict family's properties and turn on his heel and head back to London and his lonely London townhouse. Lonely as it had been these past years.

But not as it had been these past few days, with her.

Because of her.

And as he was being honest with himself, it was why he'd turned his mount about and waited for the conveyance to catch up.

But he was not glad, and he was not calm.

Not when the carriage finally reached him and the song that came from within those dark walls did, too.

One that ratcheted up a tension, coiling all his muscles into knots, twisting his lungs in a vise and squeezing so that it was impossible to make a breath or a sound.

Despite the chill of the early winter morn, sweat slicked his palms and dotted his brow.

Val gritted his teeth.

Must she always sing?

Only, she didn't always sing. She was determined to sing those Christmas carols, ones that he'd not heard since his wife's death. It was his late wife whom he should be thinking of and recalling in that moment.

God forgive him, however. It was not.

Somehow his mind had become all confused, with memories of the past tangling and twisting with the vines of an imagined future.

One where Myrtle, who now sat inside that carriage with the same dog who'd sat inside another, was tossed through an open door while he remained hopeless to catch her. To keep her from flying out.

Val squeezed his eyes shut so hard his head ached, and he concentrated on the pain, welcomed it, preferring that physical suffering, for surely it would prove a diversion and break the hold of those imaginings that now haunted him.

Only it didn't.

He still saw that tableau of terror, in his mind.

Not with Dinah, but with Myrtle, Myrtle who was always laughing and chattering and teasing, silenced forever, her broken body sprawled in the snow with her legs twisted at odd angles under her.

A tortured moan gurgled in Val's throat.

Under him Lady whinnied, the horse growing restless and tense.

"Easy, boy," Val whispered, as much for himself as to the animal. He stroked the loyal mount on his withers as he so loved.

Then, miracle of miracles, the memories ceased. The haunting stopped.

For an instant.

And then he felt it. Because the devil was determined to torment him this night and every night . . . a bit of moisture. It touched his nose, wet and cold, and brought his mind waltzing back to that long-ago night.

He clenched his eyes, willing the song to stop. Pleading with God to win the battle over the dark lord so that Val might know some—any—peace.

But he proved as alone as Jesus himself had been in those forty days spent trudging through the desert, tested by his father. The lyrics of that German song his wife had softly sung right before the world had caught fire reached from within the carriage and spilled out into the countryside.

> "Stille Nacht, heilige Nacht,
> Hirten erst kundgemacht
> Durch der Engel Halleluja . . ."

"Will you stop?" he rasped, the command barely audible to his own ears.

> "Tönt es laut von fern und nah:
> Christ, der Retter ist da!
> Christ, der Retter ist da!"

"I said, 'will you stop,'" he thundered, his voice booming around the sprawling, empty countryside, made all the quieter by the winter morn.

The driver instantly yanked on the reins, bringing the carriage carrying Myrtle to a dangerously jarring halt, one so quick it sent Val's heart racing all the faster and nausea turning in his belly, as it careened left and then right in a moment that lasted forever and then stopped.

"Not you," Val bellowed, even as he knew it wasn't his brother's driver's fault. That he'd been responding to what he'd believed had been a directive sent his way. It didn't help. Fear at the sight of that carriage carrying Myrtle listing back and forth still unleashed more of that dread inside.

The door popped open, and Myrtle appeared in the framed entrance. "Worry not." Standing up and stretching on tiptoes, she arched up in a bid to see the man on the box. "He was talking to me. I, for one, am glad you stopped." With that ominous pronouncement, the lady hopped down.

With a happy bark, Horace leapt down, and landing on all fours, he proceeded to dance a happy circle about the earth.

Cursing, Val swung his leg over and dismounted. Not breaking stride, he headed over to meet her. "What do you think you are doing?" he barked.

"Coming to speak to—"

"No."

"Y-you." Cold rather than fear lent a tremble to Myrtle's voice, and she rubbed her palms vigorously together. "It is cold out here."

He grasped that offering she'd held out. "Precisely." Val took her lightly by the arm and proceeded to steer her back.

Or attempted to, anyway.

Attempted and failed.

Myrtle slipped her slender arm from his grasp and folded her hands in front of her. "I will g-get into that carriage—"

"Good," he said, reaching for her again, but she took a step back.

"Uh-uh, I did not finish. What I was going to say before you interrupted me was, I will get into that carriage"—she brought a finger up, accentuating that which she clearly felt was the most important part about whatever this was—"if"—she wagged that long gloved digit at him—"you join me."

His mind went completely blank; the matter of his brain went to black in that moment, as what she suggested, what she asked, stole all ability to think.

Which was preferable, because at least in this way he wasn't recalling an unreal-for-now image of him climbing inside that conveyance and joining her while she sang, and then him wanting—needing—to silence her by dragging her onto his lap and kissing the song from her lips and—

Val stilled . . . aware of Myrtle's voice moving in and out, some of her words slipping into focus.

"You are a stubborn man, and I know . . ."

He'd not imagined her dying in this moment.

Nay, in this moment, the memories had twisted, taking another path, a different one, one that included him alone with Myrtle, making love with her.

"Respectable and honorable . . ." Whatever soliloquy she gave on his honor and respectability, his improper thoughts now made the greatest mockery of as he remained unable to shake the tempting images that had taken root.

Ones that hadn't involved her winding up dead and him hunched over her, and there was a giddy relief that his mind hadn't gone to the darkest of dark places.

It was because of her. This woman.

On the heel of that came the realization, one which hit him square in the chest . . . that this deviation in his thinking was dangerous in its own right.

"Val. *Vaaal.*" Her query, his name, came with a slightly greater emphasis, bringing him back to the moment with a whirring *whoosh* in his ears.

"Hmm?" he said.

She slipped her gloved fingers through his, twining their hands, and giving them a squeeze. "I said, I do not fear being alone with you, Val," she said softly, her voice a near whisper that still carried clearly to his ears. "In fact"—she drifted closer—"I would . . . welcome the company. Horace and I both would."

His black snout buried in the snow, Val's dog picked his head up, and barked his agreement.

And then a second truth hit him in that moment. That was why she wished for him to join her. Given all the peril she'd faced this same morning, he should have thought of it sooner.

He'd been determined not to set foot in a carriage ever again.

He detested the things.

They were conveyances that conjured death and tragedy and recalled in his mind the memory of his wife's broken form, sprawled in the snow, a bright splash of crimson satin upon the stark white.

It had been years since he'd done so.

And after this journey, it would be a lifetime more before he ever put someone inside a carriage and climbed inside one himself.

But this time, he would, and for one simple reason only . . .

"You're afraid," he said gruffly.

Chapter 18

He'd asked if she was afraid.

And she was.

She had been since he'd informed her of his plans to escort her to her family's Scottish estates.

But it wasn't the fear he likely thought it was.

This dread that had gripped her and continued to grow with every inch of the countryside that the fast-moving carriage had put between her and London had nothing to do with the thieves who'd attempted to rob her family and harm her.

Nay, it had everything to do with being parted from this man before her.

Because when he left her with her family and rode off, they'd part ways . . . for good. And she'd never recover from the loss of him.

Gloved fingers came up to stroke her cheek in a light, tender caress; that quixotic touch brought her lashes fluttering, weighting them down until her eyes closed and her body became all the more attuned to the feel of his light caress.

"Forgive me," he murmured, his voice a deep rumble, and as close as he was, his chest nearly pressed against hers, the vibration of that apology thrummed within her. "I should have thought you would be afraid and joined you."

Let him think that. Let him think that because then he will.

She knew as much.

And she was so very desperate for any scrap he might hand over to her that the devil inside coaxed Myrtle, urged her to let him believe she was afraid so that he remained.

Alas, she could not.

She did not want him this way.

And with that, the hold he had over her lifted, and she managed to take his hand and lower it. "I am not afraid, V-Val," she said, her teeth chattering from the cold. Not in the way he thought, anyway. "I just"—unable to meet the searing intensity of his gaze, Myrtle dropped her eyes briefly to Horace, who happily bounded back and forth upon the old Roman road, before forcing them up to meet his—"don't want to be alone."

He eyed her with an inscrutable stare, one so opaque she could make nothing of it.

And then he grunted. "You have Horace. Furthermore, it would be inappropriate—"

"Nothing about these past few days has been appropriate, Val," she interrupted him. "It's all been scandalous. But neither does that mean you have to suffer through the cold."

"I don't ride in carriages," he gritted out.

"Yes, I understand most men prefer their mounts. My brothers both always—"

"No. No. It is not . . . that," he said tightly, and then dragged a hand through his hair, knocking his hat loose.

With a restlessness to his movements, Val stalked over to the black garment resting upon the ground and swiped the article up. He beat it several times against the side of his leg. "My wife." Myrtle stared blankly at Val, but she may as well not have been looking at him. For his gaze remained locked, fixed firmly above her head, his eyes off in the distance, staring at a sight only he could see. "She was killed in a carriage accident."

And then she drew back, her entire body recoiled away from that revelation. "Oh, Val," she whispered. And here she'd been so self-absorbed. "Forgive me," she said. "I'm a blunderbuss. I did not think . . ."

"No, no. It is fine," he said gruffly. "It is silly."

She swept over and took his hands. "It is not." Myrtle squeezed his long fingers in her own. *"It is not,"* she repeated, this time more emphatically and applying another bout of pressure. "It makes sense." And then another thought slammed into her, nearly knocking her feet out from under her. Here she'd been so consumed in her own misery at their nearing end and mourning the loss of the time with him. All the while, he had been trapped in the hell of his past. Haunted by memories made stronger by carriages, of the wife he loved.

I am the worst . . .

The ghost of a smile formed on Val's lips. "No, you aren't, Myrtle," he said quietly in an affirmation that she'd accidentally spoken those thoughts aloud. "You are all that is good." His smile withered, faded, and then died, leaving his features solemn and ushering in a cold to rival the one hanging in the winter air. "It is why I'd see you nowhere near me."

Myrtle traced her gaze over each cherished plane of his beloved face, committing those harsh angles to her memory to store away for a later time. "Is that what you think?" she murmured, drifting closer once more. "That you were somehow to blame for what happened?" *To your wife.*

She couldn't bring herself to utter those words that made her ghostly foe real, but she loved Val too much to refer to that same nemesis for his affections in the past tense.

"I know I am, Myrtle," he said, and a sound of frustration escaped him as he stalked off. "If we hadn't been making the journey to my mother's affair, then she would still be here."

And he and Myrtle would not.

And yet, that did not mean anything to him.

Not as it mattered to her, and how she wished it to mean something to him.

But this moment . . . it was not about her.

Myrtle started over to him, then stopped just beyond the edge of his shoulder.

"When I was to turn thirteen, my brother was set to make his first journey." She hugged herself, recalling the envy she'd felt. "How I wished I could join him," she said wistfully. "He was going to the Americas. His closest friend in the world has a shipping business, and they intended to make a journey together." She knew the moment Val's demons had fled, and the moment he'd begun listening to her. "I entered his rooms, where he and his servants were packing his things, and insisted that it was not every day that a young girl became a woman." Because she'd been so certain she'd been a woman the moment she reached those teen years that had put her that much closer to eighteen and her first London Season. "I begged him to remain with me because our parents had begun speaking about me leaving the following birthday for Mrs. Belden's, and . . . he stayed. His friend, however, did not. The ship he was to sail upon, the one his friend did sail upon . . . went down at sea."

Val's body drew taut, and she tightened her arms reflexively around herself.

"When I learned of it, I spent days crying, because it was my fault Jeremy had perished. Jeremy had been like another brother to me, and I'd failed him."

A guttural groan escaped him as he turned back and took her in his arms, and she accepted all the warmth that came in his embrace.

"I'll have you know, he did not perish," she said, grateful when he did not release her at that admission, though she felt him draw slightly back.

"He didn't?"

That question was met with the same wonder she'd felt upon learning of Jeremy's return from the grave.

"No. He was rescued at sea, and the day he appeared on our doorstep, informing my brother of his survival, I threw myself at him and pleaded his forgiveness." Myrtle tipped her neck back so that she might meet Val's eyes. "Do you know what he said to me?

"He said, 'Myrtle, you are not Boreas. You do not dictate the North Wind. You are not Amphitrite—you do not control the tides of the oceans.

"You are a remarkable woman, Myrtle." His gaze touched on every part of her face, his eyes moving slowly over hers, as she'd searched him moments ago before he ultimately locked his gaze with hers.

And she held her breath, waited for him to say more, nay, to say *the* more that she so desperately wanted.

A forlorn wind howled, recalling his attention to the land around them, and he looked away.

The moment shattered.

"We should go," he said gruffly.

"Yes," she said, unable to keep the sadness from creeping into her reply. "We should."

Val handed her inside the carriage, and whistled once.

Horace immediately jumped inside. He gave his big head a shake, dislodging drops of snow, before settling onto the floor.

Val shut the door behind them.

Myrtle gave the dog's damp head a distracted pat, and she waited for the elegant, gleaming conveyance to lurch back into motion almost immediately.

Only, it didn't.

There was a brief exchange between Val and his brother's driver, and her heart hammered.

Surely he wasn't sending her on her way, alone. Surely—

A moment later, the carriage door opened, startling a gasp from her.

Horace's head popped up, and he released a happy bark.

"Val," she whispered as his broad frame filled the entryway, blotting out the grey winter skies at his back.

"I thought I would join you, after all," he said gruffly.

She stilled. Every part of her stopped.

Well, that was, with the exception of her heart. That organ thumped so very loudly, so wildly in her breast that surely Val heard the excited hammering.

"It is snowing," he explained.

It was . . .

Frowning, Myrtle caught the curtain, and looked outside.

Sure enough, between the moment he'd deposited her for a second time that day in the carriage and spoken to the driver and seen to his horses, the skies had unleashed a flurry of tiny white specks that fell down, swiftly coating the earth.

Her heart fell.

You stupid, naive, pathetic, pitiable fool . . . And here you thought he'd had a sudden change of heart because he wanted to be with you . . .

Val cleared his throat. "Unless you'd rather I n—"

"No!" she exclaimed. "I . . . It makes sense," she finished lamely. "That you would not ride."

"It doesn't," he said gruffly.

Myrtle angled her head.

"I . . ." Val's gaze slid away from hers, and he moved it over the carriage. "I've not stepped inside one since . . . since . . ."

Her heart suspended its function once more. "Since your wife's passing," she said softly.

He gave a jerky, uneven nod. "Yes. Since her death."

He looked ready to bolt.

Worse, he looked ready to cast up the contents of his stomach.

And likely he was.

Given what he'd revealed about how his wife had perished, how would he ever feel comfortable setting foot inside a carriage again?

Yet he intended to do so.

"You won't be alone, Val," she said gently. Myrtle stretched a hand out. "I am with you. Horace and I both are."

Val stared at her fingers, then slid his palm into hers.

And this time, as he squeezed himself past his dog and shut the door behind the three of them, they rode off . . . together.

Chapter 19

He was going to die.

Val knew it, and he cared not at all.

He didn't care about the Aragon title, and not even because he was confident his brother would do right by the line, the estates, and the people and staff dependent upon him.

He didn't even care about himself, or the certain pain that would come at the end.

Rather, it was her.

Myrtle.

Myrtle, with her bright rose cheeks and penchant for off-key singing and smiling and teasing and finding mischief and making mischief.

And she was going to die.

Snowflakes mixed with ice, and pinged against the window, punctuating that thought, taunting and terrifying Val with the threat.

She would die.

And there was absolutely nothing he would be able to do to bring her back.

A low moan stuck in his throat, and Horace, somehow squeezed onto the bench beside Myrtle, whined and sniffed in Val's direction.

"Are you all right, Val?" Myrtle's gentle query slashed through the fear that gripped him.

"Fine."

Just then the carriage hit a patch of ice and slid forward, before his brother's driver managed to regain complete control of the team.

"Just fine," he gritted out as his churning stomach made a liar of him.

Myrtle took his hands in hers, and he gripped them hard, squeezing them more than he should. He forced himself to lighten his hold, and he clung to them and her as the lifeline they were.

"I find singing is a welcome distraction."

It was on the tip of his tongue to say it wasn't—songs, particularly the familiar Christmas hymns always falling from her lips, recalled past terror and always present grief.

Only . . . he stopped.

Yes, initially, when he'd first heard her outside wassailing herself all the way back from her jaunt through London alone, he'd been transported back to that tragic moment years earlier.

The past few days with Myrtle, her chipper, off-key singing of those songs had chased away the sadness.

Now he fixed on the sound of her voice, the joyful sound of her singing, even when the tune contained a trace of solemnity.

It was her voice, and that song that kept him sane.

"Es ist ein Ros entsprungen,
aus einer Wurzel zart,
wie uns die Alten sungen,
von Jesse kam die Art

"A rose has sprung
tender from one root,
as the ancients sang to us,
from Jesse came the kind . . .

"Und hat ein Blümlein bracht
mitten im kalten Winter,
wohl zu der halben Nacht.

"And brought a flower
in the middle of the cold winter,
probably for half the night."

Alas, God appeared determined to deny Val any and all peace this night. A violent gust battered against the carriage, and his stomach lurched left and right along with the sway of the conveyance.

Val cursed.

Myrtle promptly stopped singing. "You do not like my singing."

"No," he gritted out. "I like it just fine." He liked it more than just fine.

His mind, however, struggled to plow its way out of a place of terror.

She wrinkled her nose. "You are a terrible liar, Val. It is fine. Mrs. Belden informed me that I'm a most horrendous singer, and that I should always forgo singing, because—"

"Don't you dare listen to that advice," he commanded. "Mrs. Belden is a twat," he said bluntly, this time thoroughly and completely distracted at the mention of her. "You'd be wise to part ways with any lesson or piece of advice imparted by that old harridan."

Myrtle's entire face lit up, from her eyes to the color that filled her cheeks, because of him. He'd brought that happiness. It was foreign. He didn't bring anyone happiness, any longer. He was a miserable, cold bastard. But this woman, somehow, with him, smiled and laughed and . . . He'd forgotten what it was to make a person feel that way. He'd not believed himself capable of it.

And soon she'll be gone.

Darkness filled every corner of his chest, and the Lord, determined to punish him for sins he still could not sort out that had been so bad to merit this depth of His Savior's disfavor, sent another gust of wind swelling outside.

Sweat popped up along his temple.

"Will you sing again?" he asked hoarsely, determined to steal these last moments of joy with her so that he might bottle them away and recall what they had been like.

She sat upright. "Do you have a preference?"

He opened his mouth.

"Because I really do love them all, and—"

"Any song, Myrtle," he gritted out when the carriage lurched precariously to the right. "The last one." Any of them. Just to hear her voice.

She promptly broke into song. It was that unfamiliar-to-him one, the one with lyrics in German, the ones that required him to pull from long-ago German he'd learned first from tutors and then been instructed on during his years at Eton and Cambridge, but beyond those times had never really used.

> "Das Röslein, das ich meine,
> davon Isaias sagt,
> ist Maria die reine
> die uns das Blümlein bracht.
>
> "The little rose that I mean
> of which Isaias says
> Maria is the pure one
> who brought us the flower . . ."
>
> "Aus Gottes ew'gem Rat
> hat sie ein Kind geboren

und blieb ein reine Magd.
or: Welches uns selig macht.

"From God's eternal advice
she gave birth to a child
and remained a pure maid.

"Das Blümelein, so kleine,
das duftet uns so süß,
mit seinem hellen Scheine
vertreibt's die Finsternis.
Wahr Mensch und wahrer Gott . . ."

He stilled, his mind lingering on those lyrics, even as she continued on to the next.

"The little flower, so small,
it smells so sweet to us
with its bright shine
drive away the darkness.
True man and true God . . ."

It was Myrtle. A delicate flower, so sweet and vibrant she chased away the darkness. In her life, she proved that God was real, because only a Lord of Might could create such a wonder as she.

And delicate though she might be, she was not fragile. Never had she wilted: not when she'd been alone, and not because of him, not even when, in those first days, he'd met her with his usual ugliness and gruff demeanor. Nay, much like the petals of those blooms that remained strong during summer storms, even as the harsh, unforgiving wind battered and whipped at them, she remained resolute, unfurling and remaining untouched by the tempest, bold and strong through it all.

"O Jesu, bis zum Scheiden,
aus diesem Jamerthal
Laß dein Hilf uns geleiten

"O Jesus, until the parting
from this Jamerthal
Let your help guide us."

She sang of that parting, a lyric that served only as a reminder he did not need of the coming of the end of his time with her.

The wind howled its mournful wail, the angels weeping. The carriage shook as the Lord thundered his discontent.

"Hin in der Engel Saal,
In deines Vaters Reich,
da wir dich ewig loben:
o Gott, uns das verleih!

"Go to the angel hall,
In your father's kingdom
since we praise you forever:
Oh God, give us this!"

Suddenly, the carriage swayed.

Val shouted, gripping the side of his carriage bench with one hand, even as he reached for Myrtle with the other.

A gasp burst from her as he wrapped a powerful arm around her, and pulled her onto his lap.

"V-Val?" she called, her head, buried against his chest as it was, lending a muffle to her voice. "Are you all—"

"No." He shot a fist up, pounding hard on the roof, instructing the driver to stop.

Which the man did.

Too quickly.

His brother's conveyance went skidding down the old Roman road.

Tensing, Val braced his booted feet upon the carriage floor to brace himself, and held Myrtle tight as he could, for all he was worth.

Praying.

And he remembered how.

Praying.

Because it was all he had power over in this moment.

Praying.

For this ride to end, and for Myrtle's safety.

And then, it appeared the Lord had not abandoned him, after all.

The carriage stopped.

Even so, he did not release her. He continued to hold her, breathing in the scent of apple blossoms that clung to her, fixing on that safe, innocuous detail. She was alive. He'd not killed her.

"Val?" she asked, angling her head back and looking him in the eyes.

"You smell like apples."

She tipped her head at a funny, endearingly sweet angle. "I . . . It is a perfume. I found it in my sister's room and pilfered the bottle," she chattered, as was her way. "I felt, given the fact she and the rest of them forgot me"—that prattling which had once annoyed him—"I was entirely within my rights to avail myself to whatever they'd left behind"—but now that he so very much loved. At last she stopped, for a moment. "Do you not agree?"

Val couldn't help it. She was so refreshing and pure, and he tossed his head back and roared with laughter.

Myrtle scrunched her nose, and then as if mirth were contagious, she added her laughter to his. The sound of it, clear and bell-like and ringing so perfectly with his, infused even more lightness within. "I . . . uh . . . yes. I shall take this as agreement."

Gathering her hands in his, Val raised each to his mouth, placing a kiss upon the tops of them, one at a time. "You are a treasure."

And treasures were to be cherished and protected.

He'd failed in the past, but he'd not fail where this woman was concerned.

The driver knocked on the door once, and Val immediately disentangled his hands from Myrtle's, just as the young man drew the panel open.

"I would have us retire to the nearest inn for the night," Val said, "and proceed . . . more slowly, tomorrow." He didn't care how long it took, just that they arrived safely and with Myrtle in one piece.

The young man doffed his hat. "As you wish, Your Grace." With that, he dipped a bow, closed the door, and then a moment later the carriage dipped slightly as he hefted himself onto the driver's box.

As he wished, the servant had said.

If he were to truly have any wish he wanted granted, he'd have himself be the man he'd once been, not the gruff, brooding arsehole whose wit had become at worst macabre, and at best drier than a French wine. He'd be a man deserving of Myrtle. Nay, she deserved a man who wasn't broken in all the ways he was, a man who'd somehow reassembled the jagged pieces of himself that had remained after that long-ago night.

As it was, he would be content to steal the remaining moments he had with her.

It would be enough.

It had to be.

Chapter 20

They arrived some twenty minutes later. Myrtle, Val, and Horace.

As they walked the snow-covered path, her arm twined with Val's while in his other arm he carried her valise, the jubilant sounds of unrestrained laughter rushed to meet them. Horace panted rapidly as he bounded back and forth down the path, expending repressed energy and barking happily as he raced about.

With every step they drew closer, the din coming from the establishment grew. As did the swirl of snowflakes falling around them.

She blinked as those bits of white flecks landed on her lashes.

A cloud of smoke billowed from the chimney as the fire's glow inside the inn illuminated the frosted windows, the figures on the other side blurred by the iced glass.

They reached the front of the stone inn, and Val drew the door open, a swell of noise rushing to greet them.

A great cacophony of merriment, laughter, the whine of a fiddle, and stamping feet.

Val motioned her on ahead, and Myrtle stepped inside with Horace following suit. As she pushed her hood back, she did a sweep of the room. The very *crowded* room.

For Myrtle and Val had arrived . . . but so, too, did it appear that every other person in the countryside, from near and far, had.

A tall, generously rounded fellow with kindly eyes and a fiddle positioned at his shoulder danced around the guests in his path, literally playing his way over to Myrtle and Val.

The cheerful smile on his ample cheeks, flushed red with both his efforts, and the happiness of the room, proved contagious. Myrtle moved her gaze over the tavern, taking it all in, from the pair of serving girls filling tankards with ale to the one-legged man near the hearth, playing away on a second fiddle. Couples danced in time to the music, roughly clad men twirling their partners wildly while those women's wool skirts flew high about their stout, durable black boots.

At last, the innkeeper reached them through the swarm of patrons.

"Good evening to you, good sir," the bear of a man shouted, making his voice heard over the din. "I am Gus, the owner of this fine establishment."

Myrtle stared at the fiddle. "You are the owner *and* you play for your patrons?" She didn't bother to conceal her admiration or her awe.

If possible, the fellow, some two inches taller than Val's impressive height, grew even more. He brought back his barrel chest and played a quick tune. "Indeed. Perhaps you've heard some of my works? 'Rakes of Madeley'?"

She straightened. "'The Rakes of Mallow'?" she asked excitedly.

He shook his big head, knocking his sandy-brown strands from behind his ears. "'The Rakes of Madeley.' Redid the piece, I did." Myrtle shook her head. "Or . . . 'Laffy Was a Welshman'? See, I changed that one, too, because 'Taffy' really isn't the kindest—"

Val cleared his throat. "Excuse me. Do you happen to have two rooms for my wife and I?"

Two rooms . . . for my wife and I . . . His was clearly the introduction that needed be given—otherwise she'd be ruined. A lady didn't go gadding about the countryside with a man who was not her husband or family. Even so, her heart doubled its rhythm at hearing those words fall from his lips about her.

Of course there would be two rooms; he was too honorable to book just one.

The innkeeper shook his head. "I'm afraid I cannot do that." He pointed his fiddle over at the room. "Snow turned fierce, and the mail coach was forced to stop. I've only got the one room remaining." He held a single finger up.

"That will do," Val said without hesitation.

That would do . . .

He'd not sought to lord his title over the servant. He'd not dangled money that would see other men and women displaced this evening. Instead, he'd let the kindly innkeeper believe he was nothing more than a mere "sir" and accepted that lone remaining room for them.

As Val finalized his arrangements with the smiling innkeeper, Myrtle's mind wandered.

There'd be . . . one room that they need share. Which also meant one bed for the two of them. Myrtle's pulse pounded as she recalled shared kisses and the longing that had not left her for more of his embrace. The sound of her name as it had fallen from his lips while he'd kissed her.

A name which she'd always thought hideous until she'd heard it spoken by this man.

Myrtle.

Myrtle.

"Myrtle? . . . *Myrtle?*"

Wait . . . that was not her rememberings. He really *was* calling her.

A blush burning her cheeks, Myrtle whipped her gaze over to Val. *"Hmm?"*

He stood with his arm outstretched, a question in his eyes.

She immediately slipped hers through his once more and allowed him to escort her to that lone room they'd share.

They followed the rotund fellow abovestairs and down a long, narrow hall, one that contained a surprising number of doors, as if the rooms that had existed here had been chopped in half to double their capacity.

Humming the tune of "Good Christian Men, Rejoice," the innkeeper, Gus, at last brought them to a stop at the last door at the end of the hall. The hall was too narrow to comfortably fit the three of them, so Myrtle hung off to the side as he removed a rusty key from the ring at his waist, jammed it into the lock, and then let them inside. "Here you are, sir," the man said, handing the key to Val, who hovered at the entryway beside him.

Val pocketed the key, and as he arranged for a meal and a bath to be brought, Myrtle ventured deeper into the space with Horace following in along with her. A warm fire raged, and Horace immediately trotted over to the hearth and paced himself a path in that narrow area before settling onto the floor.

Myrtle took in the room. It was not as small as she'd expected, but yet still modest enough that the bed, the biggest piece of furniture present, commanded the space.

Perhaps the size isn't what's got you focused on it, a voice taunted. Nay, it wasn't the sole reason her eyes went to that piece.

It was not grand like the Venetian St. Mother of Pearl headboard and frame she slept in at home.

It was a simple, functional piece designed of pine, with no embellishments and even less frill. Nothing but the mattress and white coverlets upon it.

Rather . . . it was the fact that she'd share that bed with Val. They'd sleep there *together*. Her body warmed and her cheeks fired hot at the wicked thoughts turning in her head.

Memories of his embrace filled her mind, swelling the way a symphony did just before a production commenced.

Every part of her had burned hot from his kiss, and the feel of his hands, powerful and hard, but gentle at the same time, too, upon her

And you may be a force of nature, but you are not Kymopoleia, goddess of violent storms, and well, if the Greeks had snow, you would not be that god of snowstorms.' We are just humans, Val. We are living in a world where so much, where most, is beyond our control. You did not cause that accident. That accident just . . . happened. And I did not know your wife, but I suspect she wasn't a woman who would ever want you shutting yourself away from the world and blaming yourself for . . . for what happened that night." She paused. "Ullr," she blurted. "You're not Ullr."

He stared blankly at her.

"He's a Norse god of winter, god of snow. Jeremy told me of—*oomph*." The remainder of those words emerged as nothing more than a little grunt as Val folded her in his arms, holding her tight, squeezing her with all he was, for all he was worth, and she brought hers up so that she might hold him in return.

"Thank you," he whispered harshly against her temple.

"You still don't believe me," she remarked because she knew him. In their short time together, she'd come to know him so very well. "But if you think about it—what I said, Val—you will. It makes sense, you know. We are mere mortals. Though I wish we weren't. Because if I wasn't, I would—" She immediately made herself stop talking.

Val trailed his fingers along her jawline, bringing her gaze up to meet his. "If you weren't and were a goddess, what would you do?" he murmured.

I'd be Aphrodite, and I'd make it so that you fell so very deeply in love with me that you couldn't bear to be apart from me.

But even then, she'd have him in a way that wasn't real. She'd have him in a way that was engineered and orchestrated by her with no feelings from him, and that would not bring her the full joy of what she wanted—him completely and hopelessly all hers because he wanted to belong to her as much as she wished to belong to him.

"I would ask to be a mortal," she said softly. "Because I want to live a real life, even with all its pain and flaws and blemishes, with all the heartbreak and suffering—I want to feel it all."

hips. But then he'd stopped, and she'd been left with only the whisper of wonder at what came after.

And she wanted that.

She wanted—

"Myrtle?"

She whipped around. *"Hmm?"*

Val stared concernedly back . . . as did the innkeeper.

Both men looked at her.

And she looked at them.

Oh, drat. An answer was expected of her. They'd put a question to her, but she'd been so lost in her improper thoughts she had no idea what they had said.

"That would be lovely," she blurted.

Gus's brow dipped, and the ghost of a smile danced at the corners of Val's lips. "You heard the lady. I will have my belongings sent to the stables."

He'd have his belongings sent . . . ?

"No!" she exclaimed.

Gus wrung his hands together. "I'm sorry. I've not another room. The gentleman offered to head to the stables and spend the night." So that was the important piece she'd missed. Splendid. "But I could see that it is turned out comfortable enough." Her panic spiraled. Val would go, and she'd be here alone, not having even this one night with him. "There is a cot—"

"No!" she quickly interrupted. "Forgive me. I'm afraid I was not clear . . . I meant the room is perfectly lovely. Certainly sufficient enough for my . . . husband and me." Her tongue tripped over that lie, even as her heart, mind, and soul embraced the illusory idea of it. "Beyond sufficient. It is one of the nicest inns I've ever stayed in." Then she remembered the ruse and blurted out a correction: "We've stayed in. Together. Because we're married, of course."

Behind the innkeeper, Val had the look of one who wanted to hit himself in the forehead.

"But even before we were married, I'm sure." She glanced to Val once more. "Isn't that right, husband? Isn't it perfectly lovely?"

"Perfectly," he uttered, and she smiled.

The innkeeper, however, positively beamed from the praise she'd heaped upon him and his establishment. He snatched his cap from his forehead and held it close to his chest. "I'm honored. It is not every day I have a lord and lady wife as my patrons."

And he hadn't. A little pang hit her heart.

She made herself smile for his benefit. "We shall tell everyone we know about your establishment," she vowed, and Gus's spine grew several inches under that promise.

"Many thanks to you both. Many thanks. My daughters will be along shortly with the bath you've ordered."

With that, the man bowed and let himself from the rooms.

Myrtle stared after him.

She'd given him a lie, however. Neither she nor Val could breathe a word about this inn or any part of these passing days. They were destined to dwell in her memory but otherwise be unspoken of for all time.

Val leaned a shoulder against the frame. "And here I thought you were banishing me to the stables." There was a relaxation to the way he stood, and she drank in the sight of him, catching a glimpse, she suspected, of the charming rogue he'd likely been before he'd found love and married . . . and lost.

"Never," she said quietly.

He'd called her a treasure.

They'd been words that, in the moment, had made her heart learn a new tempo, one that was galloping wild and wonderful.

Until they'd arrived at the crowded inn and he'd paid for the last remaining room and joined her abovestairs.

"You are . . . *leaving*?" she asked, hurt and disbelief a perfect underscore to her question, one she could not conceal. Nor did she want to. She didn't want to pretend in any way with Val.

"I'll be just outside," he vowed. "The innkeeper's daughters will help you and keep you company."

I don't want the innkeeper's daughters to help me and keep me company, she silently screamed at him.

She wanted him.

The great big dunderhead.

Alas, he was determined to be rid of her. She folded her arms around her middle, hugging herself tightly.

"Myrtle," he murmured, caressing her cheek once more. "I'd never let myself be separated from you."

A thousand butterflies danced within her stomach, thrilling, wonderful butterflies unleashed from the joy of—

"You don't have to worry. I'll be close so I might ensure you don't find yourself harmed while you are in my care." He turned to go, and a fresh swell of panic crested in her breast.

Myrtle took a frantic step toward him. "And then after that, whatever happens to me matters naught," she said, unable to keep the trace of bitterness from her response, even as she knew it was petty and wrong.

He turned back, a frown on his hard lips. "That is not what I meant. I'd never see you hurt, Myrtle."

He sounded stricken. And she'd never heard him sound that way. Now he did . . . because of her.

Her response had proven her petty and small. "No. I know that. I do," she said on a rush. "I . . ."

Val crossed over to her, his long legs and even longer stride all but swallowing the small distance imposed by the room. He stopped beside her.

Myrtle drew in a breath, attempting to clear her thoughts, which always grew muddled at his nearness. "Forgive me," she said, unable to meet his eyes, studiously examining the hardwood floor. "I did not mean to offend you."

Val brushed his knuckles down the curve of her cheek, lightly dusting under her chin and then raising it so that she met his eyes.

The sheer beauty of those dark-blue pools sucked the air from her lungs. They always had.

She suspected if there'd been more tomorrows with him, they always would.

"I care about you, Myrtle," he said gruffly. "My sense of concern for you and about you will not end when I bring you to your family."

Myrtle bit the inside of her cheek hard. That should be enough. It wasn't. She wanted more than his concern. "I . . ." *Love you. Most desperately. Most ardently.* His black brows came together, stitching in a single line of an unspoken question. "Care about you, too," she said lamely.

His gaze, if possible, grew even more opaque.

He opened his mouth, and her heart lifted with the hope that he would say something else. Something beyond simply "caring about her."

KnockKnockKnock.

That perfunctory rapping broke the moment.

Val let his arm fall. "Enter," he called out.

A moment later, a young man entered with a small wooden tub that he set by the fire.

On his heels came a flurry of young serving girls with buckets of steaming water, all of whom bore a striking resemblance to one another, and the blondish-brown shade of their hair marked them as the innkeeper's daughters.

They worked to fill the tub. Entering, leaving, and then promptly returning.

She counted seven daughters in all.

The small army of them, on a parade of seeing to her bath, ensured that there was no time to be alone with Val . . . until the last bucket of water was thrown into the tub and the youngest and smallest of the women dipped a curtsy, and collected coin from Val.

Left, so that she and Val were once more alone.

Suddenly, the feel of the bed against her legs sent her heart into a wild hammering; the furniture grew thrice the size for all her sudden awareness of it.

Stop. This is not the first room you've been in alone with Val.

It felt different this time.

Why? What was it about this moment that made it unlike the others that had come before?

Val cleared his throat. "You require help."

He was staying!

"I'll fetch one of the women to return and help you," he said, and disappointment flared in her breast.

"Wait!" Desperation lent a panicky pitch to her voice.

His eyes darkened, and he cleared his throat. "Yes?"

"I . . . I . . . wanted to thank you," she finished weakly. "For everything."

Of course he could not remain while she bathed. Except . . . he had before. That had been before, however, when there'd been absolutely no servants about and she'd been completely to her own devices, with only him to serve in that role.

"And then you'll return," she said softly, needing to hear that anyway. To remind herself that he'd come back.

"I'll not leave, Myrtle." His always gruff voice lent a harsher quality to that low baritone. "I'll remain outside the whole while."

Relief swept through her. "Thank you. And then we can dine together, and there really is more than enough room—"

Something in his eyes. Nay, not something. Horror. Horror cut her ramblings short. "You don't intend to come back in," she whispered, her voice stricken to her own ears.

His features grew strained. "Myrtle, I cannot—"

"You did before! You and I . . . We . . . shared a room, and—"

"That was when you and I were completely alone," he said with a gentleness that she'd never heard from him, and it caused a deep ache of mortification and shame that sent her toes curling sharply into the soles of her feet.

Myrtle fell back on her heels. Unable to meet his eyes, she slid her gaze to a point on the door just beyond his shoulder. "Of course. I understand."

And she did. Even as hope and joy all withered within her breast, it could not fully erase the longing for more time with him.

Chapter 21

Seated on the floor just outside her room and next to her door, Val stared at the opposite wall and thought about the meal that would be coming. And his surroundings. And . . . anything beyond the young lady singing softly to herself in the room at his back.

Especially, he fought the thought of her as she was in that moment, naked, her creamy white skin likely flushed red from the heat of the tub and the roaring fire in the hearth.

His body stirred, and he drew a slow, unsteady breath through his teeth.

Suddenly, she broke out in song.

As she invariably did.

> "This endris night I saw a sight,
> A star as bright as day,
> And ev'r among, a maiden sung,
> 'Lully, bye bye, lullay . . .'"

A wistful smile brought his lips up as that boisterous, loudly sung song briefly tempered a relentless desire for her. Rather, it roused a different hungering for her . . . one that was more dangerous, for it moved him onto a plane beyond mere physical yearning and to that emotional connection he'd forged with Myrtle.

Val had known from the moment Myrtle had entered his life that there would be a finite set to the time they spent with one another.

In those first moments she'd exploded into his existence, there'd been nothing but sheer annoyance, and hungering to be free of her and her chattering and cheer. But everything had . . . changed from their earliest days together.

"This lovely lady sat and sang,
And to her child did say,
'My son, my brother, father dear,
Why liest thou thus in hay?'"

Their earliest days?

There'd been only days. Yet, how could that even be possible?

How had she turned his whole world inside out in just . . . *days*?

How had he learned to smile again and laugh again and to talk . . . ? And care about her?

His mind shied away from anything more, from anything deeper that would leave him exposed to a level of grief that this time he'd not recover from.

"My sweetest bird, 'tis thus required,
Though I be king veray,
But nevertheless I will not cease
To sing 'Bye bye, lullay.'"

As if fate sought to serve up a reminder that he shouldn't need, Myrtle sang that discordant lyric about goodbyes.

Nay, he'd loved and lost. He'd not be so foolish as to commit himself to that same fate for a second time.

Soon she'd be gone.

Only, that didn't carry with it the relief it should.

As if fate sought to taunt him with his sudden melancholy, there came a faint giggle, accompanied by a deeper chuckle, and he looked to the end of the hall.

A young couple wound their way down the hall, their arms twined like ivy and their bodies angled toward one another; they stared up at each other, their gazes locked, as they continued walking past Val—Val, who was forced to draw himself impossibly tight to the wall and his legs closer so they didn't trip over him—oblivious.

Oblivious to anything but one another and their love.

Val wrenched his gaze forward, allowing them their privacy.

Then there came the quick click as they shut the door on the world.

Val gripped his knees hard. How he envied them. How he envied that level of joy. And yet he was not the man of his youth. For he pitied them, too. He pitied them for the pain that would invariably come to them, because ultimately one would be left behind here on this cold, unforgiving earth, and all that would remain was the agony of memories of what joy had once been.

It was also a much-needed reminder for Val about how essential it was to get Myrtle out of his life and back to hers.

Because this? This caring about her as he did—his yearning to hear her laugh and see her smile, and to listen to her as she sang—was the stuff of danger, more perilous than even carriage rides in the middle of snowstorms.

And he didn't want it. He didn't want to feel this way.

Val squeezed his eyes shut and banged the back of his head silently and slowly against the wall, wishing he could rid himself of the thought of her.

Then, as if she sought to ensure that he couldn't shut her out, Myrtle raised her voice louder in song.

"For all Thy will I would fulfill—
Thou knowest well, in fay,
And for all this I will Thee kiss,
And sing, 'Bye bye, lullay.'"

Suddenly, the door opened, making her voice soar even more out into the narrow corridor.

Heart racing, Val hopped up.

The young woman who'd been helping Myrtle stepped outside, drawing the panel shut behind her.

But not before he caught a glimpse of Myrtle.

Oh, God.

He looked up at the ceiling. "Thank you for helping my wife," he said roughly, his mind balking at how easily those words fell without so much as a stumble or sense of betrayal. When there should be. And they were a lie, at that. But it was a lie that felt dangerously too easy to speak.

The young woman smiled and sank into a curtsy. "Happy to help, Your Lordship. Her Ladyship is a kind one. She likes to sing. Invited me to join her"—he couldn't tamp down the smile—"but I dinna know the songs she sang. Didn't know there were people who celebrated Christmas."

There were many who didn't, and some who did. Aside from his family, he'd never known another family who knew the ancient traditions, and ones learned from distant lands . . . until Myrtle. "She is quite special," he murmured.

"And she is lucky to have your love, too," the serving girl said. "Not every husband and wife find that kind of love like my ma and da did."

Love.

His stomach muscles seized, and his facial features froze.

The young woman, seeming wholly unaware of the tumult she'd wrought, offered another curtsy, and then humming the tune of the carol that Myrtle continued to sing, she headed down the hall, belowstairs, and disappeared, with Val frozen to the spot where she'd left him, motionless, fearing if he moved he'd break apart.

He didn't love Myrtle.

He couldn't.

Yes, as he'd told her, he certainly cared about her. But that was different. Why, he cared about Horace and Jenkins.

You don't feel about her the way you do Horace or Jenkins, a silent voice in his head jeered. *And you've certainly never kissed either of them.* Through the tumult, Myrtle's singing drifted in and out of focus.

> "And in thy arm thou hold Me warm,
> And keep Me night and day."

Her song came so clear, his awareness of her so keen, that her voice grew louder in his mind. It was as though she were right there.

> "And if I weep, and may not sleep,
> Thou sing, 'Bye bye, lullay.'"

The door opened quickly.

And then she was there.

It hadn't just been in his mind.

He stared dumbly at her. Attired in a proper white wrapper and nightdress, there was nothing scandalous or wicked in what she wore, only in that she wore it before him. And still with that, it was as though a siren had stepped into the entryway and called to him, drawing him hopelessly out to sea.

She smiled. "I thought you might join—"

"No," he said before she'd even finished speaking.

"Me." She concluded the thought anyway.

"Are you afraid?" he asked gruffly. He was a bastard. He should have considered the impact left by the pair of brutes who'd invaded her home and attempted to harm her.

"If I said yes, I expect you'd join me, but . . . no. I'm not afraid. I just"—she glanced down at her palms—"do not want to be alone."

"You aren't alone," he pointed out. "You have Horace."

Horace, who proved wholly uncooperative, rolled onto his side and proceeded to snore.

"Horace does not sing," Myrtle said.

"No, he does not. Though he does *howl* fairly well."

She laughed, merriment adding a sparkle to her eyes, her amusement contagious, and he joined in.

Where had that ability to tease come from? It was still there within him, apparently, one more thing stirred from the ashes by this woman.

He let his laughter and smile both fade, and it was as though doing so had extinguished her joy. "I don't sing, either, Myrtle," he said gruffly. Not anymore. Though he could now listen to the sound of those carols without pain. What did that mean?

Once more, he refused to let his mind linger on that.

"No, I know . . ." She sighed. "I wanted to spend our last night *together*."

Her words sent a jolt through him, and his body jerked.

"Not like that," she whispered furiously. "In an intimate way. That is, *not* in an intimate way."

Every meeting they shared proved intimate; intimacy was an emotional connection, and one he feared more than any other kind.

"I don't think that is a good idea, Myrtle," he said quietly. In fact, he knew it was a deuced bad one.

The worst. It was a manner of temptation far greater than the mere apple held out in that fated garden.

"Please," she whispered. "I . . . We will never see one another again." And then she proceeded to ramble. "I will have my London Season and you will certainly not attend any of those balls or soirees."

The truth of that, the realization, cleaved him straight through like a battle-ax, slicing through his middle and rending his heart right in half. And if that weren't further reason to politely decline and urge her back inside that room alone, he didn't know what was.

"And I'll marry Lord Who Knows, who won't understand me or my Miss Austen"—she let her hand fly through the air, slashing at it, cutting close to his chest—"but some *gentleman* who wants me to be nothing more than an arm ornament."

Oh, God. And he wanted desperately for her to stop, not because of the earlier annoyance he'd felt from having his solitude stolen by her, but because of the words that fell from her lips, ones that painted a scene of her married to some other man.

"And then I'll go . . . Lord knows where." Pain twisted her features, and he keenly felt and shared in that misery. "I mean, it might be the wilds of North Yorkshire or Wales, or mayhap even Scotland."

And she'd be far away from Val, and beyond his reach forever.

He should be relieved.

So why, then, did he want to toss his head back and snarl like a feral beast?

"Fine." He flung that harsh capitulation out to make her just stop with the scenes she painted. Alas, he was hopeless where this woman was concerned. At some point, somehow, he'd cracked open the door to feeling just enough for this one to wend her way in. "Fine," he gritted out a second time. "I'll . . . join you."

Myrtle smiled widely. "Splendid!" And spinning on her heel, she all but floated into the rooms and headed for the fire.

Val entered, turned, and closed the door, locking it, using the action as a moment to put his thoughts to rights, fighting to free himself from the torturous imagery she'd painted of her off in London, dancing with some undeserving fellow who'd make her his wife and take her away and . . . He growled and turned angrily back, determined to tell her he was not staying. Because this was both improper and a mistake and—

The words stuck on his tongue.

Myrtle sat before the fire with her knees pulled close to her chest, drawing her fingers through the cascade of dark curls; they hung like a midnight curtain around her shoulders, falling all the way to her waist. And hunger licked at his insides. A yearning to drag his fingers through those curls, worshipping the satiny texture, and then pushing them back and lowering his lips to her shoulder.

"Would you mind terribly retrieving my hairbrush from my valise?" she asked, her innocuous tone penetrating those desirous musings.

Wordlessly—and grateful for the distraction—Val strode over, grabbed the valise, opened it, and fished around inside.

His fingers collided with the harsh bristles. Grabbing the handle, he yanked it out and headed over to where she sat beside Horace. "Here," he said, thrusting the silver brush at her.

Myrtle tipped her head back and beamed at him. "Splendid."

There was that word again.

As she set to work brushing those strands, he contemplated her and her response.

It was a word choice he would have mocked days ago, because he'd been so very certain there wasn't anything good enough left in this world to merit that selection.

But that had been before.

Before her.

Because he'd come to appreciate her and saw the world in her eyes; she still found it wondrous and great, and for her, it would be. Or that was his hope. When they parted, he prayed that she'd never lose that infectious joy that lived inside her . . . even as he knew that day was inevitable. For there would come a time that happiness was crushed by the reality of life's cruelty, and he didn't want to be around and see when that day came.

He didn't want to witness the moment she stopped humming in that happy little way.

Or singing . . .

As if she followed the cue of his thoughts, Myrtle broke into song, her voice quieter than usual, but still she managed to pack the same exuberance and cheer she always did into the carol that sprang from her lips.

> "Christians, awake, salute the happy morn,
> whereon the Savior of the world was born,
> rise to adore the mystery of love,
> which hosts of angels chanted from above . . ."

And wonder of wonders, as Val watched her, his lips began to move in a silent song.

> "with them the joyful tidings were begun
> of God incarnate and the Virgin's son . . ."

His eyes remained locked on her.

Myrtle looked up, her eyes landing on him.

Had she felt his stare? Was she as in tune with Val and his movements as he was acutely aware of her?

The thought should terrify him; it was further proof of this deepening connection to her.

So why, then, did he not look away?

Why, then, did he continue his noiseless recitation of those lyrics as he joined his silent voice to her still quiet soprano?

> "He spake, and straightway the celestial choir
> in hymns of joy, unknown before, conspire,

the praises of redeeming love they sang,
and heav'n's whole orb with alleluias rang,
God's highest glory was their anthem still,
peace on the earth, and unto men good will . . ."

Myrtle let her song trail off, and he closed his mouth, also allowing it to die upon his lips.

"You were singing," she remarked softly.

"Is that what you would call it?" he asked drolly. Unable to meet the intense emotion pouring from her expressive eyes, Val wandered restlessly over to the window and peered out, intent on severing this growing connection.

Alas, the feat proved impossible. "You were singing the lyrics, Val." Even in the pane, his eyes went not to the storm that raged outside, but to her still seated on the floor. "I saw you."

He felt his cheeks go warm. "I don't sing anymore."

"Because of your late wife."

"Dinah," he said sharply, needing to say her name as a reminder, because he'd not thought of her, because he was forgetting her.

"And you don't sing because of Dinah?"

"Yes. No." He yanked his fingers through his hair, tousling the strands, and loosening them from the queue at his nape. "I don't sing because my happiness died with her."

Myrtle jumped up, brandishing that brush as she spoke. "Happiness only dies if you let it, and even then, Val," she continued in an earnest way, "it is always inside you, resting like the banked embers of a fire." She angled herself closer and rested her fingers on her chest, touching herself in that place where her heart beat, and the cadence of his own increased. "But if you nurture it and allow it to breathe, it can grow again. Your wife, your Dinah, would not want you to be sad."

Her use of his wife's name, the resurrection of that ghost who deserved his allegiance, scraped like nails upon a board. "You don't know that," he said sharply. "You didn't know her, and you don't know . . . what she would have wanted."

"You're right. I don't." Myrtle paused. "You, however, did. As such, you tell me, Val . . . *Was* she the manner of woman who'd have wanted you to never again sing or smile?"

"No," he murmured, a new type of hurt hitting him square in the chest at those words, but not for the reason they should cause this pang. Myrtle wasn't wrong. Val didn't sing or smile; Myrtle deserved a man who could do both of those with her. "She used to insist if anything were to happen to her that I not become one of those brooding dukes." Yet that was precisely what he'd become. Until Myrtle.

Now . . . now he reflected on that discussion his late wife seemed to always raise. "I told her I would never forget to smile and laugh because . . ." Tears filled his throat, and he swallowed around that lump.

He registered the slight groan of the floorboards and the delicate fall of Myrtle's footsteps as she joined him at the window. "Because?" she gently urged. And he felt her hand as it came to rest upon his shoulder. Felt it with the same awareness he'd somehow always had with this woman, and he took strength and found comfort in it.

"I told her I would never forget to smile and laugh because all the joy I found with her would be enough to carry me through the rest of my lifetime and into the beyond."

"Oh, Val," Myrtle whispered, and she leaned into him, laying her cheek against his arm.

Val stared unblinkingly at the frosted window, through the small patch of glass he'd cleared with his palm.

"You are right," he said quietly, his voice surprisingly steady despite the groundbreaking revelation he'd made in this moment with her. "She would not have." She'd have been disgusted with the man he'd become. She'd have pitied him and mourned the fact that he'd shut his family and her family from his life.

"It is not too late for you to honor that promise you made to her, Val."

Thoughts of his late wife slipped forth like a specter floating past for a final time from the place where they'd last dwelled, and he turned to Myrtle.

The air shifted.

Something hovered between them, all around.

He moved his eyes over a face that had come to mean so very much to him, taking in the sight of her, drinking in all of her.

Val lifted a palm and cupped her cheek.

Her thick lashes fluttered as she leaned into his touch.

"Thank you," he murmured, emotion hoarsening his voice.

"Do not thank me, Val," Myrtle said, opening her eyes once more. "We are friends."

Friends.

"Is that what we are?" he murmured, the question one he asked of himself as much as he asked it of her. Val continued to cradle her cheek. "Friends?"

A little frown puckered that place between her eyes. "I . . . thought we were. I mean, we've shared so much these past days. Or I have. I—"

Val kissed her.

Chapter 22

Myrtle had been so very determined to commit the memory of Val's kisses to her mind, to sear them there for all time.

Because she'd been so very certain that was the last time she'd ever know his kiss.

Or passion in the arms of a man.

Certainly, passion in the arms of a man she loved.

She'd been wrong.

And she was so very glad for it.

Stretching up on her tiptoes, Myrtle leaned into Val, accepting his kiss.

She whimpered. "Val," she begged him without words, with only his name, to not stop this time. To continue.

"Open for me," he pleaded against her mouth, and she let her lips part, and he swept inside, his tongue a firebrand against hers.

The fiery heat of him, the rush of desire as he tasted of her and she explored him in like measure, sapped her of the ability to stand.

Only, Val was there to catch her. He scooped his palms under her buttocks and drew her deeper into his arms.

Myrtle met every thrust of his tongue in a dance more entrancing and forbidden than the scandalous waltz she'd been so very eager to learn.

Only, there was no dance like this one, and she knew there never would be.

It was with every glance of that hot flesh against hers, a fire was set to each part of her person until an inferno threatened to consume her whole.

She registered Val's hands shifting between them, and his fingers at work as he loosened the belt of her night wrapper. He slipped the garment from her so that she stood before him clad in nothing more than her nightshift.

Val drew back, and she bit her lip to keep from crying out and begging for him to not stop.

Only, he passed a heated gaze over her frame. "You are so beautiful," he murmured in that baritone that had gone husked with desire.

Her belly fluttered. "I'm really at best passably pretty, Mrs. Belden s-said," she said, passion making her voice falter.

He growled. "Mrs. Belden is a twat." He repeated his opinion of the old harpy a second time, and Myrtle leaned up, twining her palms about his nape and lifting herself so that she could touch her nose to Val's.

"Thank you," she murmured.

She knew the moment another shift had occurred.

She felt it in the way Val's tall, powerful body tensed against hers.

Sensed the connection had been severed, and she clung tightly to him, determined to hold on to him and this moment. "Please, don't," she entreated.

"Myrtle." And worse than begging him, he pleaded with her. "I don't know much, but I know two things with a certainty: you deserve more than settling for some pasty-faced, dull English fellow who won't appreciate you and your smile and your wit." Her lips parted and a sigh slipped out. "And you deserve more than a night with me."

She cut him off. "I deserve to have a man honor and respect what I want." She tipped her chin up a notch, angling her head back to better meet his stare. "And I want . . . this," she said softly. "I want this with you."

She saw the fight that glinted in his eyes; it was a battle that he, a man who was honorable, fought with himself. And determined to conquer that feeling he carried and steal this moment for the both of them, Myrtle touched her lips to his.

He remained still, unparticipating as she moved her mouth over his, and then a low, tortured groan escaped him.

Val deepened the kiss, deepened their embrace. This time, as she parted her lips for him, there was a raging intensity to it, one that made her quiver as heat pooled in her belly, and lower, in that place between her legs.

She should be ashamed or horrified. Or she suspected a proper lady was expected to feel those sentiments.

For Myrtle, there was no regret; there was nothing more than a wanting that redoubled with his every kiss.

Val shifted his attention, his lips grazing the corner of her mouth as he kissed a path lower to the curve of her cheek and down to her chin, and lower still.

Myrtle bit her lip and angled her neck intuitively, knowing where his quest went. He nipped lightly at that flesh, suckling, and she moaned.

"Your skin is like satin," he praised, his voice hoarser than she'd ever heard it. And then he shifted, placing his lips against her collarbone and moving onward in his quest.

He paused, and holding her eyes with his, he lowered the straps of her nightshift, and then ever so gently, tenderly, he kissed her shoulder.

Myrtle's eyes slid shut.

It was an innocuous part of her person.

Or that was what she'd believed.

She'd never seen her shoulder as a part of her body to inspire desire or capable of making her feel . . . everything she now felt.

She'd been so very wrong.

Her breath hitched as he continued to place the softest kisses upon that flesh, and it was as though she were a goddess whom he sought to properly revere. The ache between her legs grew unbearable, and she shifted in a bid to alleviate that sharp burning there.

Her efforts, however, were in vain.

"Val," she whispered, pleading with him all over again.

He swept his arms under her, catching her to him, and carried her to the bed.

That lone bed she'd yearned to share with him.

In all those yearnings she'd had when she'd spied the furniture moments—a lifetime?—ago, she'd never dared allow herself this dream, the one now coming true.

Val laid her down and then came over her, framing her in his arms, shielding her from the cold.

He stopped, his dark eyes moving over her face. "You are certain . . . ?"

Myrtle stretched up and kissed him again.

She'd have this moment with him, without an expectation of anything more. And when this night was over, she'd protect him, too.

And as he returned that kiss, deepening it, she'd never been more certain of anything in the whole of her life.

❄ ❄ ❄

Myrtle didn't sleep.

It had been two hours since Val had awakened her body in all the ways it could be awakened, two hours since he'd opened her to the most magnificent pleasures.

He snored when he slept.

Nor was it that snoring which kept her awake long after he'd made love to her.

Curled against his large, slumbering form with her chin resting on his chest, Myrtle continued to study him in slumber. His rugged features, always carefully drawn in a mask or in a scowl, were soft in sleep. As if this were the time when he was freed from his sadness and anger, and he looked so . . . peaceful.

Another shuddery snore split the quiet, and she smiled wistfully.

It was one detail she'd wondered about him . . . just because she'd wondered so much where he was concerned. It was also a question she'd thought she'd never have an answer to.

Only she had.

She touched her fingers to his cheek, and he moved against her touch.

Myrtle bit her lower lip.

And she wanted to memorize this moment, every part of it, every aspect of him and her time with him. She wanted to commit those memories to her mind so that when they parted and she was living a life without him, and he was continuing on without her, she might pull forth this image of him, rested in slumber after he'd made love to her.

He'd do right by her.

She knew that.

When the sun rose and a new day reared its head, Val would be who he'd always proven himself to be: a man of honor. Even with her heart crying out to take him however she could have him, she'd not have him this way.

Tears threatened, and she did not fight them. She let them fall until his visage grew blurry, and then she blinked those drops away because they were stealing these last looks she'd have of him.

Myrtle inched over to the edge of the bed, and then ever so slowly, she carefully swung her legs over the side until her feet touched the chilled hardwood floor.

She stood, and the mattress dipped ever so slightly, so faintly as to barely move, and yet Val stirred, shifting and stretching an arm out for her, as if in his sleep he sought her out.

But then he rolled onto his opposite side, his other muscle-hewn arm flung to the far side of the mattress so that his fingers hung down.

Tiptoeing over, she shifted that limb to rest comfortably on the mattress so that when he did awaken, the muscles wouldn't tingle with numbness.

She stood there several more moments, making sure he slept, torn between wanting him to awaken and needing him to stay precisely as he was.

Myrtle, however, could not remain here with him. Fighting a fresh wave of tears, she headed over to the cloth that contained traces of her blood, that cloth he'd used to tenderly clean her. Catching it, she walked to the hearth, where Horace slumbered like his master.

The dog suddenly popped his enormous head up.

"Shh," she whispered, urging him to quiet. Myrtle favored the beloved pet with a final scratch behind his ears. "He needs to sleep."

Horace whined in canine disapproval.

Behind her, Val stirred, shifting on the mattress, the netting that held it creaking.

And she held her breath, waiting for him to go motionless once more, waiting for the noisy rumble of his snores . . . that eventually, blessedly, came.

When she was assured he was deep in sleep, she looked to Horace; he shoved himself up on his back legs and stared at her with big, accusatory eyes.

"Please," she begged the dog, and sinking to the floor, she wrapped her arms around him, whispering close to his ear. "Do you not know this is hard for me, too?"

He whimpered.

"Fine, impossible," she said in that same quiet way. She drew back enough so that she could still meet his eyes and touched a finger to her lips. "I need you to be quiet. And I—I . . ." *Oh, God.* Myrtle squeezed her eyes shut. "I need to do this," she said, her voice catching, and to keep from sobbing aloud, she buried her face against Horace's thick neck and wept against him.

She allowed herself to indulge in only a moment of misery, knowing each second she remained was a moment she risked discovery. Taking a slow, quiet, steady breath, she released Horace but remained there on the floor beside him, looking him in the eyes. "You must look after him. He loves you very much." Horace lifted a paw and slapped it against her chest.

She stared down at it, then shifted her focus back to his pointed gaze. "He does not love me," she insisted. "He doesn't." She loved Val with every fiber of her soul, and would until she drew her last breath, but those feelings . . . They weren't returned. He'd loved too completely, too deeply, to ever give his heart to another. Loving him now as she did, his devotion, even in death, made sense.

Never would she feel like this again.

Not for any other man.

It was that reminder which gave her legs back the will to stand.

She straightened, and before her courage deserted her, before she let herself remain and allowed Val to join into a union he did not truly want but would enter into anyway, Myrtle headed for her valise.

As she proceeded to dress and then brush and plait her hair, she kept a close eye on him in that bed.

At some point, he'd ceased snoring, and his breathing had settled into a smoother, even cadence. Having finally sorted out the tangled mess of her hair, she affixed a ribbon to the end.

Her dress complete, Myrtle returned her brush to the valise and fished around for the piece of charcoal pencil she always traveled with.

She did a search for something with which to write upon, her eyes landing on a small leather book.

Drawn to the book she'd not even known he'd had in his hands when he accepted her invitation to enter the room, Myrtle stopped at the table.

She hesitated a moment, then picked up the copy.

A piece of parchment remained tucked at the back of the book, and she stopped.

This meant . . . he'd read it.

She flipped through the pages of *Pride and Prejudice* to that marker in the tome she'd given him.

Myrtle chewed at her lower lip, contemplating her words—nay, not just any words, a goodbye. How did one aptly capture everything she felt, all the depth of her love and feeling for him?

He doesn't need to know.

It would only make his sense of guilt—and worse, his pity—that much greater, and she wanted his guilt and pity even less than she wanted his sense of obligation to wed her.

Myrtle quietly turned to the front of the book and proceeded to write. She paused to read and reread the handful of sentences there before signing the note and closing the book with a silent click.

Grabbing up her nightdress, she held it close, and then added it to the fire. She watched the flames lick at the white fabric, rending a black hole bigger and bigger until sparks burst and her nightdress was swallowed up by the blaze within that grate.

And with that, Myrtle donned her cloak, grabbed her valise, and after one last pet for Horace and one last look at Val, she left.

Chapter 23

The first thing Val registered was the chill. It penetrated a slumber which had been so thoroughly empty of either dreams or nightmares.

Nay, it wasn't a chill.

It was a quiet but incessant whine.

Horace.

Horace, who was used to rising when the sky was still dark, and Horace, who would need to go outside and have his usual morning exercise.

Val forced his eyes open, and immediately a pair of large blue, accusatory ones met his.

And also Horace, with the handle of Val's satchel stuck between his teeth.

Val, however, couldn't recall when he'd last felt this . . . sated after sleep. He closed his eyes once more. "A few more minutes," he mumbled.

Horace dropped the bag, and it hit the floor with a noisy thump.

Val had started to drift off when Horace released another piteous whimper.

Oh, bloody hell.

Rolling onto his side, he unlatched the bag and fished out one of the gifts his brother deposited on his desk every Christmastide Season. "Here," he muttered, handing it over.

The dog ripped off the light cloth wrapping, and a peculiarly crafted ball attached to a rope fell out of the packaging.

Val peered at the oddly shaped object.

Horace briefly nosed around the peculiar toy, then slapped a large paw on the side of Val's mattress, which sagged slightly.

"Not even that will make you happy," he mumbled, and then abandoning all hope of sleep, he proceeded to withdraw and unwrap gift after gift, until a series of crudely made but specialty dolls lay at Horace's feet.

Val stared at the collection.

His brother . . . had had toys made for Horace.

Emotion welled in Val's throat, making it hard to swallow.

It was one of the damnedest, most thoughtful gifts Sidney could have ever given, and Val had been a miserable lout to him every time.

Still, his brother had returned again and again, eager to welcome Val back into the folds of their family, and he'd resisted.

Only, those same walls he'd erected that had managed to keep his brother and mother out had been effectively toppled by a curly-headed pixie who'd managed to fell a pair of thieves and was never without a carol on her lips, and who'd also cried his name to the rafters over and over throughout the night as he made love to her.

His body hardened at the memory. He'd marry her, of course.

The terror he expected that should accompany such a thought did not come. Instead, he felt a mystifying lightness throughout every corner of his previously dark soul. It spread inside, leaving him almost giddy.

He wanted Myrtle not just in his bed. He wanted her in his life, and in his home. He wanted to sing carols with her, and find a renewed joy in Christmastide and in simply . . . being alive.

They'd made love . . . and yet that was not the reason he'd ask her to wed him. It was because he loved her.

In the short time they'd spent together, she'd hammered away at the protective walls he'd built about his heart, smashing them into fragments of dust, obliterated so completely that she'd left him utterly and completely hers.

He loved her.

Myrtle, with her smile of sunshine and the freeness with which she spoke about anything and everything.

Val flipped onto his side to tell Myrtle—

Myrtle, who was missing.

And then he registered . . . the absence of her body next to his.

So that he wondered if he'd merely dreamed that he'd made love. Or mayhap these past days had been nothing more than imaginings conjured of his loneliness. Myrtle, a woman so bold and vivacious and lively and joyous.

For she'd certainly been the stuff of dreams.

His gaze landed on the spot of crimson upon the white mattress, indicating the loss of her maidenhead.

He frowned, his joy briefly tempered.

Of course, with her endearing antics, she'd even foil the moment he intended to proclaim his love and ask her to be his wife.

Horace's whine cut into his musings.

Val swung his legs over the side of the bed. At some point the fire had died and a chill had settled over the room. "You should have not let her go belowstairs alone," he chided as he padded over to his things.

Horace yelped.

"No, no. I deserve that," Val allowed, bypassing the tub that still remained from last night. Water that he'd used to clean her, and then himself. "I certainly should have awakened and accompanied her myself." With a smile, he reached for his shirt and pulled it over his head. "But I intend to see that we are never parted again."

Horace jumped up, and while Val attempted to step into his trousers, the dog did a frantic circle about his legs.

Val finished buttoning the placard on the front of his breeches and reached for his jacket, and then stopped.

His gaze locked on the valise Horace had held in his mouth moments ago.

The *lone* valise present.

Val's heart beat a dull thud against his chest as he did a slow turn about the room.

She wasn't going.

He frowned.

She wasn't going . . . because she'd already left.

What in blazes?

His heart hammered, thundering away in his chest and knocking so loud in his ears the sound of that beating proved nearly deafening, maddening.

Gone.

Her garments that had littered the floor at some point had been cleaned up.

Her valise was gone.

The small serviceable boots she donned.

She was gone.

Nay, that could not be.

And yet, he frantically searched every corner of the small room, looking desperately for some hint of her and finding none. And even as he knew it was futile, Val stormed over, nearly tripping on Horace as he went, and stripped the blankets off that bed he'd shared with her.

This time, the terror he'd expected to feel earlier did consume him. Like rushing water, it swept over Val, a great big wave that threatened to drown him in his own fear, not at the prospect of wedding her, but at the thought of losing her.

He concentrated on breathing and on trying to think.

It couldn't be.

She couldn't be gone.

Some of the tension left him. Surely she'd just . . . gone belowstairs to the floor of the tavern and taken her things with her? His gaze snagged upon the copy of *Pride and Prejudice*, the gift she'd given him . . . and a lone scrap of charcoal pencil that had not been there last evening. His heart and stomach both tensed as he made himself walk over to that book.

Val stopped beside the table, and then opened the book.

> Dearest Val,

She'd called him "dearest."

> I cannot thank you enough for the past days. You've brought me more joy than I've known in so very long. I hate goodbyes and, as such, decided to spare myself that.
>
> I also know if I remain you'd try to marry me because of what we shared, and I do not want that . . . for either of us.
>
> So I shall simply say:
>
> Happy Christmastide to you.

He stared incredulously, reading and rereading the words that confirmed she'd gone.

His gaze flew to the window, where the snow still came down, though more lightly than it had when they'd sought out the inn last evening. "Oh, God," he whispered as the implications hit him.

She'd gone off . . . alone.

Sheer terror he'd thought to never again know ate him alive—images of her hurt or in danger cannibalizing all reason.

The moments following were a blur as, sometime later, with his boots on and Horace safely secured with his brother's driver, and details from the innkeeper about the lady's whereabouts obtained, Val leaned over the mane of his mount and urged him on through the thick, powder-soft snow. Lady's hooves kicked up a cloud of the white flakes as they went.

She'd boarded a mail coach.

In this weather, with snow still falling and covering the ground in a thick blanket, she'd climbed inside with the strangers who'd sung and danced merrily last evening and taken herself off.

Val gritted his teeth so hard pain radiated along his jaw, and he welcomed it because then he wasn't thinking about her being flung from a carriage, her body broken and bleeding and—

He thrust aside the thoughts now threatening to drag him into the realm of madness and concentrated on getting to her . . . and then what he'd do when he did reach her.

He was going to kill her.

Or kiss her.

Nay, he was definitely going to kiss her.

But then shout his head off over her foolishness.

Because how could she go?

Worse, how could she not know? How could she not know that she was the reason he'd been resurrected from sorrow, taught by her to again smile and laugh, and with her not in his life, he'd be restored to darkness?

She doesn't know because you never told her. You let her believe she was a burden.

Val's throat moved, and he leaned lower over Lady's head and pushed him onward, faster.

He wanted her in his life, forever.

He wanted to wake beside her every day and find her resting next to him.

He wanted to watch her as she read and underlined the passages that resonated and ask her questions about why.

And he concentrated on those thoughts. Because they gave him life and hope, and saved him from thinking of—

Shards of fractured wood strewn about the countryside.

Val drew on the reins of his mount so quickly the creature whinnied and reared, pawing at the earth before landing. And Val sought to regain control of his reins, and the moment Lady landed on all fours, Val nudged him on.

Trunks littered the snow, stark slashes of brown and black upon the white.

And—Val brought his horse to a stop and stared—mail.

Little sheets of folded parchment danced as the winds carried them over the earth. They were everywhere.

Val's eyes slid shut, and he squeezed them to keep them closed, to keep from thinking, to keep from descending into a pit of misery from which he'd never pull himself.

It was not her carriage.

There could be any other conveyance carrying such papers.

It could be a lord and lady on their way to celebrate the holiday season.

Except it was the wrong thought, one that thrust him back to another time.

Only, it wasn't his late wife's face that he saw.

It was Myrtle's.

Myrtle lying on the ground, her body broken, the lifeblood ebbing slowly from her veins, her heart slowing and her breath growing shuddery, fainter and fainter, until it was no more.

A tortured moan, garbled as it stuck in his throat, choked him, and Val gasped.

Mad. He was going mad.

Or mayhap he already was.

The world came rushing back on a whir, and with a shout, he kicked Lady on ahead, continuing just over the rise . . . and then he yanked on the reins once more.

This time, Lady maneuvered the abrupt stop.

Val scanned the tableau, similar to one of the past, but different.

Unlike that dark day of years past, there wasn't a lone woman lying upon the earth.

A handful of dazed women *stood* about, and a fine-dressed gentleman had his back to the crowd. A coarsely clad man wrung his cap in his hands, while the women quietly wept.

I am going to throw up . . .

Swallowing back bile, Val jumped down, frantically skimming his gaze over the passengers surrounding the overturned coach.

He dragged a hand through his hair, searching her face out of that crowd, wanting to see her standing because then it would mean she was not lying there with the life draining from her.

A sob exploded from his lungs, and tossing his head back, Val roared to the early-morn sky just one word.

"Myrtle," he cried.

One word that was her name. And it was a prayer, to her, for her.

And then, as if God had heard his calls, Myrtle stepped out from behind one of the passengers.

Disbelief rocked Val, nearly knocking him off his feet.

The hood of her familiar cloak had fallen back, revealing a dark plait. At some point during the melee, several strands had come loose and hung about her shoulders.

He didn't blink. He didn't move, afraid if he did, she'd vanish from his life and this earth, leaving him empty and lonely once more.

Myrtle cocked her head in that way that was so very her; joy propelled him forward. Slowly, and then faster, he churned snow up as he went. "Myrtle," he bellowed, his feet flying as relief melded at last with fresh anger at her for leaving and putting herself in harm's way. He was going to shake her.

And then kiss her.

Mostly kiss her. But shake her, too.

He was reaching for her before he even got to her. "What in hell were you thinking?" he begged, squeezing her arms lightly to prove to himself she was standing here, alive and real, before him.

"It is fine," she murmured in soft tones that managed to penetrate the horror of that accident. "It looks worse than it is. We hit a patch of ice and skidded, and the trunks were not secured properly, and it looks terrible, but it is just a mess. I'm fine." She held his eyes. "I am fine."

She was fine. She was not hurt. She would not die.

And in this instant he knew—even if one day life tore her from him, if he lost her, it would be worth it for a single moment more spent with her.

And perhaps this was one of the Christmas miracles that had long been written of and handed down through time. Myrtle, who with her song and spirit and the purity of her heart, had given him faith again to laugh, and love . . . and live.

His hands spasmed upon her arms, and Val's eyes slid shut. When he opened them again, he took in the detail he'd previously failed to note.

The tall, frowning gentleman who flanked her shoulder, standing protectively beside her, his fingers twined with Myrtle's, his hair dark, those brown eyes familiar.

Familiar because they were Myrtle's eyes.

Val instantly released her.

Dumbfounded, he lost all the words in his head, along with the ability to speak.

Frowning, he looked from Myrtle . . . to the man at her side.

It had better be a brother, because if some stranger dared twine his hand with hers, Val would sever it from his person with a blunt blade. "Who is this?" he clipped out between his tightly clenched teeth.

As if she'd heard the thought and feared it, Myrtle disentangled her fingers from the dark-haired gentleman's. "This is my brother Dallin."

One of the brothers.

One of the ones who'd forgotten her had gotten to her.

He and the other man eyed one another up and down.

A lifetime ago, Val would have cared about proper introductions being made. Now, he looked away, dismissing the gentleman and putting his attention where he wanted.

Myrtle, safe. She had her family. Everything was all confused in his mind. She wasn't supposed to be with them. She was supposed to be alone. They were supposed to be alone.

But this . . . It was as if reality had returned and he'd been presented with a reminder that she was a young lady who'd not had a London Season and would. And . . .

"Is there . . . something else you want?" she asked.

Did he imagine the hopefulness in the uptilt of her question?

"I . . ." *You. I want every tomorrow unto my last tomorrow with you. And then a million tomorrows after that.*

Tell her.

Alas, her brother hadn't been so jaded as to care so very little for formalities. The gentleman took a step forward. They'd never met, and he didn't imagine the gentleman was home enough to clearly recognize him. "And just who, may I ask, is *this*?" the other man asked, confirming as much while also turning Val's own words back on him.

In the end, it was Myrtle who made the formal introductions.

"Dallin, this is His Grace, the Duke of Aragon; Val, this is my brother Dallin, the Viscount Crichton."

Suddenly, the gentleman's eyebrows drew up as he placed Val. And Val remembered what the world knew him to be—a recluse, shut away from the world, icy cold and miserable. And because of it, certainly not the manner of man ever worthy of a woman as good and joyous as Myrtle McQuoid.

The other man found himself first. He sketched a bow. "Your Grace."

Incapable of a returned greeting, Val managed only to incline his head.

He looked to Myrtle, floundering, because when he'd imagined finding her, he'd seen playing out in his mind first the offer of marriage he'd make her. And then there'd been all the worst possible scenarios—ones that, by the state of the mail coach, had nearly come true. But he'd not imagined . . . her family with her.

Val cleared his throat. "I wished to be sure that you are well . . . and I . . ." Myrtle stared at him with those gigantic eyes; they were large circles. "And I . . ." He didn't have the words. And in the end, Val dropped a bow. "I am so very glad you are. I should . . . see to the other passengers. If you would?" With that, he stalked off, leaving Myrtle speechless for the first time in all the time he'd known her, standing there and wishing he had the right words . . . for her.

Chapter 24

Her brother spoke with their family's driver, Kinley.

Dallin had ridden like mad on horseback to reach her, he'd said, but at some point, the servant who'd been driving the carriage had caught up.

It was not her brother she watched, however.

Her gaze remained on Val's retreating figure.

Val, who paused periodically to ask after the passengers, who nodded when he spoke. And the sight of him, ensuring the well-being of those strangers . . . It was impossible for Myrtle to love him any more.

Tears threatened.

That was why he'd come for her.

Because he'd wanted to be sure she reached her family without incident.

She'd intended to spare him that sense of responsibility, and now she thought about the terror that must have plagued him when he'd come upon the scene of the accident.

Finishing up his discussion with the driver, Dallin drew the door open and offered Myrtle a hand to help her inside.

She lingered, her gaze following Val as he offered his help to the people who'd been riding in the carriage with her when it hit an icy patch and careened off course.

He'd come for her.

And it should mean everything to Myrtle.

But it didn't.

Because he'd not really come for her. He'd come to look after her. For if he had come for her, he'd be with her now, and she'd not be joining her brother inside their family's carriage.

Myrtle willed Val to look back.

He did not, however.

Why should he? a voice taunted. *He's always been determined to see after you only as long as your family was gone.* Now they'd returned.

Reluctantly, Myrtle let Dallin help her inside.

He followed, drawing the door shut behind them. "The chap is as strange and taciturn as they say," he remarked as he rubbed his hands together.

That was what he'd say? "He is not strange," she said sharply, glaring at her brother. "He is a good man. Honorable, and he is the one outside helping—"

She caught the glint in her brother's eyes and made herself shut up.

Her cheeks flamed hot, and unable to meet that knowing stare, she looked away.

"Are we going to talk about it?"

She pulled her gaze from the window and stared blankly at her brother.

"The gentleman who showed a shocking familiarity to you?"

Alas, with how this day had gone, she should have expected her brother would make her speak about Val.

"He is our neighbor." She shrugged. "That is all."

Only that wasn't all. He was Val, a man who'd urged her to find her happiness, and who'd helped her to see what she wanted in life, and it was him, and—

"That is all?" her brother drawled. "Do you want to tell me why our neighbor is going about calling you by your given name?"

"He helped me these past days," she said softly. "He showed me the same kindness he would have shown any other person."

Myrtle felt him probing her with his gaze. "You're certain nothing untoward happened? Because the gentleman seemed very concerned for—"

"You're making something of nothing," she cut him off impatiently. A tear fell. "He's as worried about all the other passengers, is he not?" She swiped a hand in the direction of the scene outside.

"Ah, but he didn't come thundering for any of them, calling them by *their* given name." Her brother caught her hands in his and squeezed them. "I'm not going to go about expecting you to marry the fellow because of . . . whatever transpired these past days when you were alone," he said, his tone faintly chiding.

"*Nothing* happened."

Dallin searched his gaze over her face as if he sought the veracity of that assurance.

In a way, though, she spoke the truth.

For *everything* had happened. Mayhap if she'd still a relationship with him and her other siblings, she might have spoken about it. She might have shared just how desperately and hopelessly she loved Val. Her family members, however, were strangers to her in so many ways.

Unlike Val. Val had been the first person in such a long time whom she'd been able to speak freely with and to, and the fact that she'd not have that time with him again ripped her heart in two.

"I am so sorry." When her brother spoke, his voice was thick with emotion she'd never heard from him.

For a moment she believed he'd gathered the true nature of her relationship with Val, and the regret he spoke of was over the pain of her losing him.

Nay, she'd not lost him. She'd never had him. And that hurt the worst of all.

"We each assumed you were in one of the other carriages," her brother said quietly. "And then we were separated by a storm, and it wasn't until the last conveyance arrived at Spynie that we realized our . . . mistake."

Their mistake.

Of course. This was what they'd speak about. This was the reason he believed her to be distraught. It was the safe assumption, for so many reasons.

"It is fine, Dallin," she murmured, her gaze sliding back to the window, and she watched blankly as Kinley led her brother's mount over, stringing it to the team, concentrating on that to keep from thinking of Val and how very much she loved him and would miss him.

Dallin rested a hand on hers, forcing her eyes back to his.

"It is not fine, Myrtle," he said gently but firmly. "You are a special young woman. One who survived these past days without so much as a maid to help you. You deserve more than being forgotten by your family." He drew his hand back. "It is my hope you can forgive us."

And in that moment, through the blinding grief of the end of her time with Val, came a sense of triumph. She'd earned their family's respect. Oddly, that didn't quite fill her the way it ought. The way it would have before this. "There is nothing to forgive," she said softly. And there wasn't. Their failure to remember her had been the reason she'd had these days alone with Val, and they would forever be the happiest, most wondrous moments of her entire life.

Of their own volition, her fingers moved, and she drew the curtain back a fraction so that she might see him, so that she could catch one more glimpse.

But he was gone.

The life slipped from her fingers, and she dropped that fabric; it fluttered forlornly back into place.

Myrtle drew in a slow, uneven breath.

The windowpane revealed her brother's intense scrutiny on her, and she reluctantly looked at him once more.

"Myrtle, I know—" And then he abruptly stopped. Shock filled his features, and he glanced from Myrtle to the window, and then back again to her. "Why do I think your upset is . . . not with our negligence?"

She sank her teeth into her lower lip and shook her head.

"Is that because you're denying it or, rather, you don't wish to talk about it?"

The latter. It was decidedly the latter.

Her brother proved relentless. "You *care* about him."

Yes, she cared about Val, but it was so much more than that.

She loved Val.

"Myrtle?" he urged.

"There is nothing to say, Dallin," she said, her voice threadbare as, with her eyes, she begged him to let the matter rest. "We . . . were together. He helped me." And she proceeded to share with him all that had transpired since their family carriages had pulled away and she'd been left alone. She shared about Val's wife and the reason for his reclusiveness. When she finished, Myrtle shrugged. "As you can see, it was merely a sense of responsibility that brought him after me."

Dallin sat with the silence for a long while. "Myrtle, I saw the way that man looked at you, and he looked like a man possessed when he saw you."

"It is because his wife perished and he feared I'd met that same fate." And she hated herself for having inflicted the terror of this scene upon him.

Her brother snorted. "I've never been in love, but I do expect if I were, it would look something like the way that man looked when he came upon the scene looking for you, believing you'd died."

"Just stop," she cried. "It is over." And as if fate sought to mock her with the truth on that finality, the carriage dipped as the driver climbed atop the box, and then he sent the conveyance slowly into motion. "He is gone." And she was never going to recover from this loss. At last, she understood the pain that had sent him fleeing from the world and why he'd locked himself inside that townhouse with Horace.

Oh, God. Horace.

"But—"

"I don't want to talk about it anymore, Dallin! So if you would please just—"

There came a loud bellow from the driver, and Kinley yanked on the reins, halting the conveyance.

Her brother frowned and yanked the curtain aside. "What in thunderation . . ." And then he stopped.

Myrtle reached for her own curtain, and she went absolutely still, her heart forgetting its job in her breast.

Like a dark warrior of old, Val came striding forward, trudging through the snow. "Myrtle McQuoid," he shouted in that rough way of his, and she reached past her brother, pushing the door open.

"Val," she whispered, drinking in the sight of him. "You came—"

"You left," he said accusatorially.

She touched a hand to her breast. "I . . . You did," she corrected.

"I wanted to look after the other passengers."

Of course he had. That was the manner of man he was. Her heart swelled all the more with her love for him.

"You forgot this," he said, his voice sharp. He brandished a book.

Myrtle's eyes went to the familiar tome, and for a second time that day, hope faded. "I . . . gave the volume to you," she said softly. "That was a gift."

His nostrils flared, and he rocked back on his heels. "You misunderstand. You promised we would discuss it."

"What is the meaning of this?" her brother demanded.

Myrtle and Val ignored him.

"I want that discussion, Myrtle," Val said, shaking the volume at her.

"Now?" she asked.

Her brother strained at her shoulder.

"Not now," Val said, taking a step toward her. And another. And another. Until he stopped just a pace apart. "In the future."

"I don't know . . ." She didn't understand what he was saying or what he was asking. It was all confused in her mind, clouded by a hope that refused to be fully extinguished. Myrtle shook her head.

Val turned the hand holding that book up, revealing the gold lettering upon the top of the copy. "I'm never going to be the best man because there is no man who'll ever be worthy of you. But Myrtle, you have bewitched me . . . In vain I have struggled. It will not do. My feelings will not be repressed. You must allow me to tell you how ardently I admire and love you."

With a sob, Myrtle flung herself from the carriage.

Val was there to catch her, folding her in his arms. "From this day on," he finished that treasured quote, burying those words against her temple.

"You read all of it," she sobbed as Val held her close.

"Are these tears of happiness because of that? Or because I'm asking you to spend the rest of your days with me, Myrtle?" he asked, and with an aching tenderness, he brushed the tears from her cheeks.

A half laugh, half sob escaped her. "B-both." Her voice broke. "But decidedly more of the latter."

"Dare I hope then that you'll agree to give me your heart, making me the happiest per—"

"Yes," she said between laughter and tears as he stroked her cheek. "But only if you agree to the same, Val."

He smiled, and then touched his brow to hers. "It seems we are in agreement, my love."

And as their laughter mingled, filling the countryside, Val drew her closer into his embrace, and she held tight to him and the promise of all the happiness that was to come.

Epilogue

Kent, England
One Week Later

When Myrtle had been a small girl, she'd known certain things as absolute truths.

Someday, when she married, she'd do so at Christmas.

There would, of course, be snow falling, and it would be a chilly, snow-covered morn, and despite that, she'd be walking down an outside aisle to meet at the other end a man who loved her most ardently and passionately, as she loved him.

They would be surrounded by the loving folds of their families, who'd be boisterous and exuberant in their gaiety.

And, of course, there would be the grandest of celebrations after.

Nearly every aspect of that imagining had come true. In its own form, and in its own way.

There was that winter wedding on Christmas Day, but the storm raging outside, rattling the windows, made an outdoor ceremony an impossibility.

Instead, Val had the idea to move the ceremony to the glass-enclosed conservatory, so they could be wed as close as it was possible to being outside, while the wind battered his—and very soon their—household.

"Here it is, my lady." One of the Dowager Duchess of Aragon's maids came rushing into the room, her voice raised to be heard above the din of Myrtle's sisters and cousins, who remained with her while she was readied for her wedding day.

The young woman stopped and looked about . . . for Myrtle's lady's maid.

But there was no lady's maid. Because Myrtle had arrived home from finishing school just before her family had been to depart, and it was a detail they'd failed to oversee.

At one time—a time not so very long ago—she'd been filled with bitterness and resentment.

On this day, with her boisterous family joined with Val's in the conservatory, awaiting their nuptials, she at last realized . . . the dreams she'd carried as a girl were only just that—dreams belonging to a small child. This day, this moment coming with Val, was so much more splendorous than any imaginings she'd once carried.

"I will see to that," Myrtle's mother murmured, and stepped forward.

She accepted the headpiece from the young girl, who dipped a curtsy and then saw herself out.

All around, the clamor of her sisters' and cousins' laughter swelled around the room.

Standing at the vanity, Myrtle remained still as her mother brought the headpiece up and arranged it just so upon her head, fixing it with pins, and then stepped back a pace and assessed Myrtle.

The white, high-waisted, high-necked dress may as well have been any dress she'd worn any number of other winter mornings in her life.

Myrtle's always riotous hair had been drawn into a semblance of an elaborate coif, with diamond snowflake combs gifted to her by Val's mother. Her mother had once lamented Myrtle's untamable curls. And even on this, her wedding day, her curls had not been tamed. They had, however, been arranged into an enormous coronet of tresses that were perfect because they were hers.

The white, long-sleeved satin day dress with a lace overlay was no finer than any garment she'd worn for any holiday before.

And yet it was perfect, for it wasn't about the gown or the trappings or the imaginings. She knew that now. Rather, the dress was perfection because of what it symbolized. Because of what this *day* symbolized—the union of her and Val's love, and the start of their future together as husband and wife.

Her heart sped up.

Her mother gave a loud clap of her hands.

That had no effect on the boisterous swell of the ladies present.

Her mother clapped a second time, this time harder and louder, and added her voice to the din. "Ladies!"

All the young women instantly fell silent and looked over.

"If you will await us belowstairs. Cassia, inform His Grace and your father that Myrtle and I will be along shortly."

Her sisters and cousins instantly resumed their happy discourse and bantering as they filed one by one from the room.

Myrtle's mother looked to her devoted lady's maid, Dorinda, who'd helped with Myrtle's preparations that day. The young woman hurried over to the gold-painted French vanity and plucked a long box from the top.

Dorinda stopped before them.

"Thank you, my dear," her mother said with her usual affection for the young woman, who'd been with her since before Myrtle's birth.

Perplexed, Myrtle puzzled her brow as her mother removed the top and set it aside.

Reaching inside, the countess carefully lifted out—

Myrtle gasped.

The satin emerald cloak in her mother's hands shimmered and gleamed with movement as the countess gave it a light snap.

"Lovely, is it not?" her mother murmured.

Incapable of anything more than a nod, Myrtle took in the article. The cloak was almost too beautiful to touch. *Almost.*

She stretched out a reverent hand and caressed the velvet-trimmed neck. And it was beyond lovely. Both the collar and hemline of the full-length cloak were trimmed with a garland of red roses and white amaryllis.

"The gloves, Dorinda," her mother said, and the young woman immediately hastened over with a pair of delicate gloves, a perfect match to the cloak.

Myrtle shook her head. "But . . . how . . . when . . . ?"

"Come, my little star," her mother chided, calling forth that endearment she'd bestowed upon Myrtle long ago and stopped using just before sending her off to boarding school. "Did you think I'd not have recalled your favorite color or your favorite time of year or holiday?" Her mother directed her gaze upon the cloak and smiled wistfully at the luxuriant article. "I'd imagined you wearing it on Christmas Day; I just never imagined it would also be your wedding day . . . or that you would leave me so quickly." She murmured that last part more to herself.

Myrtle startled. Leave her so quickly . . . ? "I don't understand," she said softly, because she didn't. Any of it.

This . . . the thoughtfulness of the cloak, or her mother's melancholy.

"What?" her mother asked. "Did you think I forgot your love of Christmas, and that I'd not have a special gift just for you?" She grimaced. "Though I can certainly see—with the mishap in our departure and our inability to get to you once we realized our mistake because of the snow—why you should think this way."

Only . . . it wasn't just her being left alone. "You sent me away," Myrtle said earnestly.

Her mother drew back. "You thought we sent you away because we didn't want you about?"

"Didn't you?" Myrtle asked, her voice steeped in all the confusion she felt.

"Oh, little star," her mother murmured, caressing her cheek. "Why did you think I should have called you by that name since you were just a babe, toddling about? Because you were and are this great light . . . and deserving to be held high above and appreciated, and in a household as wild and unruly and big as ours, I knew we could not give you the attention you deserved, and so we sent you away." She dabbed at the corners of her eyes. "It was the hardest decision I'd ever made, and now I have you home, and I don't even have you for your London Seas—"

Myrtle tossed her arms around her mother before she could complete the rest of that word. "I didn't know," she whispered against her mother's shoulder.

Her mind spun. And all these years, she'd believed it had been what her family had seen as her failings that had gotten her sent off, never imagining, never believing, that it had been an act of . . . love.

"I did the best I could to see you happy, and clearly, that you are not confident in my love, I have failed miserably in that regard," her mother said, drawing back slightly and rubbing Myrtle's shoulders. "But as parents, we do the best we can, and sometimes when we have big families, well . . . You will see when you have a half dozen babes of your own. Now, come . . . We have your duke waiting for you."

Her duke.

Val.

He was so much more than his title. He was all her heart and the other half of her soul.

"I know that smile," her mother murmured. Another one of those wistful smiles danced on the edges of her lips. "Even as I will lament never having had the time spent with you for a London Season, I will be content in knowing you found the only thing I'd hoped for you—love." She looped her arm through Myrtle's. "Now, come along."

"I love you, Mama," Myrtle said when they reached the front door.

Tears welled in the countess's eyes. "And I love you, little star." With that, she pressed the handle and led them from the rooms. As they walked, her mother sighed. "There's still Cassia for another Season, and there will be Fleur, and though it will not be the same as having the time with you . . ."

Myrtle smiled. "Thank you, Mama."

When they arrived at the end of the hall leading to the conservatory, her mother brought them to a stop. "Are you ready?"

As a young girl and then even as a young lady at Mrs. Belden's contemplating her future, she'd expected she'd feel some sadness . . . at leaving her family. Only to have failed to realize then that there'd be no sense of leaving; rather, it felt like she was . . . coming home.

"I am," she said softly. From the moment Val had first shown up with an armful of wood, she'd dreamed of this moment.

Her mother peeked around the corner, then looked back at Myrtle. Leaning down, she kissed her cheek. "It is time, little star," she whispered, and rushed off.

A moment later, her father stepped around the corner . . . joined by—

"Horace!" Myrtle exclaimed, falling to a knee.

The dog immediately covered her face with kisses.

"I would kiss your cheek, dear daughter," her father drawled. "But alas, I fear I must pass at this moment."

She laughed as he held his arm out; she looped hers through, allowing him to lead her onward.

As she made the slow walk into the conservatory, converted into a magical winter wonderland resplendent with flowers and garlands and Christmas trees, she drank in the sight of her family and Val's, both beaming, as radiant in their joy as she was.

And then she looked at him . . .

Standing at the end of a makeshift aisle with his brother beside him, Val kept his gaze locked on her. On only her.

"I love you," he mouthed.

Tears filled her throat. "I love you, too," she said silently in return.

And that moment, as she reached Val and her father placed her fingertips on her husband-to-be's arm, Myrtle found herself with the greatest Christmas wish she'd ever carried at last fulfilled—a lifetime of love with the man before her.

Horace yapped happily, and she looked down.

And a dog, of course.

Acknowledgments

To my editor Alison Dasho. It's always a joy when one's editor has the same enthusiasm and excitement for one's characters and story as the author herself. From romps to gritty dramas and pure ballroom romance, you've never not supported my vision. Thank you for that gift and trust in me.

About the Author

Photo © 2016 Kimberly Rocha

Christi Caldwell is the *USA Today* bestselling author of eleven series, including Wantons of Waverton, Lost Lords of London, Sinful Brides, Wicked Wallflowers, and Heart of a Duke. She blames novelist Judith McNaught for luring her into the world of historical romance. When Christi was at the University of Connecticut, she began writing her own tales of love—ones where even the most perfect heroes and heroines had imperfections. She learned to enjoy torturing her couples before they earned their well-deserved happily ever after. Christi lives in the Piedmont region of North Carolina, where she spends her time writing and baking with her twin girls and courageous son. For more information visit www.christicaldwell.com.